SECOND
TERM

SECOND TERM

A THRILLER

J. M. ADAMS

OCEANVIEW (PUBLISHING

SARASOTA, FLORIDA

ISBN 978-1-60809-591-9

Published in the United States of America by Oceanview Publishing

Sarasota, Florida

www.oceanviewpub.com

10 9 8 7 6 5 4 3 2 1

PRINTED IN THE UNITED STATES OF AMERICA

Dedicated to the heroes of the Capitol Police force whose courageous actions and uncommon valor on January 6th, 2021, protected not only members of Congress, but also helped our nation preserve the very pillars of our fragile democracy.

The object of life is not to be on the side of the majority, but to escape finding oneself in the ranks of the insane.

MARCUS AURELIUS

PART ONE

BENGHAZI

CHAPTER 1

September 10, 2012
Mediterranean Sea, North Africa

A HEAVY BREEZE rolls off the Mediterranean Sea pushing away the stench of the city slowly dying around me. The deep salty air offers a snippet of comfort although I have no idea why. There are no childhood memories of the sea. I grew up in western Colorado and southwestern Virginia. Maybe it's the brief respite from the taint of chemicals and human waste that's embedded itself into the pores of this city. I feel like I'm constantly gagging on smoke from the unseen forest fires that raged in Colorado when I was a kid.

The buildings around me are pockmarked with bullet holes. Sandbags stand watch in front of every entrance with piles of rubble towering from thirty to fifty feet high. This place is a giant landfill waiting to fall into the sea. I walk another block and come across a building that looks like something took a mammoth crescent-shaped bite out of it. Rebar splinters off in several directions like webs constructed by a giant spider.

There's no way to underscore the toll of human suffering here. My line of sight follows another tower of rubble going up to the second floor where a little kitchen comes into view. On the left side of the room there's vibrant yellow wallpaper, a Roman numeral wall clock, and a table topped with a bright floral Persian table runner. On the right, the walls are stained with blood and black scorch marks. There are more weapons than food in this cursed city and the reminders are everywhere.

Western leaders continue to fool themselves into believing that the death of Muammar Gaddafi would have brought some semblance of sanity or stability to this region. The Brother Leader's forty-year reign of terror against his people might have ended, but death and chaos rule this city with an iron hand.

Libya is a slave to its violent history, and no one is looking for a way out. But what do I know? I'm just a covert foot soldier for the American Department of Defense. I can't begin to understand why Washington believes that with Gaddafi gone, it's nothing but butterscotch and ponies here in North Africa.

I have a wake-up call to deliver to my superiors that may realign some of that thinking, but only if I can make it to the CIA installation in one piece. I've been collecting intel for the past two months posing as an English teacher for a wealthy family living in a chateau in Derna.

Derna was the perfect place for undercover work. The charming Libyan port city is about 200 miles east of Benghazi and doesn't begin to fit in with the rest of Libya. It's one of the wealthiest areas in the country, a quaint little town nestled into beautiful green mountains rich with exotic sea cliffs and waterfalls. Two days ago, I obtained information that forced me to blow my cover and run. There was no way to securely transmit the sensitive information I've gathered without landing in a cell never to be seen again.

My pickup time is slated for the conclusion of the Muezzins' call to Fajr prayer. The Fajr is the first of five daily Muslim prayers broadcasted from speakers atop the mosques that are still standing around the city. They stick to strict schedule and this morning's devotional is set for 4:58am (the true dawn) although the sun won't rise until after 6:30 this morning.

I emerge from the shadows of the long-abandoned Benghazi Cathedral. It's ironic that one of the most prominent structures in this old Muslim city is a decaying Roman Catholic Church. I have little time to get to the parking lot at the 7th of October Hospital without drawing attention to myself. Good luck with that, I laugh out loud. Hopefully my baggy clothes, hat, and short haircut can fool anyone who doesn't get too close.

I pull the wide brim of my camouflage bucket hat lower to cover more of my face. My oversized camo jacket is untucked over a dark t-shirt hanging over black jeans. The street is still deserted as I execute what I like to call my husky "man-walk."

I emit an audible sigh of relief rounding the corner by the burned-out Hamzawi Café. I'm less than a hundred yards away from the hospital and have a straight shot to my destination where I can hole up until my ride arrives. At the same time, two militiamen turn the corner and are coming my way. So much for a smooth escape. Why aren't they preparing for morning prayers?

I ease my Cressi finisher knife into my right hand spinning the blade backwards against my forearm to keep it out of sight. The sharp pinprick of the blade against my skin provides some small comfort. The knife is specifically designed for underwater hunting, but it's always done the job for me. Five inches long with a deadly stiletto tip.

I have zero interest in any confrontation, but that pipe dream is starting to evaporate.

"*Asalaamu alaikum*," I say in my practiced husky "man-voice" trying to sound masculine friendly, but in a hurry.

Thankfully, both of their AK-47s remain slung to their backs.

The guy on the left is slightly built, with a camo hat that looks a little like mine. He's not paying any attention, but the bigger man closer to me answers with a slight edge to his reply, "*Wa alaikum salam.*"

His eyes are alert and suspicious underneath bushy caterpillar eyebrows and a tangled mane of black facial hair.

I try to politely pass them on the right when the hairy man lashes out seizing my shoulder and reaching for a compact revolver from his belt. I wonder what prompted him to grab me at the same time I plunge the length of my blade deep into his armpit underneath an outstretched arm. His eyes pop wide open in horror. He grunts in confusion as I turn my blade twice before yanking it out of his body and jabbing two explosive thrusts deep into his throat.

Blood erupts from the neck wound covering my hands as I step forward to his companion who is in the clumsy process of unslinging his rifle. I dispatch him quickly with a sweeping arc of my blade and survey the area for witnesses. I'm just lucky that this unfortunate incident took place in the cover of darkness. We are the only people on the street, and our encounter made very little noise.

The entire altercation took less than ten seconds. My arms are covered in bright red arterial blood with one of the men gurgling bubbles from his open neck wound at my feet. I lean down and try to leave as much of the mess as I can on his jacket. I switch jackets with my second victim as the loudspeakers crackle to life around the city signaling the start of the morning prayers. Any sane person would want to sprint from the scene, but my training forces me to walk casually away from the dead men lying in the street. I walk into the hospital parking lot. There's a black Mercedes. The plate matches the numbers I'm expecting as I throw open the passenger door and slam it behind me.

"That's a good way to get shot," says the smiling driver in place of a greeting, his hand resting on the Glock 19 in his lap. He studies me with open curiosity.

"If you don't want company, you should probably keep your doors locked in a neighborhood like this," I answer.

"Jesus," he asks, voice rising in concern as he stares at the blood-soaked jacket on my lap. "You hit?"

"It's not mine. I had a run-in with a couple of locals around the block," I say quietly.

"A run-in? You're covered in blood," he says.

I nod.

"Those two militia dudes? Big shaggy guy?"

I nod my head again.

"We need to get out of here," he says.

"Better wait until prayers are over," I answer. "We shouldn't be on the streets during prayers."

"Muhammad will have to see his way past our sins," he says slamming the car into gear and pulling out onto the empty street. "I'm Deckard by the way. Welcome to Benghazi."

I nod, scanning the streets for anything out of place.

"There's wipes in the glove box. You should clean up the best you can. We should be back at the ranch in fifteen to thirty depending on roadblocks. You sure you're OK?"

I reach for the wipes as a violent cough escapes my lips. The worst thing about Benghazi isn't the people waving guns; it's the never-ending cloud of macabre dust that dominates the air here. North Africa is hot, the air is thick, and it's only rained once since I got here two months ago.

A bottle of water appears in front of my face, and I suck it down in two gulps.

"The station chief told me to look for a seasoned operative. You don't look old enough to drink. Are you Langley? Everyone else here is."

Langley is shorthand for CIA. I wonder if he's going to prattle on all the way to the station.

"Something like that," I say.

"So what should I call you?" he asks with a twinkle in his eye. "Jane the Ripper?"

"Jack is fine," I chirp back. "Got another water?"

"You don't look line any Jack I've ever met. Anyway, the station chief has a hard-on for you already," he says handing me another water. "Says you're compromising the Agency's mission in Benghazi and you shouldn't be coming in at all."

I lean my head back and close my eyes. The last thing I need now is some sad little station chief crying to me about his little slice of turf in the desert. I need to talk to Washington and get the American ambassador out of Libya or at least stop him from coming to Benghazi.

CHAPTER 2

September 10, 2012
Benghazi, Libya

I HAVE TO ADMIT, the driver is quite competent, and that's high praise coming from me. He's avoiding the main roads and driving around in haphazard circles. The last thing he needs in life is to be caught up in one of the impromptu militiaman road-blocks with an armed woman scrubbing blood off of her skin. There is no rule of law here. It's survival of the fittest and open season on Westerners.

People are shot dead in the street every day. Benghazi is inun-dated by a tsunami of guns, rocket launchers, and grenades, cour-tesy of the raided Gadaffi stockpiles around the city. Once Gadaffi was dead, the grand prize was a leaderless country where everyone suddenly had access to military-grade weapons.

"You got a change of clothes?" I ask.

"In the duffle behind the seat."

I climb into the back and start rummaging through his bag.

"Please," Deckard says dryly. "Help yourself."

I pull off my jacket and shirt, happy to see my sports bra didn't catch any blood. I only have one more in my possession. I pull on his shirt, about two sizes too big, and tie it up at the bottom. I ball up my blood-covered jacket and hand it up to him. "Get rid of this, please."

"Pockets empty?" he asks.

"No, just a blueprint for the U.S. Consulate, signed confession, and the bloody knife."

He chuckles at my amazing wit and tosses it out the window.

"How's my face? Any blood?" I call up to the driver looking at him in the rearview mirror.

Silence answers my question.

"Are my breasts distracting you?" I ask. "I'm asking if there's any blood on my face?"

He colors with embarrassment, causing him to change the subject. "Listen up, Annie Oakley. We need to clean you up before the station chief sees you. You can't come in hot like this and tell him you chopped up two friendlies with a steak knife during morning prayers and left them to rot on the main road by the hospital. He ahhh . . ." he pauses, searching for the right words. "He wouldn't understand."

"Deckard, right?" I ask patiently. "I'm not remotely interested in what you're station chief has to say. I need to make a call on a secure line before I speak to anybody. Can you hook that up for me?"

He nods with that smile again as we pull up to the security gate. A fetid smell hits my nostrils inside the CIA installation, at least twice as bad as downtown Benghazi. Jesus, I hate this place already!

"Are the locals running security here?" I ask Deckard.

"Feb 17th Militia," he says as we watch them run mirrors underneath our vehicle to make sure we didn't bring back any car bombs or IEDs—Improvised Explosive Devices—into the compound.

This little government hideaway is supposed to be covert, but it's the worst-kept secret in Benghazi. Armor-plated vehicles with rugged-looking American men going in and out at all hours of the day doesn't exactly blend in with the local landscape. Not to mention that members of the February 17th Martyrs Brigade aren't famous for keeping their mouths shut.

"Comm center?" I say looking over Deckard. I can tell he's been around the block, but I'm sure my arrival and attitude has thrown him off balance. Warrior females don't exist in his world. Or anywhere in the world for that matter. We are a breed apart.

He answers his phone. "Deckard."

He nods and says, "She's on her way."

"Station chief?" I ask.

He looks at me, shrugs his shoulders. "I told 'Tom,' the station chief, that you were on the way—I didn't say when."

I like this guy.

He sets me up on the secure phone in the communication center and tells me he'll wait outside the door to make sure I'm not interrupted. A moment later he pops in with a fresh box of wipes, a bar of soap, and a small bucket of water.

It takes almost three minutes on hold before I'm connected with Josiah Timmons, the United States Assistant Secretary of Defense for Global Strategic Affairs aka ASD (GSA).

"Bronco?"

Bronco is my code name.

"Sir."

"Is the line secure?"

"I would be shocked if this call isn't being recorded or actively monitored here and back at Langley," I say giving myself a bath with the precious baby wipes Deckard gave me.

He pauses, thinking about how our conversation should proceed.

"Give it to me straight," says Timmons. "We don't have time for subtleties."

"We groomed that family I stayed with in Derna because of the father's ties to Ansar al-Sharia Militia. I had the house wired."

"I thought we agreed not to do that," says Timmons sharply.

I ignore his rebuke.

"Did you break down your network before you fled?" he asks.

"Yes, sir. All traces of my presence disappeared with me," I reply.

"And thanks for the trust, sir," I say silently to myself and continue my briefing, shaking my head.

"The group's leader, Walid Al-Kataani, dined with the family two nights ago. They are planning a September 11th strike against American interests in Benghazi. Ambassador Sullivan's name came up multiple times during their discussion."

The silence on the phone stretches on for nearly an entire minute before he speaks again.

"I understand that Ambassador J.T. Sullivan is in Tripoli. His visit to Benghazi is supposed to be a closely guarded secret," says Timmons. "And the agency screened the Ansar al-Sharia Militia and found no ties to Al-Qaeda."

"You don't need ties to Al-Qaeda to kidnap or kill an Ambassador," I say.

"Goddamnit!" says Timmons who rarely swears and never takes the Lord's name in vain.

"Any more details?"

"Not many."

"Stay there with the CIA. Brief the station chief. Give him everything. I want a condensed report sent to me by four p.m. my time. That's"—he pauses. "You have ninety minutes. I'll be in touch."

The line went dead. No orders except stay put and make the case for keeping the Ambassador out of the city. I tent my fingers noticing dried blood in some of my cuticles.

I walk over to leave when the door flies open in front of me. A portly ruddy-faced man, about my height, with graying curly hair stares at me with eyes blazing. "So sorry to disturb you," he says, voice dripping with sarcasm. "I'd like a word in my office? Is *now* OK?"

This must be Tom, the CIA Station Chief. He doesn't have a clue that we've met before in Afghanistan.

We enter the office. He sits down behind his desk and glares at me like an angry boy who lost his decoder ring. I slide a chair back, sit down, and cross my legs.

"Did I ask you to sit down?" he asks with a snarl.

The prudent thing to do would be to stand, but I'm not what you would call a shining example of a people pleaser.

"I don't know who you think you are, little lady. But—" He stops, staring at my hands. "Is that dried blood on your hands?"

I ignore his question and plunge ahead. "Sir, there's a credible threat against Ambassador Sullivan, and it must be assessed before he comes to Benghazi. I've been asked to brief you by ASD Timmons. Do you want to call some of your analysts in here while we speak?"

"Your intelligence is missing the mark or dated," says the station chief stupidly. "Sullivan arrived at the Special Missions Compound last night."

"Here in Benghazi?" I ask, dreading the answer.

Jesus—What a nightmare. My face gives nothing away. He's looking for a reaction, but there's nothing to be gained by giving it to him. But I have to raise the point of security.

"Sir, I would like to assist your operation with its plans to safeguard the Ambassador," I say, feeling the gravity of the caustic situation begin to corrode around me.

"I'm afraid those plans are classified," he says with a smug smile.

"Sir, the Secretary of Defense has instructed me to brief you," I say, trying to help this man see some sliver of reason.

"Then brief me," he says studying the papers on his desk. The meeting is obviously over, but I have my orders.

"The Ansar al-Sharia Militia has plans set in motion for tomorrow. September 11th. The Ambassador's life is in danger," I say.

He looks up from his paperwork. "Grave danger?"

You're kidding me, right?

"Is there any other kind? We need to evac the ambassador and neutralize the threat."

With great conviction, he says, "That's preposterous. Ansar al-Sharia worked with us to bring down Gadaffi. Walid Al-Kataani and his people may not love America, but they have no plans on attacking our interests either."

"Are you willing to bet Sullivan's life on that theory, sir? Tomorrow, as you most certainly know, is the anniversary of the 9/11 terrorist attacks. American lives in Benghazi are in danger," I say. "Especially Ambassador Sullivan."

"And where were you on 9/11, kid?" he asks, back to the personal attacks again. "Grade school? You're out of your depth. Stay out of the way and let the grown-ups handle this."

He forgot to say *little lady* again. My mouth hangs open for a second, but no words come out. There is no point. But I know exactly what I have to do. Track down the Ambassador and convince him to bail out of Benghazi before the shooting starts tomorrow.

CHAPTER 3

September 10, 2012
CIA Annex Building

I TAKE A SECOND to control my breathing before smiling at him with a nod. "It's been educational."

I casually walk out of his office wondering why I let him keep all of the teeth in his mouth.

The sound of clattering keyboards continues to bang off of the office walls even though several analysts are staring at me and not their screens any longer. I look to my left and Smiley is standing there waiting for me. He leads me out into the courtyard, and I try not to wretch all over again as the potent cocktail of rotting animals and feces punches into my nostrils like a pickaxe.

I close my eyes and breathe through my mouth, letting the punishing desert heat try to calm my stomach with little success.

"Want to talk about it?" he asks quietly.

I sure as hell can't do anyone any good without support. I would be violating multiple protocols by giving Deckard the full sitrep—situation report—but I have no choice unless I decide to sit on the sidelines and let the terrorists have all the fun.

"I have some tough decisions to make," I say.

"Seems like Tom didn't dig what you had to tell him during your intelligence briefing," he says.

"He's a charmer. Off the record, his real name is Jack Dempsey," I say. "But instead of a heavyweight champ, he's saddled with a little man syndrome that casts a long shadow. I'm a threat to his little slice of heaven. He knows his operation here is missing the big picture and I just spilled the real-world situation to Washington," I say. "Rather than acting on my information, I'm sure 'Tom' is doing everything under the sun to discredit me."

"He's a world-class tool," he says looking off toward the slaughterhouse. "Let me give you the five-cent tour and let you meet the rest of the GRS—Global Response Staff—operators. You can decide if there's any intel you'd care to share with me or the team. By the way, I still don't know your name."

He looks at me expectantly.

I smile at him for the first time and his face lights up. "I'm sure you'll think of something, Romeo."

"We're about a half a mile southeast of the diplomatic Special Mission Compound across the Fourth Ring Road," he says, pointing over the comm center to his left.

I make a snap decision because I have to trust someone. "Tom told me that Ambassador Sullivan is here in Benghazi."

"Yeah, he's staying right there, at the Special Mission Compound," he says. "We're providing security for him this afternoon for a speech he's giving at the Mayor's office. It's a last-minute thing—they just dropped it on us last night."

That's the first piece of good news I've heard all day. "Can you please make sure I'm part of that security detail?"

"I can make that happen," he says as we walk to the middle of the courtyard. "So you just came out of Building C, which is obviously the communications center and intelligence think tank.

"The annex is comprised of four buildings, A, B, C, and D." He points to each structure. "The local slaughterhouse is there behind building B where you see all the sheep grazing in the dirt. It's also where that wonderful smell comes from. We call that area Zombieland."

I nod as I knock another fly out of the air before it can land on me. "It's nice here," I say. "The flies, the ever-present stench of death. It's paradise really."

He ignores my sarcasm and continues, "Off subject—Your reflexes are stunning," he says with a smirk. "I'm serious. We're smacking flies away all the time. You knock them out of the air before they can land. You think like a fly."

"Everyone has at least one talent," I say while we make our way toward the security staff quarters. I hear music, video games, and loud raucous conversation.

I walk in behind Deckard and the room suddenly falls silent as five pairs of eyes lock onto me.

"Jesus, ain't you Gomers ever seen a woman before?" he asks the room as they eye me curiously.

"Simmer down, boys, this is—" Deckard begins his introduction but is cut off by a giant cowboy standing at attention in the center of the room.

"This woman needs no introduction in the civilized world," he says in a deep baritone voice that shakes the walls. "This woman is Cora Walker. Ma'am, can I shake your hand?"

The four men stare at the cowboy as their mouths fall open.

"Ahhh, sure. Um, you seem to have me at a disadvantage, sir," I say trying to recover from this man's bewildering familiarity with me. I know we've never met, but he sure as hell knows who I am. My cover didn't last thirty friggin' seconds in Benghazi.

His muscular hand looms toward me like an oversized catcher's mitt trying to snag a wild pitch. I grasp his hand, and he delivers a firm but very respectful handshake.

"Austin J. Barton. At your service, ma'am. Great grip by the way," he says beaming at me.

The rest of the team looks back and forth between us with shocked expressions that probably match my own. His forehead wrinkles as he looks around the room, his presence and charisma reeling us all in.

"Gentlemen, you are in the presence of greatness," he says with a hint of awe in his voice. I don't know this grizzly bear, but there's no doubt—He's been in the desert sun too long.

"Mizz Walker here won the 2008 Interservice Pistol Championship at Fort Benning. The god-damnedest shooter who ever picked up a weapon, excuse my language, ma'am."

Oh shit—busted. I feel my face coloring and smile like a befuddled prom queen. Of course now I have a new problem—my cover is completely blown.

"Mizz Walker demolished eighty-four of the military's best shooters right there at Fort Benning, Georgia. I know because I was there. Correct me if I'm wrong, but you shot a score of 27-60 out of a possible 28-hundred points. The highest score ever and largest margin of victory in the history of the competition."

I nod my head and the men gawk at me like I've just discovered fire, cured cancer, and thrown the winning touchdown in the Super Bowl. Or they could just be staring at my chest.

"And I heard a rumor, but I could never get it confirmed," he says looking at me expectantly. "Can I ask you something?"

"Shoot, cowboy," I say feeling an instant comradeship with this team of warriors although slightly uncomfortable with all of their adulation.

"One of the shooters from the competition told me you were right-handed."

It was a question, not really a statement.

"I am," I confirm and I know where this is going.

"Jeezuz-H! I knew it. So tell us, Mizz Walker. Why did you shoot the entire competition left-handed?"

"Bullshit!" one of the guys says, laughing in shock.

"No way!" says another, smiling broadly at the thought.

"Just to clarify. I did not shoot the entire competition with my left hand!" I say. "I hurt my right wrist in a hand-to-hand combat training exercise the day before the competition. But only about ten percent of my shots were southpaw."

"See, gentlemen, I told ya'll. We are in the presence of greatness!" he says with final authority. "I have never seen a finer or more composed shooter in my life. She is blessed with liquid silver in her veins."

Deckard stares at me with those beautiful big blue eyes, and I feel my stomach tangle into knots. The last thing I need is a romantic entanglement in my life.

Deckard introduces me to Jimmy Buchanan, who goes by the nickname "the Surgeon," along with Boyd McAfee and Deacon Lobdell.

"I think you got Sheriff Bart a little starstruck," says Deacon Lobdell appreciatively—referring to Austin Barton. "Hell, I'm not sure Bart has ever been able to string more than ten words together at one time."

We make small talk and they each give me a brief bio about their exploits, experience, and skills. They're a tight knit and impressive unit. A collection of former Navy SEALs and Army Rangers. Every one of them trained operators who fought in various theaters around the Middle East before joining the GRS— Global Response Staff.

These former combat vets have each other's backs. They're government contractors now, all tasked with protecting the CIA case officers who scamper around Benghazi trying to dig up actionable intelligence.

The cowboy—Austin Barton—had been the chief firearms instructor at the Federal Law Enforcement Training Center in Cheltenham, Maryland, before joining the Global Response Team two years ago. He was a decorated sniper during Gulf War Two and is the most respected shooter in the unit. I don't know how my introduction to the team would have proceeded without the over-the-top accolades from Sheriff Bart, but I'm lucky to have them.

CHAPTER 4

September 10, 2012
CIA Annex Building

I ALWAYS WONDER why my crippling remorse is always so far removed from the violence of my actions. What cog came loose inside of me to make me this way. I stand under the shower scourging my body with the industrial-grade soap Deckard gave me. I scrub the blood off of my skin watching crimson streaks from my morning execution seek refuge down the drain.

Has my moral compass always pointed due south? Did I need to butcher those men this morning? I did. Did they deserve to die? That's the kind of question I can never quite wrap my head around. I kill people, but am I a killer? I'm thankful for the hot pounding water washing away any evidence of my tears. Warriors don't cry. At least never in public.

I walk into Deckard's room trying to regain focus on the task ahead of me. He set off to bunk with someone else to make sure I have some privacy. I'm getting the royal treatment by getting a room all to myself.

I take a silent inventory of the arsenal of deadly tools neatly arranged in the corner. Deckard certainly delivered on the list of weapons I asked him to gather for me including the RPG—Rocket

Propelled Grenade Launcher. He's taking me seriously and that bolsters my slim chances of success for whatever comes my way in the next forty-eight hours.

I pick up the night vision goggles and helmet Deckard left lying for me on the bed. My short thick hair is almost dry. Even in the air-conditioning, the desert works hard to devour any trace of moisture it can find. I put on the helmet and adjust the goggles until they fit my head perfectly. The only thing he didn't deliver for me was the earplugs I asked him for.

There's a soft knock on the door.

"Room service," Deckard calls on the other side.

I throw on some clothes and put on an oversized field jacket. I pad over to the door in bare feet, opening it slowly. I feel a desire to wrap my arms around him before shaking my head clear.

He hands me a little white plastic bag like a little boy presenting me with an apple he just picked. "We're meeting for chow in thirty. You know where the mess is?"

I peer into the bag seeing five sterile sets of earplugs and smile.

"Thank you for all of this," I say sincerely.

"Earplugs?" he asks, gesturing toward the bag in my hand.

"Always," I say. "Don't engage in a firefight without them."

"What?" he says, cupping his ear, pretending he is hard of hearing.

"Funny," I say making no effort to hide the smile on my face.

He kneels in front of his bed reaching underneath. He comes out with body armor and a heavy black Rhodesian vest—a tactical assault vest.

"More gifts," he says placing them carefully on the bed.

"I also want to show you this before I post it," he says handing me a piece of folded paper from his pocket. "Looks like someone might be taking your warning seriously."

I scan the document: *Intelligence indicates that a Western facility or U.S. Consulate/Government Building in Benghazi, Libya, may be attacked within the next 48 hours.*

I fix my gaze on him. "What makes you think this has anything to do with me?"

"I figure you didn't come visit so you could lounge by the slaughterhouse," he says, pleased with himself. "See you at lunch."

An hour later, I feel like a new woman. Food always has that effect on me.

"I can't believe how good the chow is here," I say polishing off my second huge serving of *tajin mahshi*. The lamb is perfect. The tomatoes, aubergines, and courgettes are to die for.

"It's what keeps me coming back," says Sheriff Bart digging into the basket for the last *khubzit howsh*—Libyan pita.

He and I are the only ones left at the table.

"I don't suppose you guys have any APCs—Armored Personnel Carriers—sitting around that we can take to the mayor's office this afternoon?" I ask.

"No, ma'am. Apparently, our huge black SUVs help us blend in," he says, shaking his head and chuckling.

Twenty minutes later, the six of us roll out in three armored SUVs. Lo and behold, I'm paired up with Deckard. Shocker! Jimmy B. is paired up with Deacon, and Sheriff Bart and Boyd are bringing up the rear.

We're all jocked up for the Mayor of Benghazi's office where Ambassador Sullivan is to deliver a few short remarks, but first, we make a quick detour to the U.S. Special Mission Compound where he's staying.

It's a five-minute drive from the annex right into the heart of hell.

"You guys can't be serious! This area is a slum. Every other Western power abandoned Libya months ago with a note tacked to the front door, 'Back when you get your act together!' How can we be the only country stupid enough to leave the lights on here?"

"Above my pay grade," is his stark response.

"Not just that, look over there," he says. "See that stone patchwork? A friggin' IED blew a hole in the wall over there on June 6th."

That was only three months ago.

"This is so much worse than I ever imagined," I say as our black SUV convoy rolls up to the gate. A shiver goes down my back as I read the signpost in English:

ATTENTION

YOU ARE NOW ENTERING A CONSULAR FACILITY OF THE U.S. GOVERNMENT

Libyan Translation:

ATTENTION

ALL TERRORISTS PLEASE REGISTER AT THE FRONT GATE BEFORE MURDERING AMERICAN INFIDELS

There are potential hostiles all around us. Some are taking pictures with their phones and that really pisses me off. They're casing the compound, in broad daylight. Gathering intel for something big. I make up my mind. Screw protocol. I'm going to drop a full intelligence dump on these GRS guys when we get back to the Annex building. I'll tell them everything I know about the possible attack.

We climb out of the SUVs with our heads on a swivel. The gates and barbed wire around us wouldn't slow down a high school glee club.

Everyone makes introductions to the two-man security team assigned to protect Ambassador Sullivan. *Two people? Two?* I keep my mouth shut and wander away, looking for more points of weakness in this half-assed compound.

The more I see, the more I realize this entire facility is indefensible. It's a shooting gallery. Two guys with M4s aren't going to slow down anyone, no matter how proficient they are. They won't have a prayer trying to protect the Ambassador. I cut through the house to the pool in back and spot two cops standing on the top floor of a building that looks to be under construction.

I stay in the shadows watching them when I feel my stomach lurch. The cops are scanning the grounds of the compound from above. And after another moment, I realize they're taking videos and snapping surveillance pictures on one of their phones.

"Glad no one else is disturbed by any of this," I say racing back into the house. I run past the startled men inside the house and yank the front door open.

"Where are you going?" calls Deckard behind me.

I run to the front gate, Deckard hot on my heels. "What the hell are you doing?"

"That building over there." I point over the wall of the compound to the building by the back of the house. "There are two cops spying on the compound. They're taking videos of the ambassador's personal residence."

I run through the front gate with Deckard pacing me.

"Wait, goddamnit! Wait!" he shouts at me.

Several shifty men on the street take great interest in our afternoon sprint. I pick up the pace, despite the heavy body armor and loaded tactical vest trying to slow me down. It takes less than three minutes to get to the skeleton building where I saw the Libyan cops.

I take the steps two at a time, and Deck is right there with me. "They were on the fourth floor," I say catching by breath.

"You can't ambush a Libyan police officer," he says urgently.

"Actually, there are two of them. I just want to have a chat. Watch my six," I say. We move quickly and quietly up the next two flights of stairs.

I peer around the corner. The busy little beavers are totally engrossed in their mission; one is sweeping the compound and videoing with his phone, while another guy is pointing out new areas of interest. They're wearing their police BDUs, bright red berets, and sidearms. They're the real deal.

I ease the Glock 19 out of my holster while Deckard unslings his M4 and points it at the ground. He moves to my right so I'm not in his line of fire as I flip my safety off.

I stop four feet away. The idiots are still clueless to my presence. I wonder how these morons survived this long? I could gut them both and confiscate their phones, but that might be frowned upon, and I would feel bad about myself all over again.

I raise my sidearm and point it at the nearest man before announcing, "*Asalaamu alaikum.*" He starts for his sidearm and stops immediately, staring down the barrel of my gun.

"PEE-LEECE," he says in broken English. "Pee-Leece."

His right hand still has the phone in it. I switch my Glock to my left hand and take a step forward. Before he can react, I snatch the phone out of his hand and step back quickly.

"Nooo. Pee-Leece," he says frantically, as if that absolves him of his sins.

I level the gun between his eyes.

"You got 'em?" I ask Deckard.

"Roger," he says.

I step back ten feet, keeping my eyes on them. Without warning, I spike the cop's phone flat on the ground as a hard as I can.

"*Tawaqaf!*" screams the cop.

I pick up the offending device, looking at the perfect glass spider web of cracks where the screen used to be. I smash the phone with the heel of my boot and ease out my knife. I stab the center of the glass web, twisting the knife into the phone before ejecting the SIM card and stuffing it into one of the pockets in my vest.

I walk back over to the policemen, put them on their knees, and relieve them of their sidearms.

"We gotta go," calls Deckard behind me. "You're gonna cause an international incident."

I shove their weapons into my tactical vest and return his shattered phone.

"Let's go," I say, turning around and walking away.

"*Shukran*," I call back to the crooked cops, which is the proper term for "thank you" in Arabic.

CHAPTER 5

September 10, 2012
U.S. Special Mission Compound

I DEPOSIT THEIR weapons into a foul-smelling barrel of liquid at the top of the second floor by the stairs. Deckard watches me silently. I guess I'll have to wait until he finds his big boy words.

"We have a problem," he says while we walk up the street together a few minutes later.

I say nothing, waiting for him to continue.

"I get it. You don't have to play by the rules," he says, choosing his words carefully. "But when those cops report what just happened up there, while Ambassador Sullivan is staying just across the street, we're gonna be in a world of shit."

"First of all, I'll confront anyone who has the audacity to video a secure American compound in the middle of the day. I don't care if he's a Libyan Police Chief or the King of Persia. Besides, you're not thinking this through," I say without looking at him.

He stops walking and turns around. "Meaning?" he says.

I turn around and walk right up to him.

"Let me get this straight," I say, invading his personal space. "Two rugged Muslim Benghazi policemen are going to report that a *girl* snuck up on them, disarmed them, and basically kicked their asses?"

A look of understanding softens his features.

"Don't mistake my speed of action for impulsiveness—If I'm in a hurry, it's because I see a tactical window of opportunity."

"Fair enough," he says, throwing his hands up in surrender.

"I know how you could make it up to me," I say sweetly, batting my eyes and totally switching gears on him.

"I'm listening," he says, rolling his eyes.

"Get me five with the Ambassador," I say. "Before we leave for the mayor's office."

Fifteen minutes later, the door to the ambassador's residence opens and one of the members of his security detail waves me in. He appraises me carefully and smiles. "Better make it quick."

"Time is money," I quip back.

He walks out, closing the door behind him.

"Miss Walker, so sorry to keep you waiting," says Ambassador Sullivan warmly. He walks up and shakes my hand. I can tell from his body type that he was an athlete when he was younger, but he's shorter than I expected. I'm five ten and I think I got him by an inch. His charisma is unmistakable and his brown eyes bleed intensity.

"I understand you wanted a word in private," he says, getting right to the point and quickly glancing at his watch. "Are you DOD?"

I've been characterized as a "blunt instrument" in the past so I skip the pleasantries and dive in.

"Sir, are you familiar with the Ansar al-Sharia Militia and its leader, Walid Al-Kataani?" I ask. My question sounds more like an accusation, not quite the way I intended it to come out.

"I am," he says.

"Sir, I monitored a meeting two nights ago in Derna. Al-Kataani was the honored guest at this dinner and told his most prominent financial backer that their plans have been set into motion to strike a "terrible blow against the Godless Americans in Benghazi on September 11th." I take a breath and press on.

"He did not specify what form these attacks might take, but he mentioned you by name on multiple occasions along with the usual rhetoric about the 'streets running red with infidel blood.'"

The Ambassador walks past me over to the giant ornate window, gripping the windowsill. He stares out over the pool.

"Not more than thirty minutes ago, I observed—I almost said *confronted*—two Libyan policeman on the fourth floor of that abandoned building overlooking your pool. They were taking videos of you and the interior of the compound," I say.

"I actually saw them earlier and reported it," he says, still looking out the window. "I'm surprised that they're not there now. I alerted my security personnel and asked them to contact the local police chief."

I need to appeal to his ego if I can. "Mr. Ambassador, you don't want to sidetrack any of the amazing progress you've achieved here in Libya. If you're captured or worse, all of your good work goes down the drain. Don't just protect yourself right now; protect the people of Libya."

"I assume you have recommendations?" he says curtly.

I ignore his question and finish my thought.

"Mr. Ambassador, perhaps the most unsettling aspect of this potential attack is how Al-Kataani got tipped off that you were going to be in Benghazi and not back in Tripoli. He knew before the DOD knew. How would a man like that come across what was supposed to be highly classified information?"

He turns around and smiles. "State secrets never keep well in Benghazi."

"Yes, sir," I say, returning his smile. "But we have to consider the possibility that there may be forces working within our government who don't want you to succeed here."

"Hmm," he says trying to hide his distaste for my comment. "You think this may be some kind of home-cooked government conspiracy against me?"

"I didn't say that," I say, masking my frustration. "What I did say is that Al-Kataani is coming for you tomorrow, and you need to decide how you will respond to that threat. Because a two-man security team is woefully inadequate. This building is a kill box, and if the invaders come, it will be over quickly."

His forehead wrinkles at my directness. He's not used to being spoken to this way. Perhaps I'm not showing the proper deference. He tents his fingers in front of his face in thought. The scent of pine swirls around me, circulated by the ceiling fan above. I think his cologne was meant to be subtle, but it's making my eyes water. Judging by the wet hair, the Ambassador must have been in the shower when I popped in on the spying policemen across the street.

Silence dominates the room, uncomfortable for many, but not for me. He's at least processing my warning or pretending to.

"You've given me a lot to think about," he says, dismissing me. "Thank you for coming in."

"Sir, you don't have the numbers or the firepower to repel any kind of organized attack at this location. At least consider relocating to the CIA Annex for the night and staying on through September 11th," I say reasonably.

Sadly, my warning falls on deaf ears. No real shock there, I guess.

"Thank you for your assessment, but the real threat here in Libya is al-Qaeda, not the Ansar al-Sharia Militia. They fought side by side with us against Gadaffi. There's nothing for them to gain by attacking American interests."

He's probably thinking: *I've been running around North Africa for the last decade and this prom queen who's been here for all of five minutes waltzes in and tells me the sky is falling.*

"I agree sir, there's nothing to be gained by attacking any American installation in Benghazi, but that doesn't mean they won't do it. This militia group in particular is more into symbolic gestures than actual results. Your death or capture would dominate headlines around the globe."

Running around Benghazi and expecting a two-man team security unit to keep you alive is ignorance personified. It's like smacking the grim reaper in the teeth and daring him to do something about it.

I can only surmise that the Ambassador is living in denial. He reminds me of a one-armed bomb maker I tracked down last year in Kabul. The bomber told me he accepted the fact that his life might end at any minute—it was simply out of his control. He was right. I shot him twice in the chest and once in the head.

"Thank you again for your briefing, but if we don't leave now, we'll be late for our meeting with the mayor." This signals a merciful end to our chat. He's about to the open the door when he turns around and appraises me for a moment.

"If I tucked my head between my legs and ran every time some militia group or Imam threatened me, I'd wind up hiding in a drainpipe with Gadaffi's ghost."

"*Inshallah,*" I say quietly, which roughly translated means: *If it is the will of God.*

CHAPTER 6

September 10, 2012
Benghazi, Libya

OUR FIVE-VEHICLE CONVOY rolls up to the sprawling hotel nestled onto the banks of the Mediterranean. The once shining palace is in need of a serious makeover, much like the rest of the city.

The meeting between Ambassador Sullivan and Benghazi's mayor and city council is supposed to be a quiet little affair. Minutes after we escort the Ambassador into the hotel courtyard, a set of double exit doors flies open and this "low-key" meeting devolves into a Walmart Black Friday sales event where people stampede one another for matching sets of Santa salt and pepper shakers.

A crush of North African press members flood the courtyard, cutting the Ambassador off from any reasonable expectation of protection. The Ambassador's two-man security team blew it big-time. They obviously didn't gather the proper intelligence and now we're all standing around with our pants around our ankles. The smell of tension and body odor makes its way through the crowd like a thick blanket.

In an Islamic country, a lowly woman does not push her way through a mob of Muslim men. It's unheard of and is the height of disrespectful behavior. But I don't have time to show the proper deference, so I violently shove my way through the crowd until I get to the Ambassador's point man.

I push my lips close to his ear so he can hear me above the noise. "Why don't you shoot the ambassador yourself and save the terrorists the trouble? You're more than twenty feet away from him. Got a plan?"

His face contorts like I just punched him in the groin.

"The situation's under control," he yells back while we're buffeted on both sides by the press of people in a confined space.

"I can see that," I say, unable to suppress my disgust. "See that window?" I point about twenty feet up to his right.

He nods.

"I'll be up there waving my weapon around trying to look menacing. Try not to shoot me," I say.

He nods his understanding before I turn and bully my way into the hotel. We both know it's an exercise of futility at this point. I'm not going up there to hide. I'll try to serve as a possible deterrent for any potential attackers on the ground.

But anyone with combat experience knows that if someone here wants to waste Sullivan at this event, we can't do a thing about it.

The carnival of chaos mercifully ends without incident about an hour later, but the Ambassador's vulnerability is weighing on everyone's mind.

"I need to send another encrypted message," I say to Deckard who is staring aimlessly out of the passenger's-side window as we speed back to the Annex. "And I need to talk to the team. I have intelligence I need to share with all of you."

Back in the communications center at the CIA Annex, I bang out six lines to Washington and hit send:

EYES ONLY
THREAT LEVEL ALPHA

SC2—*Assistant Secretary of Defense*
AnB—*Ambassador of Benghazi*
U-P - 2 DEFENDERS—*Unprotected*

COMPOUND VIDEO/PHOTO SURVEILLANCE
UNDERWAY BY BENGHAZI POLICE FORCE

I stop to examine a fresh set of cables coming in from other points in North Africa. Five minutes later, I walk out of the communication center heading left over to the GRS outdoor workout area they call the gym. God bless Deck—they're all out there waiting for me.

"Guys," I say nodding my head at them. "Great gig over there at the Mayor's office this afternoon."

"The Ambassador needs to get his ass back to Tripoli before some serious shit goes down," says Deacon Lobdell.

They nod their heads in agreement.

"Gents, this is a Top-Secret briefing. None of you have the proper security clearance for this information, so apparently, I'm going rogue." Each of them looks at me expectantly.

"I don't want to pressure any of you, so if you want no part of this, I understand. Just walk away, but do it now," I say, going from face to face to see if there are any dissenters.

The pleasant breeze swirls around us, and I can actually smell lamb cooking in the kitchen temporarily replacing the ever-present stench emanating from the friendly neighborhood slaughterhouse. My stomach grumbles to life.

"Are any of you familiar with Ansar al-Sharia Militia and their leader, Walid Al-Kataani?"

"We know him," laughed Boyd McAfee. "Well, not personally."

"Two nights ago, Al-Kataani relayed plans to attack an American target and either capture or kill Ambassador Sullivan. He indicated that the plans were already in motion. The attack is to take place on September 11th, which of course is tomorrow," I say.

"They sure as hell don't have the numbers over there to protect him," says Deacon Lobdell throwing his hands up in the air. "Why aren't we making plans and providing round-the-clock security?"

"Great question," I say, my voice matching the group's level of disbelief. "I've relayed the same intel to Washington, the Ambassador, and the Station Chief here at Club Paradise."

Every one of them is dialed into my words.

"My warnings have fallen on deaf ears. You all saw the cable that Washington sent out yesterday reporting that a Western facility may be attacked. That's just the Pentagon trying to cover their asses in case Al-Kataani and his street thugs wipe us off the map tomorrow."

I give them a minute. I just jammed a lot of bad news down their throats, and they need a moment to digest.

"I realize that until the station chief orders you into action, you can't do anything about this potential threat. But . . ." I pause looking for the right words. "You now know what I know."

Jimmy Buchanan, the one they call the "Surgeon," is the quiet one in the group, but he raises his hand like a kid in class. It's extremely cute.

"Mr. Buchanan?" I say.

"Just to clarify, ma'am," he says, putting his hands on his hips. "The ambassador declined any additional protection?"

"Let's just say my warning was not well received. I can only surmise that he's survived this long in North Africa and has avoided any major incidents. I believe this luck has provided him with a false sense of security," I say.

"What about Tom?" asks Deckard.

I laugh out loud. "Sounds like you're asking me about the Bill Murray movie *What About Bob?* Bob, I mean Tom, assures Washington that Al-Khatani and his gangbangers are no threat to the Ambassador or to any other American interests in Benghazi."

"Typical," someone barks, but I wasn't sure who said it.

"That's not all. I reviewed the cables while I was inside the comm center regarding our neighbors to the east in Egypt," I say. "Intelligence suggests a major demonstration and potential violence at the American Embassy in Cairo to mark the September 11th anniversary. Obviously, 9/11 is a huge day of celebration for our friends here in Sandland."

I turn around looking past the Annex to the skies over the U.S. Temporary Consulate where the Ambassador is staying. It's only a half-mile to the northwest.

"We can pray that Al-Khatani gets cold feet and calls the whole thing off," I say, turning around and looking at them again. "But you saw what I saw today. Twitchy dudes snapping pictures and running around the perimeter of the American Consulate. They're whispering into their phones and making seedy plans."

Everyone in Libya is either preparing or bracing for tomorrow's shitstorm. Meanwhile, the suits here and in Washington are telling us to sit around and hope for the best.

CHAPTER 7

September 11, 2012
CIA Annex Building

I'M SITTING IN the mess hall with Deck's computer trying to look busy, but even on a somber day like nine-eleven, I can't tamp down the huge smile spreading across my face.

"Must be good news," says Deck plopping down across from me with a plate full of Libyan breakfast food.

I try to keep what I'm doing undercover, but then blurt out, "Only if you're a Broncos fan!" I accidentally announce to the room.

"Well, if you must know, my team is the Bengals," he says, shaking his head.

"The Bengals?" I say, wrinkling my nose. "I guess you guys made the playoffs last year, but that wild-card loss to Houston will sting for a long time."

"Full of surprises, aren't you? A woman who knows guns and football?" He laughs.

"You're changing the subject," I say sternly. "It's never too late to breathe in that Mile High Magic. Even after four neck surgeries, Peyton Manning went off for 253 yards, a pair of touchdowns, and even the defense scored a TD!"

Some of the analysts in the mess hall give me a sideways look. I'm too loud again, but I love my Broncos.

"You think Peyton can finish the season?" he asks, looking deep into my eyes. He's trying to participate, but he's got more on his mind than the National Football League. Dirty boy!

"Perhaps we should make a little wager?" I ask.

He throws his hands up in surrender. "We'll see. So I guess I know why your code name is Bronco."

"Guilty as charged, Romeo," I say smiling back at him.

"So if nothing more ominous comes up today, we have a *Call of Duty* tournament on Xbox at 1300 hours. Do you play?"

"Play? Some people 'play' *Call of Duty*. I can make it 'rain,'" I say standing up. I gently close his laptop and ease it over to him. "Thanks for the computer. I'm late for my morning run."

*　　*　　*

September 11th turned out to be a sleepy day for all of us. Being on edge, waiting for an attack that may or may not come, is mentally taxing. But by 1600 hours, it seems like my proclamation of doom missed the mark. There goes my credibility too. My failure would be OK if I were a man but being wrong in a man's world makes things that much harder for the next woman who comes around. Sorry, ladies!

The entire team sits down for dinner just before 1900 hours. I'm sandwiched between Deacon Lobdell and Jimmy Buchanan with Deckard, Sheriff Bart, and McAfee sitting across from us.

Sheriff Bart stands up and raises his cup of water calling for silence. "Gentlemen. I have never seen a team of shooters as talented as yourselves get your collective tails kicked so badly by a newcomer. We need to have the mirrors taken out of Building B because after that *Call of Duty* beatdown, this woman delivered to ya'll, you men will never be able to look at yourselves in the mirror again."

Hoots, hollers, and laughter fill the dining hall.

"Hear, hear," they cheer.

I stand up, take a bow, and resume my seat before tearing into a plate of lamb kebobs. Looks like my dire warning about a 9/11 attack was a false alarm. My credibility took a huge hit, but for me, my country always comes first. To tell the truth, it never felt so good to be so wrong.

I take a long and surprisingly hot shower and climb into bed around 2100 hours. For the first time in forty-eight hours, I relax and feel my brain finally doing a long overdue self-imposed shut-down. I'm somewhere between sleep and consciousness. The last little bit of combat juice in my system ebbs away into the abyss as I drift off to sleep.

Suddenly, my eyes flutter open to a rumble in the distance.

"You're hearing things, Walker," I say out loud to the empty room.

I adjust my pillow and start to close my eyes again when another soft rumble jolts me awake.

NO! NO! Not now. That's an RPG firing. And it's close. My body braces for impact, but the concussion hits somewhere else. My God, the Ambassador!

I'm out of bed in a flash. I throw on my last sports bra and full fatigues. I gear up in less than four minutes. My brain instantly fries away any vestiges from the fog of sleep. I secure my tactical vest and stow the earplugs Deck gave me into the top pocket. I run down the hall nearly knocking over Lobdell who's wearing a pair of shorts and t-shirt with his bare feet and cranked-up earbuds.

"What the hell are you doing?" I ask him urgently. "Don't you hear that? Rally the troops. We gotta go!"

He follows me as I rip down the hall smashing into the area they call the family room. Three startled GRS agents look up from their movie, staring at me with wild eyes.

"RPGs and gunfire, are you deaf? Let's roll, boys!" I bark, realizing instantly that no one else heard the faint rumbles.

Deckard comes crashing into the door behind me ten seconds later. "The consulate's under attack," he says, cranking up his radio so we can all hear:

"Tripoli, Tripoli, be advised, we have been overrun. Forty to fifty tangoes have breached the residence. Tripoli, they are everywhere. We are being hit from all sides. We're fucked! Request immediate assistance. Repeat. Request immediate assistance!"

I check my Tigger watch that I keep set to civilian time. 9:45 p.m.

"Front gate. STAT. GO!" Deck calls out.

Tom, the Station Chief, is already out front, his thumb thoroughly lodged in a place I don't care to mention while he fiddles with his phone.

"Consulate says forty to fifty hostiles," I say calmly.

"I have a fucking radio," he snaps at me, panic clipping every word out of his mouth.

I have no respect for those in authority who can't keep their head on straight when things don't go to plan. I bolt away helping Deckard load the trunk of the first armored car with weapons and ammo while Boyd McAfee loads the other one with Jimmy Buchanan.

"Where's Bart?" I ask Deckard as we work in unison.

"I contacted him before I came outside. He was doing an escort with one of the analysts. He's on his way back now," he says.

The loading op takes less than six minutes and we're ready to move out. Tom walks up behind us, hands on hips.

"What the hell do you think you're doing?" His voice cracks, going up an octave on the word *doing*.

Deckard walks up to Tom and says quietly, "We gotta go, Chief. Hostiles have taken the consulate. They need us there and they need us now."

"You don't get it," says Tom loud enough for all of us to hear. "We don't exist. We are not here. You can't drive over there blazing away like some inner-city SWAT team. We are a secret installation."

Deckard stays calm and moves his face closer to Tom's ear, speaking in a whisper. "Chief, a United States Ambassador is over there. He's in mortal danger. And I'm sorry to tell ya, everyone in Benghazi knows we're here at the Annex. You know this installation ain't exactly a state secret."

"Deckard, you and your team will stand down," says Tom. "Feb Seventeen will handle this. The local authorities will take the lead. You don't move until I order you to. Are we clear?"

"Crystal," Deckard says.

Tom walks away and I run to catch up with him.

"Dempsey, what are you doing? Don't do this," I say in a low urgent voice. His face contorts with the realization that I know his real name.

"You ignored my warning. That's fine. But American lives are at risk," I say quietly, trying to reassure him. "Don't make this worse by denying Sullivan and his people their best shot at being rescued. We can save them, but the clock is ticking!"

His look tells me I'm something he might have just scraped off the bottom of his shoe. "If I want your advice, trust me, I'll ask."

He tries to walk away, and I snatch him by the arm. He tries to pull away, but I hold him tight. His face turns a gruesome shade of purple while the GRS team looks on.

"You know the difference between a rescue operation and a recovery operation. We can *rescue* people now or we can go in later and collect bodies. Do the right thing," I beg, trying to sway him.

He yanks his arm out of my grasp hustling toward the entrance of the Annex. I can only hope the sheer weight of his shame will bring him back, but men like him are slaves to their personal demons.

"What was that all about?" asks Deckard.

"We need to go, now," I say emphatically. "This second. At the very least, let's get on the road and wait for further instructions."

"We will," says Deckard. "Tom will give the order any moment."

"He'll give the order when it's too late," I say, shaking my head.

There's no point in arguing. I'm not in charge here.

"Jimmy, go grab Salem," orders Deckard. "We need an interpreter with us."

"Do we have grenades?" I ask no one in particular.

Boyd McAfee speaks up. "I got flash bangs."

"I need four," I say.

McAfee walks over to the back of the Toyota Land Cruiser and removes a handheld ammo locker and hands it over to me while Buchanan runs up the stairs and disappears inside.

"There's more stuff in there for you," says McAfee.

I pop the locker open doing a quick inventory when I notice a slight fog of diesel fuel sickening the air around us. Burning diesel fuel—what the hell is on fire?

The pop of automatic weapons and small arms fire at the consulate grates at our patience as we sit there all dressed for the dance and nowhere to go. Every second we delay makes our mission infinitely harder and decreases the chance of finding anyone alive.

Eighteen long minutes after the first shots were fired, the radio crackles to life again with a desperate plea from the consulate. The frail voice is raw and broken, clogged with pain.

"Tripoli, do—do you read? They've set fire to the main building. Cough, cough, cough. We are dying. We're cut off. Cough, cough. Can't breathe. We're fuckin' dyin."

The radio falls silent.

"If you're coming with us, mount up now," orders Deckard. "Fair warning. None of you has to go. This is a non-sanctioned OP. So we may not have a job when we get back."

"We're all going," says Buchanan, the one they call "the Surgeon." Deckard, Buchanan, and I awkwardly slide into the vehicle with our body armor and tactical vests while Salem, the translator, climbs into the back of the other vehicle with Deacon Lobdell and Boyd McAfee.

Tom comes charging down the stairs screaming at Deckard, "Stand down. That's an order. You are not authorized!"

We all look at him, but no one says a word. Both Land Cruisers peel out of the lot shooting dust and gravel in our wake as we speed toward what's left of the American Consulate.

CHAPTER 8

September 11, 2012
U.S. Special Mission Compound

YELLOW FLAMES AND black smoke lick the sky above the United States Consulate and temporary home of Ambassador J.T. Sullivan. I pray it doesn't become his final resting place.

We're two minutes away from the front gate when everything falls apart. There's a sporadic firefight between two militia groups in front of us effectively shutting down the Shari' Al Andalus Road and cutting us off from the Consulate. Before we can engage the attackers, we need to determine who the hell is on our side. But Deckard already has the situation in front of us mapped out in his head.

"That's Feb 17th right here," he says to us. "They're the good guys." Don't shoot them and *don't* let them shoot you. Dying by friendly fire is no way to go."

Deckard keys his radio, contacting Deacon Lobdell.

"Deac, take the translator over to the commanding officer for Feb 17 and let him know we're joining the party. Bronco will provide cover."

He hands me an earpiece and small receiving device. I stick the earpiece into my right ear and place one of the earplugs in my left.

The plug expands once it's in place and the world suddenly goes very quiet on my left side.

"How do you want me to differentiate the good dudes from the bad?" I say sliding out of the vehicle.

"Godspeed, Bronco," he says, ending the conversation.

I appreciate the lack of direction. It gives me freedom of movement. I carefully flip down the night vision goggles and the world around me morphs into a muddled mass of green viscous gel. I call it the "astronaut in the ocean" effect. I hate the damn things because it kills my peripheral vision, but seeing at night is almost a fair trade-off. Almost.

I scan the area for hostiles who might take an interest in Deacon and the translator while marking targets in my mind. I break the surrounding area down into grids. There are two hostiles, 150 yards up to my right crouching in front of a shimmering green wall. My breathing slows along with my pulse rate, my stance is easy and relaxed. In my mind, I've already put them down although I haven't pulled the trigger yet.

They bring their weapons up and take aim at Deacon. I fire two quick sets of shots and green liquid erupts from their chests as they drop to the ground.

I'm in my quiet place now. Weapons come up on both sides as I engage next targets. Short bursts, no wasted shots. Methodically, I clear grid after grid, cutting down each tango.

I don't see bodies fall. The instant I pull the trigger, I'm already engaging the next target. Only my tactical awareness informs me that everyone on both sides are still shooting. I'm locked in and cleaning my fields of fire.

I stop to reload, but the damage on the other side is complete. The tangoes are either dead or have fled the area. I'm already reloaded when I see headlights swinging wildly around the corner up ahead. I identify the vehicle as a technical, basically a death wagon on wheels.

A *technical* is a pickup truck with a large caliber machine gun mounted into the bed of the truck. Lucky for all of us that this is the Libyan amateur hour. Instead of taking a slower and more methodical approach, the driver is coming at us like a madman.

His wild approach is ineffective because the shooter who's manning the gun in the back of the pickup is holding on for dear life. So instead of aiming the weapon, he's trying not to go airborne.

More calm washes through my system. I instantly calculate where the shooter will be in space. Geometry merging with situational awareness.

I fire two rounds. The second shot hits the shooter in the forehead instead of the chest. He spins like a broken helicopter blade into the air and out of sight while I lay waste to the driver's-side windshield, punching five softball-sized holes through the glass and through the driver. The technical spins out of control, hits a parked car, and pirouettes into the air spinning twice before slamming headfirst into the wall fifty yards to my right.

The entire engagement is done in three minutes. My concentration relaxes while the heavy fog of burning diesel smoke rakes my throat and poisons the street around us.

We gotta move. Every minute we jerk around out here kills our chances to find Sullivan and get him out of harm's way. Members of Feb 17 watch me with their mouths open as I climb into the SUV next to Deckard. Both vehicles shoot forward toward the compound.

"Jesus, Bronco," says Deckard, his tone dead serious as he punches the accelerator navigating through the burning cars in the street. "The sheriff told us that when he watched you shoot at Benning, your level of calm was unnerving. Said it looked like you could have been throwing a Frisbee at the beach with a beer in your hand."

I ignore him. "If we can get through the intersection up here, drop me at the building where we hit those cops yesterday. I can protect our flank, scan the back of the compound, and secure the back gate. You guys keep your strobes on, so I don't accidentally shoot you."

"Affirmative," he says, going up the road. He keys the radio. "Deac, Bronco will climb the tower by the back gate. The abandoned construction site overlooking the pool. Don't shoot her. Take the front gate—we'll hit from the rear."

"Copy," Deacon says. "Bronco, great fuckin' shooting back there. Saved my ass."

Deac and his team race through the front gate that's been battered open and is on fire. Deckard drops me off at the unfinished building we climbed yesterday and motors off toward the front gate.

I take the stairs two at a time, the heavy equipment kicks my ass with every step. I reach the top of the second flight of stairs and the view causes me to stop breathing.

I stop and stare at the raging fires inside the U.S. Consulate and I know we're too late. Sullivan tried to forge a life-long alliance between Libya and the United States, and it probably cost him his life. We waited too long. The only thing we're going to do here at the consulate tonight is collect our dead.

CHAPTER 9

September 11, 2012
U.S. Special Mission Compound

DECKARD'S SCRATCHY VOICE comes through the earpiece breaking me out of a trance. He's obviously been breathing smoke.

"Made three passes inside. No trace of the ambassador. We're bugging out."

"Copy," I say. "Be advised. Back gate to compound exposed—gate is open. I'm coming down to secure it."

I double-time down the stairs when I hear the screech of car brakes. I look down. Seven men with weapons drawn pour out of a pair of beat-up compact cars.

I key the mic. "Contact. Seven tangoes. Back gate."

At this range, I could take them out with a garden hoe.

They're huddled in a tight mass. Not an ounce of tactical awareness among them. My soul issues a pang of guilt for the lives I took tonight, but I tamp it down deep inside. Thinking like that will not only cost my life, but the lives of those depending on me.

I do what needs to be done. I refuse to shed a tear for a cadre of thugs carrying machine guns who have come to murder Americans.

I rake the drivers with gunfire and finish each one with a head-shot. I circle around the tangled mass of the dead and bleeding bodies strewn in front of the gate.

"Back gate clear," I radio to Deckard. "I'm coming in."

"Lock it up, Bronco," says Deckard trying to suppress a cough.

I secure the gate and jog up to the burning United States Special Mission compound. I stare stupidly at the flames like an impotent spectator. I know the Defense Department declined enhanced security here at least twice in the last few months. The United States was the last Western outpost here in Benghazi and the suits back home couldn't be bothered with something so trivial as protecting American lives.

I spot my team loading up a pair of black Land Rovers. I can see by how low each vehicle sits off the ground that they are armor plated. "Bronco, provide cover. We're getting the fuck out of here."

I catch movement along the hedges. I level my weapon. "Contact. Multiples coming in at my three o'clock," I say into my microphone.

Deckard joins me as the others continue to load up the vehicles. We crouch low and fire controlled bursts, putting down three more.

"You have the city grid memorized, right?" he asks.

"Affirmative," I say.

"Take Salem, Lobdell, and the Ambassador's bodyguard back to the ranch. Take the long way home. I don't need to tell you, I'm gonna anyway. No hesitation on the ride back—everyone is an enemy tonight. There are no friendlies!"

We step aside as Lobdell and one of the ambassador's bodyguards emerge from the burning Special Mission Compound with a dead body wrapped in a blanket. My eyes shoot to Deckard's.

"It's Jason DeRosa, the ambassador's bodyguard," he says, walking away and shaking his head.

It takes a thirty-second debate before Lobdell finally relents and agrees to let the little lady drive. That's me. Men!

I shoot out of the compound, impressed with the power of the Range Rover. There must be a V-10 under the hood. I head north away from the CIA Annex instead of south so I can pick up the Tariq Al' Arubah Al U'rouba Highway to the west and work my way down.

Deacon Lobdell breaks the silence. "Bronco," he says, introducing the man in the back seat. "This is Chris Alterman."

"Chris," I say staring straight ahead into the blockade with flaming cars taking shape in front of us about 150 yards to the west.

"Chris, does this thing have airbags?"

There's no reply. I need an answer immediately.

"Big guy," I say loudly. "Does this vee-hicle have airbags? I need an answer now."

"Ahhh, no, no. Ahh, no airbags," he stutters back. "Um, why?"

That's what I needed to hear. Six seconds before impact.

"Brace for impact," I say loudly so no one can miss it.

I survey the situation in front of me. Two compact cars blocking the road, but facing the wrong way to be effective. Which is good. Four men with guns, which factors out to around 650 pounds of meat blocking the four-foot gap between their vehicles.

My inner voice blurts out instant calculations as I increase our speed to 82 kilometers per hour. That's fifty-plus per hour, meaning we are covering twenty-five yards per second.

"Goddamn, Bronco. Whaddya doing?" asks Lobdell urgently.

"Hold on," I say.

I pump the gas pedal. The hostiles realize far too late that we are rocketing forward right at them and not slowing down. The two armed men in front of us go airborne as we ram through the gap like a giant bumper car without a conscience. The compact cars blocking our way shoot backwards from the collision clearing a path for us as bullets rain down on our Land Cruiser from every side.

If not for the armor-plated car and bulletproof glass, every one of us would be a smoking corpse. My ears ring from the staccato of constant gunfire that rakes our vehicle for twenty straight seconds before we finally emerge from the kill zone.

My earplugs are wedged in tight. I can't imagine what it sounded like to the men in the vehicle without ear protection. We slow down again, trying to blend in with the surrounding traffic, although a Range Rover pockmarked by gunfire isn't exactly inconspicuous.

"You are positively one hellacious individual, Bronco," says Lobdell with a touch of awe in his voice. "Don't you ever sweat, ma'am?"

I'm not one for small talk, but it's best to keep the men in the vehicle as calm as possible and hopefully ease their minds.

"What's your question, Deac?" I ask him, cracking a wry smile without taking my eyes off the road.

"As soon as you saw the roadblock, you instantly decided to just plow on through, didn't you?" he asks.

"That's a fair question," I say noticing that we had picked up at least one tail behind us.

"All right, how did you know we'd make it through? Why did you ask if the vehicle had airbags?" he asks.

"If airbags had deployed, we could have been temporarily stunned, had the air knocked out of us, or worse," I say. "Or maybe we just got lucky," I tease him.

He laughs out loud. "Well, Bronco, I am impressed."

I can see the "secret" CIA installation coming up fast in front of us.

"Deac, alert the Annex. We're coming in hot and dirty," I say.

The gates open in the distance just as our tail falls away.

Fifteen minutes later, thanks to Deckard giving A.J. Barton the heads-up, we are fully stocked with ammunition, with two-person teams stationed on three separate rooftops. Bart and I are on top of Building B overlooking the back gate when I say softly into the radio, "Contact. Convoy of ten to twelve vehicles just came to a stop at the back gate. Be advised, someone left the back gate open."

"Probably the Libyan cops who bugged out five minutes ago," says Deck over the radio.

The terrorists pour out of unmarked vehicles with automatic weapons at the ready, emboldened by the cover of darkness and the burning of the American compound a mile up the road from here. For them, and by the will of their creator, it is long past the time to purge the Godless Americans from their sacred soil.

We watch them patiently through the night vision sights mounted to our weapons. The advancing Libyans are under the deadly delusion that they're silent phantoms drifting toward the unsuspecting Americans, when in reality, they could not have been more obvious to us if they were being led by dueling heavy metal bands waving flares.

"Everyone be cool," says Deck into our earpieces. "I count forty-plus hostiles. Coordinate your fields of fire one more time. Bart and Bronco, field one; Boyd and Deac, field two; the Surgeon and Mac, you got the back. Paint them again, establish your fields of fire, and let them walk right up on us."

Libya had declared war against us tonight. This unprovoked attack displayed the same level of hatred and aggression they used to overthrow Gadaffi. But why? And then I laugh at myself. What difference does it make? We know they're here to finish what they started. Without a little air support from Uncle Sam, we won't survive the night.

PART TWO

TICKING TIME BOMB

Sixteen Years Later

CHAPTER 10

December 17, 2028
Chantilly, Virginia

WILD CURLS SPILL out from underneath the covers giving my daughter's Winnie and Eeyore pillowcase the Jackson Pollock look. She's exhausted after a full day of swimming. The sun won't be up for another hour, and I should really let her sleep in. But something wonderful happened overnight and I can't wait to share it with her.

A warm feeling of love makes me drowsy as I watch my eight-year-old baby girl sleep. I've already put in a hazardous four-mile run on icy roads this morning along with twenty minutes on the heavy bag and far too many squats and kicks for someone my age.

Abby is blissfully unaware of my madness. Her stuffed tiger is immobile, stuck in a suffocating headlock. The tiger was originally named Hobbes, from the *Calvin and Hobbes* comic, but my daughter renamed him the moment she freed him from the wrapping paper. She immediately announced to the room that her Tiger's name was *Pirate* and she was actually a girl. When I asked Abby how she knew that Pirate was a girl, she shook her head and laughed at me. That was Christmas day several years ago when we still lived in Roanoke, Virginia.

Pirate has lost some of her shine over the years, but not her status in the family. The white fur on her face and belly has a gray tinge to it now and is no longer fluffy from far too many journeys into the washing machine. The bright orange coat faded long ago, but even with Abby's menagerie of stuffed sweeties scattered around her bed, Pirate will always be numero uno.

I slide into bed watching my daughter's chest rise and fall. Out of nowhere, a tsunami of guilt sours my stomach. My lousy job is stealing all of my time from her. She needs her mom so much, and I'm stuck in security briefings hour after hour as the Federal Bureau of Investigation dukes it out with the Department of Homeland Security.

The outgoing President, Terrance B. Locke, put the call out to all of his followers to come to Washington D.C. in a couple of weeks for his national "Keep the Peace March." It's billed as an event to showcase the unity of the American people on the eighth anniversary of the deadly 2021 Capitol Riots. This generous invitation to the District of Columbia shocked the nation because it came shortly after it was determined that Locke lost his reelection bid by nearly twenty million votes.

Despite the President's kind gesture, Homeland Security is gathering intelligence that points to a second Capitol Insurrection. DHS insists that the President is planning a coup that's shaping up to be infinitely worse than what took place eight years ago. DHS reports that the Capitol Insurrection of 2021 was nothing more than a dry run and this time our democracy will shrivel up like a slug plopped into a saltshaker.

On the other side of the fence, the FBI leadership is applauding the President for his KPM—Keep the Peace March/Movement. The Bureau is accusing the Department of Homeland Security of manipulating small snippets of information and drawing all the wrong conclusions.

At this point, it's impossible to decipher who's telling the truth and why our Idiocracy can't just work together.

Nothing gets decided, hours tick by, another day is wasted while the feud between the DHS and FBI escalates. Meanwhile, I've missed another snuggle, another swim meet, and another dinner with Abby.

My guilt turns to tears—being a lousy mother is the only thing I seem to excel at anymore. I had a sick mother with a debilitating drug problem. I wonder if I'm any better at parenting than she was. I took my job on Capitol Hill to make a difference, fooling myself that I would be able to strike a balance between being a good mom and protecting the Speaker of the House.

I stroke Abby's arm and snuggle into her from behind, tears stinging my face. My little girl is like a warm bath, the greatest gift in my life. I need to rest my eyes for just a second.

"Good morning, ladies, today is not the day you want to sleep in," says a soft voice from somewhere beyond my dreams.

I blink for a moment realizing that I must have fallen asleep the second I took Abby into my arms. I've been out for more than ninety minutes. My little girl doesn't budge.

"Good morning, Gertie," I say without turning around, not ready to rouse Abby.

"I don't know about ya'll, but I'm starving this morning," she says warmly, stepping around the bed and pulling open the curtains.

Gertie Nunley has been looking out for me since I was a fifteen-year-old kid—after my father had died back in Colorado, and I fled the area fearing that I'd be put into the Colorado foster care program. Gertie was the first person I met when I got off the bus outside of Rocky Mount, Virginia. She's always been there to pick up the pieces no matter what life threw at me.

We never lost contact, even during my overseas adventures, as she likes to call them. Gertie was over the moon when I returned home and told her I was done with government service and enrolled at Virginia Tech. Even when I became a single mother, it was Gertie to the rescue. She moved in with my new baby and me and saved my life all over again.

She looks at me with that perfect smile on her round face. "Baby girl is just gonna fall out when she sees what's waiting for her outside."

My little princess spy, who's obviously been awake since Gertie came in, pipes up immediately. "What's waiting for me, Nanna?" she asks with obvious delight. "Let me up, Mom, I have to see."

She wriggles out of my arms, springs out of bed into the air, and plants a perfect landing that would make any gymnast envious. She nearly bursts into flames when she catches sight of the scene waiting for her outside.

"SNOW," she says with her voice near the breaking point.

She looks at me and then up to her nanna and says it again, in a sacred whisper, "Snow."

She gives her nanna a long, sweet hug, races around her, and begins flinging winter clothes out of her drawers chattering like a loquacious spider monkey. Ten minutes later, without so much as a sip of coffee, we're swarming the snowy hill in our backyard.

A tangle of curls with flecks of red peek out from beneath her floral hood. The incoming figure takes flight from three feet away. I brace for impact with the hopes of cushioning her landing as she crash-lands on top of my body. I let out an exaggerated "ooomf" upon impact and shower her exposed forehead with several kisses.

She squeals with delight and squirms away as we continue our assault on our mini mountain. Our Venom snow discs have carved a fast path for us that dead-end into an ominous patch of pine trees at the bottom of the hill.

"We'll go faster if we ride together, Mom," she says, eyeing the trees at the bottom of the hill. "It's not gonna be a soft landing. C'mon. Go, Mommy. Go!" she says flipping over and molding herself into my lap with the rounded black snow disc beneath me. I wrap my arms around her tightly. I raise my legs and gravity does the rest. We rocket down the slope with no regard for personal safety, parenting at its worst.

She shrieks with delight as the chilly wind nips at our faces. I push my boots out for stopping power as we crash into another pine tree that dumps a truckload of fresh snow onto on our heads in protest.

The snow was wet and heavy last night and our continued assault on the hill leaves more grass than powder in our wake. We shake the snow off of us like dogs emerging from an unwelcome bath.

I hear the back window open at the house. "Girls! Breakfast!" shouts Gertie. "Ya'll got ten minutes to come in and clean up."

"Awwww," bleats Abby.

"OK, Nanna," I call back. "We're on our way."

"Do we have to go in?" asks Abby. "Wasn't that the best? I'm hungry, are you? What do you think Nanna is making for breakfast? Can we come back out and do some more disc? Did you know Christmas is on Monday? Not tomorrow, but the next one. Can we sing at breakfast? I know the whole twelve days of Christmas song, all of it!"

The smell of bacon assails us before the garage door is halfway up.

"Hmmm," we say together. "Bacon."

We shed our coats, and I help Abby yank off her snow boots.

My phone is already buzzing before I get to the breakfast table. I intentionally keep it facedown and toss it onto the living room couch before returning to the breakfast table. Lucky I already got my snowy four-mile run in this morning. If Washington is burning down right now, it should be nothing but ashes by the time we finish breakfast.

I can feel the gravitational pull of my phone, daring me to ignore it with every bite of food. This is family time, not phone time, I scream silently at myself while Abbs delights us with wildly exaggerated accounts of our bravery and brushes with death on the snowy peaks behind our house.

My baby can spin a tale. I try to enjoy the moment, but I feel like the vibrating phone is pulsing hard enough to knock the house off of its foundation. Like all of idiot America, I'm addicted to my damn mobile device. I tell myself I'm not like other people who can't put the damn thing down, but I'm no different. Maybe I'm worse and the confirmation of that thought comes far too soon.

"Is everything OK, Mom?" Abby asks, interrupting her story.

You're such a jerk, Cora Walker. "Everything is perfect, my love. Aren't the biscuits sooo good?"

"It's your phone, isn't it?" she asks. Her bright hazel eyes are filled with all the love and understanding in the world. "You can get it. It's OK. Don't feel bad."

I nod my head sheepishly, feeling ten times worse than if she had been angry with me.

"I promise, my love. Whatever they want, it can wait." I can feel her eyes carefully appraising me as guilt sets fire to my forest. She has to be the most dialed-in eight-year-old on the planet.

She looks over at Gertie, who's sitting at the end of the table. "Nanna, may I be excused for a moment?"

Gertie lets out a soft chuckle. "Of course, baby girl."

She leaves the table and Gertie finds my eyes and whispers, "It's OK, Cora, she understands. You have a very important job."

I can't say anything. Everyone is covering for me. They're giving me a pass I don't deserve. And then comes the deathblow. Abby returns with my phone and places it on the table facedown next to my hand and says, "Up, please."

I pull her up onto my lap and squeeze tightly. The country can go to hell. I mean it this time. But the words ring hollow in my head and everyone at the table knows it.

CHAPTER 11

December 17, 2028
Washington, D.C.

THE DRIVE INTO D.C. is mercifully uneventful.

Even the 14th Street Bridge is giving me a break this dreary afternoon. There's nothing like a little snow to keep everyone off the streets in Washington, D.C. Five missed calls from the head of HSEMA, pronounced H-Seema, leads me to once again abandon my family and venture back into the swamp on another Sunday.

My eyes track the frozen pellets pinging off the windshield, spiraling away like albino popcorn kernels as I wonder for the twentieth time today how I ended up careening down this particular rabbit hole. The last ten years of my life have been a whirlwind since my departure from the Defense Department. I grabbed a Bachelor's from Virginia Tech, finished a grad degree at American University, and brought home the little girl who would change my world forever, my baby, Abby Walker.

I thought I was on the right track. I got my first real civilian job as a television reporter in Roanoke, Virginia, and spent nearly two years there reporting on violence, not becoming part of it. I had just been offered a television reporting job in Philadelphia when I was thrust back into government service to undertake a suicide mission I didn't want along the international border between Mexico and Texas.

After that fiasco was over, I planned to revive my journalism career, but the government came calling again and my convoluted career path brought me to Sarah Vasquez, the Speaker of the House. She was in desperate need of a competent press secretary who could also handle a diverse range of extracurricular activities. In short, they needed an educated, well-spoken attack dog with tactical experience and a heightened sense of combat awareness. I was recruited as part of a deep cover program known as the Political Protection Initiative, but I turned my loyalties directly to the Speaker of the House.

I crack the driver's-side window because the glass on the windshield is starting to fog up inside and glance at the light snow resting on top of the Jefferson Memorial. I remember how excited I was the morning after President-elect Drew Hayden had soundly defeated President Terrance Locke a few weeks ago.

*   *   *

There was a renewed sense of hope for the country, but it turned out to be a trick of the light. It was obvious now that the results of the election were irrelevant.

Baseless accusations of voter fraud permeated the airwaves and the nation's leadership made the egregious moral plunge from election denial straight into the depths of election subversion, once again fully discounting the will of the voting majority.

Locke's legions lined up behind him eager to topple the last domino of democracy. Not that there's much left at this point. President Locke is the architect of domestic immigration policies that have led to the death of more than a half million migrant workers.

Since his election in 2024, more than two million immigrants have become modern-day slaves, rounded up by the government's reformed Immigrations Customs Enforcement Strike Squads, known as "Ice Squads," and forced to work the fields all over midwestern and southern States.

Mass graves hold the bodies of those who've died of disease, malnutrition, and torture although the government denies all of it with the cry of "Alternative Facts" and "Fake News." Locke's administration policies have often been compared to the crimes of the Khmer Rouge purges that took place under Pol Pot, the Minister of Death, and Prime Minister of Cambodia during the 1970s.

President Locke's reign of terror swept over the nation like a second pandemic during the past four years. Incarceration levels in the United States tripled since he took office in 2024 leading to the construction of an additional 300 prisons across the country to try and keep up with the crush of new inmates.

More than 200 journalists who spoke out against Locke are in prison charged with civil crimes although none are facing any criminal charges. Another 1.6 million immigrants are being held captive in what Locke affectionately calls "Sanctuary Camps" scattered throughout the border states. The country now boasts north of 700 mass shootings per year and anyone foolish enough to express confusion about their sexual identity is forced into mandatory sexual rehabilitation clinics. African Americans aren't in the back of the bus yet, but restrictive voting measures have effectively squelched their voices across the country. The American flag looks the same but has morphed into the stars and bars of the Confederacy in four long years.

The only person who *wasn't* behind bars was the former President of the United States who tried to overturn the election results from the 2020 election. This was impressive because after the Capitol Riots, he was eventually convicted on two felony charges. He wound up with a suspended prison sentence and twenty years of probation. The conviction shattered his aura of invincibility and scattered his followers to the wind. For a man who bragged about winning so much, he was now derisively known as the nation's first "Probation President," but anyone in his or her right mind would take him back in a hot second. Russian and Chinese leaders shake their head in envy as the United States has shown the world what a true police state can really look like. Locke and his administration use deranged conspiracy theories to fire up the base and promote their unique brand of lawlessness, leaving the country mired in fear and desperation.

President "Terry" Locke is a world-class alpha-predator who's waged an overt burnt-earth campaign against the educated and middle class for more than twenty years now. The irony is that Locke is Ivy League educated with a law degree. He's cold and calculating and infinitely more cunning than the *Probation President* ever dreamed of being. He games the system with a vast array of master-class Orwellian skills. But when the economy tanked over the summer, so did any chance of him being reelected. But his party was locked in on how close they came to overturning the election results in 2021 and understood that this time, the will of the people could effectively be snuffed out once and for all.

*   *   *

My thoughts are interrupted as the car begins to slip and slide. Apparently DPW neglected to salt the roads this morning. Being a Colorado girl, I never understood why snow and ice present such a hardship for so many communities south of the Mason-Dixon Line.

As my car eases through the security gate at HSEMA, I give a long look at the armed security man who's waiting outside my car for me. I drain a large water bottle and check my reflection in the mirror. I look like a mom who could use a long vacation in the south of France.

HSEMA stands for the Homeland Security and Emergency Management Agency. It's Washington D.C.'s local branch of Homeland Security nestled about five miles away from the main federal office in the heart of the city. It all gets confusing in D.C.—let's just say HSEMA is D.C.'s local Homeland Security branch and the DHS in downtown is federal.

The head of HSEMA is Jonathan Dayton. He's forty-something with salt and pepper hair and an organized mind that's always planning five steps ahead. He's the guy who's been blowing up my phone all morning. Each message he left was identical. "Walker. Dayton. We need to meet." No impatience, no sighs, just the same message.

I appreciate a man who gets to the point.

The front desk people are very tight on security, but I'm starting to become a fixture in this office. The man behind the desk lights up when I walk through the door.

"Looks like my own personal ray of sunshine just walked through the door," says the security man with a wide, toothy grin. He's got close cropped hair, former military, and probably pushing past his retirement age.

"Afternoon, Damian," I say returning his smile.

"The big man told me not to chat you up this morning. Told me to rush you in past security," he says.

He activates a door release behind bulletproof glass. A swoosh of air and series of clicks activates a first door. I walk through and it closes behind me trapping me inside an enclosed full body scanner. I raise my hands. It's like going through TSA Security at the airport, except you don't get out until the person monitoring the scanner is satisfied you're not carrying or concealing any objects that might turn everyone inside into a charcoal briquette.

The second door opens and two armed guards zip me into Dayton's office and shut the door behind me. He looks up and motions me toward a chair with his left hand, his right hand cradling his office phone. He looks exhausted, probably been up for days. You really don't want to be the head of any government agency when the President of the United States is planning a second coup in your backyard.

"Yes," he says pausing to listen. "Yes. Confirmed. Five Eastern. Invite everyone and let's see who shows up." He places the receiver down and in the same breath says, "You checked your social media feed lately?"

"No, is another Kardashian auctioning off a pair of King Kanye's used boxers?"

"Even better, the President of the United States issued a threat against Congress last night. Told his followers and some select extremist groups to come to Washington in January and finally get the justice they've been looking for."

I've read it several times already and Dayton knows that, but I open my phone pulling up the feed for Terrance B. Locke, the outgoing Commander and Chief.

Twitter.

TERRANCE B. LOCKE
@realTerranceLocke

Get it in Gear and Get to Washington to support ME,
*   your President!!*
I need a million #PATRIOTS side by side for this march
Together we can KEEP THE PEACE on SUNDAY -
*   January, 6th, 2029!*
Patriots Only! #KPM #LockeAndLoad #SOA #GWM

#SOA is the hashtag for the *Sons of the Apocalypse* and #GWM is *God's White Militia*. Inviting extremist hate groups and domestic terrorists to a "Keep the Peace" march is about the same as welcoming vegans to the grand opening of a meatpacking plant, but I can't help but play devil's advocate.

"I don't see any mention of Congress at all," I say. "Maybe the President really is proposing a march for unity to show that he's not such a sore loser after all."

"Didn't that kind of talk land you in prison a few years ago?" he deadpans back to me.

"Your friends over at the Hoover Building insist that the President is inviting everyone to Washington to hold wreaths and sing Kumbaya," I say trying to milk a reaction out of Dayton.

He ignores me.

"The President's tweet went viral, and his followers are barking at the moon," says Dayton, rubbing his forehead slowly. "His backers are all over Twitter issuing threats and organizing 'field trips' to the District of Columbia."

"Already more than eighty thousand retweets and over two hundred thousand likes in just fourteen hours," I say. "The comments are nothing short of inspirational. Listen to this: 'Are you ready to fight for your Prez? You heard your President—*Locke and Load and hit the ROAD! Hey Patriots, TIME TO WAKE THE F*** UP!!! #FIGHT.'* No shortage of enthusiasm on their end."

He looks at me with his piercing green eyes. I never know what the hell this guy is thinking.

"I need you on this call at five," he says.

I just nod my head and picture my feeble phone call to baby girl in my head.

Me: "Abby, it's Mommy. I know it's a Sunday and we should be on the hill out back, but you know I'm not too good at the mom-thing. I'm gonna miss another dinner."

Abby: "I'm sorry, who is this?"

The sound of him banging the keys of his keyboard snaps me out of my funk.

"Who were you talking to on the phone when I came in?" I ask.

His left eyebrow twitches at my directness, but he answers directly. "James Talbot. He heads the Fusion Center out of Chicago."

Fusion Centers are state-run intelligence operations that fall under the authority of the Department of Homeland Security. Fusion Centers gather and share intelligence on threat-related information. They were created after the 9/11 terrorist attacks to coordinate and enhance the information flow between federal and state government officials. They have also been on the receiving end of a landslide of public criticism and under constant attack by the president.

"And what is he saying?" I ask.

"It's not what he's telling me, Walker, it's what everyone is telling us. Do you know how many Fusion Centers are operational in the United States including our major urban areas and domestic territories?"

"Umm, last I heard there were a hundred and two such branches up and running," I answer.

"One hundred and three. We opened a new one in Pennsylvania a month ago, and honestly, we almost never agree on everything. This is different. A brave new world. We have complete agreement and confirmation from ninety-six out of our one hundred and three branches that World War III is coming to the nation's capital in two weeks. Warning bells are blaring from Guam to Boston to San Francisco and it's time to hit the panic button."

"So what's the problem?" I ask. "Revoke travel to Washington D.C. Call in the National Guard and lock down the city."

Apparently that's not a great idea because he just keeps on speaking. It's not a state secret that men have a very hard time hearing the voice of a female, even if I happen to be sitting right in front of him. He must have to get it all off of his chest at once.

"All over the country, extremists aren't talking about *attacking* the Capitol this time—they're going to *occupy* it. These extremist groups are gathering weapons for the big event. Men with violent criminal histories are making plans to come to D.C. for what they're calling the 'Sledgehammer Check-In' event on January 6th," he says stopping to take a bite of a stale bagel, probably left over from breakfast.

He chews and takes another bite and continues with his mouth half full.

"An FBI informant in Seattle says Locke supporters have been smuggling guns into Washington D.C. for weeks so they can lay siege to the Capitol and then take over," he says. "He insists that the Patriots have vowed to get it right this time."

"For what purpose? Are they looking for lodging? What does anyone accomplish by taking over the Capitol?" I ask.

"It's a dog chasing the car scenario," he says throwing his hands up. "What would a dog do if it actually caught a car? They don't have a clue."

I don't buy it. Nothing was accomplished the first time, why go through the hassle all over again?

"These groups have identified five focal points around the country from where they plan to caravan to Washington to meet the day before the election certification on Saturday, Jan five. The frigging election certification is on a Sunday, so this is quickly morphing into a holiday weekend for the diehards."

He stands up unsteadily. "I need a goddamn cigarette."

"I agree with everything you said, Walker. Lock down the fucking city and restrict travel. There's just one tiny problem," he says. "The feds don't wanna hear it."

I wait for him to continue.

"Let's take a walk," he says moving toward the door. "I haven't moved from that desk since five this morning."

We squeeze out the back entrance. The door hasn't even closed before he's lighting a cigarette and sucking in the smoke with everything he has. I maneuver to stay upwind of his deadly fumes.

"The FBI, the National Guard, the Joint Chiefs, the Pentagon? None of them want to hear a goddamn word we're saying. We have more than twelve hundred confirmed tips. You can see it on a map. There's a hurricane crawling toward Washington D.C. and the federal government, under presidential orders, is going to let it play out all over again. Welcome back to 2021!"

CHAPTER 12

December 18, 2028
Oval Office, the White House, Washington, D.C.

TERRANCE LOCKE, the President of the United States, feels his blood pressure rising as his son and personal attorney jabber away on the couch from across his desk. He slides open his desk drawer and removes a bottle of cough syrup that is actually filled with bourbon. He tops off his coffee before sliding the bottle back into his desk and takes a long, healthy slug of presidential courage. He looks up from his phone and gives them each a dirty look. *Fucking retards*, he thinks, shaking his head. *They can't fix this mess. It's up to me. What a fuckin' surprise.*

He takes two more healthy swallows of his special coffee just as a text message flashes across his phone. He reads it slowly and then explodes.

"No wrongdoing? That son of a bitch," says the President. "Did you see him last night? Stupid son of a bitch."

The President's attorney, Jamie Cipriani, and his son, Artie Locke, exchange nervous looks. They obviously have no idea who the President is referring to or what just set him off. Welcome to Monday morning.

"There's no way I lost in Wisconsin; everybody knows that. You get him on the phone this morning. You hear me?" bellows the

President. "I'll fix his ass. How can he say there was no evidence of voter tampering in Wisconsin? Remind his worship that the Waupun Correctional Center is only an hour north of Madison."

"Uhhh, who would you like me to tell that to, Mr. President?" asks the attorney bracing for a stream of insults.

"Philip Fucking McKey, the idiot from Wisconsin. Look him up under 'D' for dummy!" snaps the President. He reaches back into his desk for another double shot of cough medicine.

"I'll get it set up," says the President's attorney, typing furiously into his phone.

The President takes a long pull on his special morning coffee, checks the message again, and clicks a link that takes him to a conservative website with an article about Philip McKey, the Secretary of State from Wisconsin, and the stolen election.

"You make sure he understands the gravity of his situation. Our enemies have been shredding ballots, apparently dead people voting. Dead! Tell Phil I'll make an example of him for the world to see."

"You're right, Dad, and there's more good news," says Artie Locke. "I've been talking to some people. Dad, we got this. We have complete control of every path to get you back into office." He stops and takes a breath. "Technically, you don't even have to have more electoral votes than Drew Hayden to win the election."

"I can't wait to hear this," says Locke, slamming his phone down on his desk. When no one speaks up, his temper flares. "Knock, knock. Anyone home?"

"Ahh, Jamie's got this one," Artie says, trying to look busy by diving into his phone.

"Mr. President, we've already initiated more than eighty lawsuits challenging the legitimacy of the election results. All in the swing states. We can actually stop the states from certifying their results," says Cipriani.

"They tried that bullshit last time. Half of them have already been thrown out of the goddamn courts," growls Locke. "Did you forget I was a trial attorney? We're spinning our wheels here."

No one would ever dare to challenge the fact to the President's face that he was an entertainment attorney and not a trial attorney.

"We only need one of these lawsuits to catch fire," says Cipriani nervously.

"The Supreme Court will absolutely rule in your favor. Once the first domino falls, the legal challenges will take hold in the other states. We just need one verdict in our favor. The majority of these legal challenges are being heard by at least twelve federal judges who were personally appointed by you, Mr. President."

"Ungrateful assholes who never miss a chance to pervert the law," snaps the President. "These people have a patchy history of letting the law interfere with what they are tasked to do. You can bend the law if you do it for the right reasons. I've proven this time and again."

"Forget the courts, Mr. President," says the President's stepdaughter and Chief of Staff, Cecilia Danforth. She's been standing silently in the corner of the Oval Office working on her phone. She looks up from the device for the first time in twenty minutes. "Not one of those verdicts will come back in our favor. Not one."

"I'm well aware of that, Cecilia. So please remind me, why are we wasting our goddamned time?" asks the President, his voice dripping with venom.

"Optics, Mr. President," says Danforth. "The people have to know you're fighting for them and for the country, and the press is salivating over every legal challenge. You're getting 24/7 coverage."

"That's exactly what I'm doing. I'm fighting for America. In the courts and in the streets," says the President, warming to the suggestion, puffing out his chest. "Hell, with my background I should have just joined the Supreme Court."

This comment causes the Oval Office to erupt into a flurry of comments effusing praise for the President: "Of course you don't, Mr. President. You saved us all, Mr. President. The American people are blessed to have you, Mr. President. America needs you now more than ever, Mr. President."

Satisfied with the response of his staff and mollified for the moment, the President presses on. "So when the courts fail us, what's next? Because, if you people can't figure it out quickly, I have people who can. The clock is ticking, people."

"Recounts," blurts out Artie. "You're right, Dad. Forget the goddamn courts, we need recounts!"

Cecilia Danforth goes back to her phone, lost in a crush of messages and already bored with the stream of dribble. Locke takes a long lascivious look at Cecilia Danforth and her long, perfectly sculpted legs. She makes him feel twenty years younger every time she smiles at him. The President knows it's only a matter of time before she gives him what she really wants and what he really needs.

"Cecilia, are you on these two morons?" the President asks his stepdaughter.

She's still busy typing on her phone and either ignores him or didn't actually hear him.

"We have the moral high ground, Mr. President," says Artie. "You've been pressing your message that the election was stolen and soon we'll have all the proof we need. Pennsylvania, Arizona, and Georgia are already conducting recounts and the evidence of voter fraud is everywhere. Everyone knows it."

"We don't need the moral high ground; we need the law on our side. You hear me, boy? Are you listening, Jamie? When I was a lawyer, we rolled up our sleeves and went to work. Get some proof. Dig some up, hire someone or bring them back from the fucking dead. I don't care how you do it. This election was a Greek tragedy, and no one is lifting a finger to do anything about it!"

"I've actually been working on another angle, Mr. President," says Danforth with a perfect flip of her hair.

"Looks like somebody bothered to show up this morning," says the President glaring at the men on his couch and shaking his head in disappointment.

The side door to the Oval Office opens, and a Secret Service agent hustles in, dutifully standing four feet to the right of the desk carrying a tray with a grease-stained bag, a fruit smoothie, and a 32-ounce Dr Pepper. The smell of greasy hash browns permeates the office and delights the most powerful man in the world.

"Looks great. Thanks, Ted."

The agent gently places the tray to the right of the President and then comes around the back of his chair and sets the fruit smoothie down to his left. He returns to his original position and waits for the President to inspect his meal composed of hash browns and two double sausage, egg & cheese sandwiches. The President finishes unpacking his breakfast and slides the empty bag to the corner of the desk and nods at the Service Agent who hustles over to remove the trash and leaves the office.

The President starts stuffing hash browns into his mouth and motions for his Chief of Staff to continue.

"I think we have a small window to throw out the election results in seven states," says Danforth, ignoring the chewing and grunting noises coming from her stepfather.

"We've hired multiple alternative electors in enough states to throw out almost 100 electoral votes. In that case, neither you nor Drew Hayden would have the 270 electoral votes needed to win.

If no one can reach 270 votes, the Congress, which we control, would be left to choose the next President of the United States."

The president's attorney gives her a sideways look. "I'm sorry, Miss Danforth. What is an alternative elector?"

"It doesn't matter what it is," snaps the President. "This is exactly what we need. Big thinking. If this doesn't work, we're going for the 'Big Bang,' in January. They'll never know what hit them. I'll show this country how to 'Keep the Peace' right before I force them to their knees to service me."

The room falls silent as the President takes in the shocked looks on their faces like a breath of fresh air. "Big Bang" is his code name for his "Keep the Peace March." He takes a huge bite out of his sandwich, leaning over the tray to catch some of the egg sliding off of his breakfast sausage.

"You people aren't getting the job done," he says with his mouth full of sausage. "They will have to pry this office out of my cold dead fingers and my flock will never allow that to happen!"

Cecilia looks at the President, still trying to decide how married he is to this plan. She wonders if it might be the alcohol talking, but with her stepfather, it's impossible to tell. She knows the nation can't afford another Capitol Riot or anything that even resembles it. The massacre at the Lincoln Memorial is anything but a distant memory. This provides an added incentive for her and everyone around the President to find an alternative path around his proclivity for violence.

"Mr. President," she says in a little girl voice, switching from the formal tone she usually reserves for him unless she really needs to make a point. His sexual desire for her knows no bounds and although she knows that he is a disgusting pig, she knows it can be an effective tool.

"Yes, Cecilia," he says, his voice strained.

"I think bringing your people to the District has a great deal of merit," she says cautiously.

He nods his head earnestly, always craving her approval.

"But," she says with emphasis. "You want to make sure this doesn't sound anything like the 2021 Capitol Riot. You know sometimes a soft-handed approach can be just as effective."

The president looks at her for a long moment with a momentary glimmer of understanding, gently sniffing the air like a drowsy beast. He appears ready to concede the point when the demon from the morning's libations breaches his seemingly calm exterior. His alcoholic rage rips him away from any semblance of sanity.

"You're kidding me, right? Who put you up to this? Plans are being made. Plans none of you know about. We're gonna put the goddamned opposition behind bars. There will be blood in the streets. By the time anyone figures out what I'm doing, it will be too late. We've been chipping away at due process for four years. Now, I make the laws! And anyone who stands in my way will be smothered by the full weight of the federal government!"

The three of them watch the President, praying for divine intervention or a place to hide until the bourbon front blows over.

"I can see it in your faces. What if the revolution fails? What if too many people die? It's time for civil war, people. I have perfected the art of demonization and turned the country against anyone who dares to oppose me," he says searching for the right words while spittle flies from his mouth.

"And the Sons of the Apocalypse and their white militias can burn their goddamn crosses on the Capitol lawn after they take care of business. My flock, my people, will force the cowards to bend the knee or they will die trying."

CHAPTER 13

December 19, 2028
Capitol Hill, Washington, D.C.

"CAN I GET you something to drink, Mizz Walker?" says the receptionist with an exaggerated Texas drawl.

"I'm fine, thank you," I say.

Her skirt is skintight leaving nothing to the imagination. If she sits down too quickly, the buttons on the back of her skirt would scatter like machine gun fire and punch holes in the office wall. "The Congressman will be with you in just a moment."

Maybe ya'll should try a little less perfume, I nearly blurt out loud as she walks past, fogging me in a trail of some ungodly Lone Star swamp flower perfume. I wave my hand trying to clear the air around my nose and politely thank her. It's a good thing Abby isn't with me, that little girl does not do well around women who bathe in perfume.

I look at the poster on the wall noting the smug look on the face of the Congressman. HERO OF BENGHAZI reads the bold letters perfectly centered over his head. I remember his campaign and the countless proclamations of his heroic deeds in Benghazi when he captured the 3rd Congressional District of Texas in a landslide in 2016. I wonder how the years since our adventures in North Africa have shaped him.

I thought about his constituency back in Plano, one of the most conservative districts in the entire state of Texas. The transformation of the Republican Party had been fast and furious since the nation propped Terrance Locke up as their Commander and Chief.

"Congressman Lobdell will see you now, Ms. Walker," calls the receptionist, breaking me away from my thoughts. "And have a very Merry Christmas."

"Cora Walker. Good Lord, it's good to see you," he says looking me in the eye and wrapping me up in a bear hug. "It's been a long time."

I'm not a big hugger. I'm sure he could tell, but it did not dissuade him in the least.

"Congressman Deacon Lobdell," I say letting out a long breath. "Is this one of those good meetings or one of those bad meetings? Considering who I work for, our current political ideologies don't exactly see eye-to-eye. President Locke lost the election and no amount of whining or coercion is going to keep him in office."

He laughs out loud with a delighted gleam in his eyes. "Always straight to the point, Bronco! I have *not* forgotten."

"Not forgotten my directness or the fact that President Rebab is finally on his way out?" I ask, my eyes boring into his.

He continues on as if I haven't spoken.

"I'm sorry it took me so long to reach out and extend a proper invitation," he says, shaking his head. "Politics is all about appearances."

"Well," I say. "Everyone wants a piece of the Hero of Benghazi. All these years later and you're still in high demand, Congressman. Your exploits took you all the way to the House of Representatives for the great state of Texas."

He scoffs at my statement.

"Mizz Walker—everyone who was there in North Africa . . ." He pauses, searching for the right words. "We all know what you did that night. I don't know how many times you saved my ass. You're one cool customer."

"Well, I can assure you, Congressman, I'm not that cool customer anymore, not even close," I say softly. "I'm not blowing through roadblocks and charging into shoot-outs. I'm an overworked mom with a nine-to-night job and I live in the burbs."

He laughs softly. "You're a warrior. Doesn't matter one little bit if you're changing diapers or selling nut-free brownies for the PTA before a school play. Whether you like it or not, you're wired differently. Stress is the cream in your coffee, Mizz Walker."

"You never had kids, so I can't really expect you to understand," I say. "It's not a criticism, it's just a fact of life. My reckless nature dried up when I started caring about someone more than myself."

"Ever thought about letting the cat out of the bag?" he says, searching my eyes. "You're a true American hero and a patriot. It's OK to let people know."

"If I wanted cheers and adulation, I would have joined the circus," I say.

"I haven't forgotten what you did for me," he says, staring deep into my eyes but somehow lost in the past. "How could I?"

We fall silent for a few minutes. And then he presses on. "That fiery roadblock you blew through still wakes me up at night. The next morning when we got to the Benina Airport, you just vanished. We thought someone grabbed you."

I can tell he's choked up and I give him another moment to reflect.

"How the hell did you get out of Benghazi?" he asks.

I think about my escape from Benghazi the morning after the attacks. I had a rug merchant on standby. He smuggled me out of the country into Algeria on a four-prop cargo plane.

"Caught a ride with a friend," I say, dismissing the question.

"OK," he says, tenting his fingers and still smiling. "Still classi-fied, I suppose? Pretty much your whole jacket is redacted. You're a daggone ghost. Hell, I'm a majority member of the HPSCI and you're entire history is still redacted. Doesn't even mention you being in North Africa at all."

"Maybe I was never there?" I say, scanning the documents on his desk. The HPSCI is the House Permanent Select Committee on Intelligence. "Aren't you also the Chair of the Counterterrorism, Counterintelligence, and Counterproliferation Subcommittee?"

His eyebrows go up in surprise and he chuckles again. "You're very well informed."

"Not exactly a state secret," I say.

Despite our shared adventures in Libya, he's a powerful and dangerous Congressman. His ideologies and fervent support of our unbalanced President directly contrast with everything I believe in. He's also an outspoken critic of my boss, who also hap-pens to be the Speaker of the House. We may have been on the same team in Benghazi, but this man and his party represent a clear and present danger to democracy.

"So, correct me if I'm wrong. But. You left whatever cloak and dagger branch of the government you worked for. Came back to Virginia and graduated from Virginia Tech. Then you earned a Master's degree in Communication from American University, had a baby, and became a local television reporter in Richmond, Virginia?"

"Roanoke, Virginia. Not Richmond," I correct him. "I guess you've been checking up on me as well."

He continues on, "Then the national spotlight fell on you when you were arrested on live television down in Nacogdoches, Texas. So maybe my question should be, how did a jailed television reporter become the Press Secretary for Sarah Vasquez, the Democratic Speaker of the House?"

I lock eyes with him, making him squirm slightly. "She offered me the job?"

"I understand that," he says. "But even a Master's Degree from American University and spending time in prison isn't what one would call a wealth of experience. That is unless some of your 'covert' skills played a role in the hiring process. Ever heard the name Josiah Timmons?"

I shrug my shoulders.

"No? The former United States Assistant Secretary of Defense for Global Strategic Affairs doesn't ring any bells?" he asks. "Hell, I heard you used to work for the man. I also heard he got you out of prison. I understand that he and the Speaker of the House have been friends for more than thirty years and that he recommended you for the job?"

I sit silently. From the brief time I spent with him back in 2012, Deacon Lobdell struck me as a competent warrior with a tendency to pontificate. Today he reminds me more of an enigmatic preacher straight off the pulpit from one of those southern megachurches where the teachings of Jesus are blended with the persecution of immigrants while members of the congregation fire off AR-15s while receiving the blessed sacrament.

He appraises me for another long moment and asks me point blank, "Who do you work for?"

"Congressman, I work for Speaker Vasquez," I say with final authority. This is far from the whole truth, but he is the last person on earth I'd choose to tell.

"Yes, indeedy," he says making a clicking noise with his mouth. "How do you feel about food trucks?"

"Congress—" I say, but he cuts me off.

"Deac," he says.

"Congressman, I don't have time for this today," I say, getting up and smoothing out my dress.

"I know you need to get out there runnin' and a gunnin', but I'm afraid I must insist, Bronco," he says. "This has to do with the election your party stole from the American people and the possible ramifications of those actions."

I nod my head calmly while my insides lurch. This newest "Keep the Peace" movement is going to give me an aneurysm.

"President Locke lost his reelection bid by more than twenty million votes," I say coolly as we climb into the back of his government-issued limousine. "He got stomped like a narc at a biker rally. Isn't that enough humiliation for one lifetime?"

We don't exchange words while the Congressman's driver crashes through a throng of puddles during the short drive to the line of food trucks crowded in front of the Washington Monument on 15th Street. We step out of the black SUV onto the curb and Lobdell tells the driver to head back to the office.

The smell of cooking meat triggers my hunger and I realize that lunch with Deacon Lobdell is now a foregone conclusion. He and I part company as we sidestep a series of puddles heading toward two different food trucks.

I get a large Greek gyro bound to destroy my stomach, but my need for comfort food outweighs any remnants of common sense. We reconnect and head off past the Washington Monument as I study his burrito packed with street meat. I envy his bravery.

"Is it just me," says Lobdell between bites. "Or has it rained every day in December? Except for that snow over the weekend."

"Another rigged election conspiracy theory?" I ask quietly after I swallow another huge chunk of lamb. I laugh derisively. "How many times can you guys pull this trick and expect a different result?"

"Those facts may or may not be in dispute, Mizz Walker," he says patiently, his mouth still half full. "But as you well know, it doesn't matter what's true, it's what the American people believe and what you can get them to believe."

I nod my head, still chewing. He's right, of course. The fifth horseman of the Apocalypse is "disinformation" and will ultimately be the final downfall of the American experiment. Locke's sycophants believe anything he says as long as he says it with conviction.

"I'm sure you've heard rumblings about the 'Keep the Peace March,' have you not?" he asks.

"I have," I say. I stop walking and look at him while two idiot joggers nearly collide with the Congressman. I watch them carefully. Something is off. They're not what they appear to be. One guy can't help but cast a look over his shoulder. They're not joggers, they're on the job, but who are they working for?

"Who're the goons?" I ask.

"You need to be careful," he says, dabbing the corner of his mouth with a napkin.

"What do you mean, *I need to be careful*?" I ask.

He starts walking again, scanning the area.

"I'm sorry to be the one to tell you. The election certification coming up in two weeks will never happen," he says, his voice devoid of any theater. "We learned a lot from that last dustup at the Capitol. It was just practice, and as President Locke has proven through the years, he learns from his mistakes."

I stop and look at the remainder of my sandwich, forgetting how it got there. I search for words, but nothing comes to mind. My mind goes momentarily blank and then his words return to me—*never going to take place.*

"*Never going to take place*?" I say, moving into his personal space. "Please enlighten me, *Hero of Benghazi*, how the hell is the election certification of our democratically elected president *not going to take place* this time?"

"Is that a note of veiled menace I detect in your voice?" he asks.

"I'm just waiting for you to enlighten me," I say, inching closer.

"Regardless of who did or did not win the election, President Locke has no intention of stepping aside and surrendering the office of the Presidency any time soon. Plans have been set in motion to keep him in place."

"That's treason," I say holding my breath for a few seconds. "Why tell me?"

"You're the hero of Benghazi, Walker. You tell me. You're the most capable person I've ever met, but you won't be equal to this task. There's too many of them and they're out for blood. The Speaker of the House and the Vice President will be swept away in the chaos and ya'll need to be prepared for that eventuality."

"You're an American," I bark, smacking him hard across the face before I can stop myself. "What in God's name happened to you?"

He made no attempt to block my hand as the right side of his face morphs into an angry bright red splotch.

"The *what's and the why's* are no longer relevant," he explains as if he's talking to a small child.

"Knowing me as you do, what makes you think I won't blow this whole thing up?" I ask.

"This operation has been sanctioned at the highest levels. The Pentagon, the National Guard, and the FBI have all been ordered to stand down, and they won't defy the president," he says. "They're gonna let this play out. Any delusions you have about stopping the rebellion will get you killed quicker than a bullet."

I laugh out loud, suddenly grasping the new reality of our nation. "Such is the price we pay for the life we lead, Congressman."

CHAPTER 14

December 19, 2028
The National Mall, Washington, D.C.

A DISTORTED REFLECTION of the Washington Monument stares back at me from a huge puddle lying in the middle of 17th Street. I study the image ruminating about our broken republic. To protect the Speaker, I must milk every drop of information I can from this man and find a way to solicit his aid. I should have thought of that before I cracked him in the face. I'm sure he's dying to help me out now.

"I'm really sorry I hit you," I offer lamely.

His deep voice rumbles as he laughs loudly. "I can see you're all broken up."

I throw my hands up, conceding the point.

"By the way, what the hell do I call you? Deac? Lobdell? Your worship?" I ask.

"I prefer *your highness*, but Deac is fine," he says completely unperturbed by my snark or the fact that I slapped his face. I'm such a child, such a complete lack of discipline on my part. The country is falling apart; this is exactly the time I need to stay calm and focused.

I can't help but wonder why he really told me about his pending rebellion. Perhaps some twisted sense of loyalty to me or something else. It's obvious that he's unsure about something and holding back. The sidewalk underneath us is cracked and unkempt, much like the neglected pond to our left. The smell coming from the dirty body of water nearly matches the stench coming from the swamp at 1600 Pennsylvania Avenue. We weave our way through a series of puddles and aquatic bird droppings littering the area they call the Constitution Gardens. The federal government must be saving money for the momentous revolt by cutting back on landscaping and upkeep. I stare absently at the line of weeping willow trees coming up on our left.

"Are you familiar with the Signers' Memorial?" I ask quietly.

He shakes his head *no*, but says nothing. Several Canadian Geese slip into the water, honking loudly to protest our intrusion. We come to a small wooden footbridge on our left leading the way to a tiny island.

"This is it, Congressman," I say. "The Signers' Memorial."

He looks down at the first stone and reads aloud, "A memorial to the fifty-six signers of the Declaration of Independence." He pauses for a moment. "Do you intend to give me a civics lesson, Mizz Walker, or ya'll gonna murder me and dump my body here for the wildlife to pick on?"

"All options are on the table."

This is perhaps one of the most neglected and forgotten monuments that lie between the Potomac River and the Capitol Building. It's in a central location, sandwiched between the Reflecting Pool of the Lincoln Memorial to the west and the Washington Monument.

Grass is pushing up through the cracks in the sidewalk and the geese and ducks have branded it as a community outhouse. The island itself would be exquisite with just a little love and care. I'm sure it will be stunning when the cherry blossoms pop in a few months. We walk tentatively over to the wooden planks, avoiding the nail heads coming up from the wood.

His smug smile isn't so pretty now with the red raised skin on his face where I smacked him. We walk down three steps that divide two groups of granite blocks, each one displaying the signature of one of the signers of the Declaration of Independence. There are twenty-eight inscribed stones on one side and twenty-eight on the other, each varying in size and arranged like crooked teeth with odd gaps. It gives the impression of a kid's block set that got dumped out but never got picked up.

The lack of symmetry always struck me as odd, like the island decided against braces at a young age, but that's not why I brought him here. I give him a moment to look around before guiding him over to John Hancock's oversized block.

"It looks like they moved all the stones here and forgot to finish the job," he says, studying the setup.

"See the giant block with John Hancock's signature on your left?" I ask.

"Kinda hard to miss." He chuckles, staring at it. "You'd think he was the most prominent person that signed the Declaration of Independence."

"Now look at the sad crooked tooth wedged underneath Hancock's stone to the left," I say.

"John Adams? You'd think the second presi-Dant of the United States would get just a little more respect than that?" His southern drawl is becoming more pronounced, and I get the impression that he's stalling.

"I agree. Actually, there aren't any monuments celebrating the life of John Adams anywhere in Washington D.C." I say studying the man in front of me.

"Should there be?" he asks with a coy smile.

"Do you know anything about the election of 1800?" I ask.

"No, ma'am, I don't," he says simply.

Despite his allegiance to Locke, I can't help but appreciate his honesty and straightforward manner.

"It was likely one of the most contentious elections in American history. Even worse than the mess we just went through. Two hostile colonial factions with polar opposite agendas spent every waking hour at each other's throats for more than a year," I say. "Each political party was committed to slandering the other and moving the country into a completely different direction."

"Worse than 2020?" he says giving me his full attention.

"The finer details don't really matter. Adams lost the presidency," I say. "But what Adams did next was astonishing."

It starts raining. Just like it had all month long. Not a gentle rain, but an onslaught of heavy precipitation mixed with snow.

"Perfect," I say. "Let's catch a cab."

He raises a hand to stop me.

"What did Adams do?" he asks.

I stop and face him as the rain grows heavier. If he doesn't mind getting wet, I don't.

"He set a precedent that endured until the 2020 election," I say. "He was the first president to peacefully transfer power to the party he fought so hard to defeat. The peaceful transfer of power to his sworn opposition. The tenet of our democracy that once made us so different from every other country on the planet."

He stares at me for a long moment, his thinning black hair matted down by the pelting rain.

"Don't let Locke destroy what's left of our democracy—our democracy, Deac. You were an Army Ranger. We fought side by side in North Africa, we spilled blood together." I stare at him feeling the desperation seep into my words.

"What do you want from me, Cora Walker?" he says, intensity flaring off of his face.

"Help me, Deac? For God's sakes, help me!" I plead with him.

He sits down on the signature of Elbridge Gerry and looks over at the crooked block with John Adams' name inscribed into it.

"Walker, I do not deny my culpability in President Locke's ascendance to power, but believe me when I tell you: I don't have the juice to derail the wheels that have been set into motion."

"Just feed me information, Deac. Everything you can. I may not be able to thwart the attack, but I need eyes and ears on these people," I say, feeling a glimmer of hope.

I see the joggers that almost ran into Congressman Lobdell fifteen minutes ago coming back down the sidewalk toward us.

"Who the hell are these clowns?" I ask, wishing I had taken my gun with me.

"They are Presidential Operatives," he says. "Roving teams that answer only to the President and a few select people of those closest to him."

"How come I've never heard of them, and why are you telling me?" I ask.

"The President calls them his S.S. They're a network of Locke loyalists sent to keep an eye on not only political opponents, but political allies like me as well."

"S.S. Like Hitler's Schutzstaffel? Hitler's secret hit squad?" I ask with a tinge of disbelief in my voice.

"I can attest to the fact that our President is a man who has never felt the burden of morality or subtlety."

"And yet you serve him?" I ask watching the joggers pass by.

"I serve at the pleasure of the voters in the great state of Texas, Mizz Walker," he said.

"I'm asking you to serve them by protecting democracy," I say, feeling the rain finally reaching my scalp after saturating my thick hair. "You think toppling the government is the answer to anything?" I ask.

He's silent for a long moment like he's grappling with a difficult decision. We're drenched. But it's only rain and clearly neither one of us has enough sense to seek shelter. And even if these Presidential Operatives have listening devices or parabolic microphones set up around us, the rain is drowning out any chance of them listening in on our conversation.

"Of course it's not," he says simply. "Why in the world do you think I brought you to my office in the first place?"

I gasp. Momentarily stunned by what he just said to me.

"If the President is successful in overthrowing the House of Representatives, of which I am a member, it will have catastrophic results. But that's exactly why I can't openly rebel."

"You want me to help you rebel against the president?" I ask, reeling from this turn of events.

"Well, I was hoping you'd catch on a little quicker, Mizz Walker," he says in his deep southern drawl. "One can not inflict change until he first grasps the reins of power."

"And do you have your eyes on the throne?" I ask

"I don't, but now you know why I reached out to you. I need your help. And I need someone quietly working in the shadows. Someone who's willing to take on the whole dang world. We have an impossible task in front of us, and time is not on our side. So let's get out of this damn rain and get plannin'. We can't do anybody any good if we're both dying of pneumonia."

CHAPTER 15

December 19, 2028
The National Mall, Washington D.C.

"Here they come, Congressman," I say. The two men finally abandon their charade of jogging in a downpour. They break into a sprint and head straight for us. They take up positions at the end of the footbridge. Their approach is uncoordinated.

"I don't suppose you have a weapon?"

"I've watched you work before. You tellin' me you need a gun for those two?" he scoffs, gesturing toward the men twenty feet away at the foot of the bridge.

They're blocking our path off of the island. The one on the left is clean-shaven, 6'2", 230, with broad shoulders. He's got about three inches on me. There's a vein pulsing at the base of his thick neck. The guy on the right isn't as pretty. The cold rain accentuates his receding hairline, matting down his mousy-brown hair. His nervous eyes dart back and forth.

"Gentlemen," announces Congressman Lobdell. "I'm afraid you missed lunch. Is there a particular signature ya'll are looking for out here on this rainy day?"

I start walking forward. The sound of the rain pelting the water is all around us, and I'm not into waiting here on the island for the cherry blossoms to bloom. The first man hesitates, perhaps not comprehending or believing that a woman would dare to challenge him face-to-face.

"Ma'am, stop right there," he barks.

Too late, he tries to reach in his jacket when I seize his wrist and bend it back at an impossible angle before ripping the Glock 19 out of his belly holster. I pivot right, locking a leg behind him and using his weight to propel him off the bridge. He crashes into the frigid murky water to my left. I step back flipping the safety off and training the weapon on his partner in one smooth motion. I give him two short whistles and shake my head no at him, communicating that this fight is already over and his next decision might very well adversely impact his well-being.

"Ease your piece out, sport," I instruct calmly.

Either the calm in my voice or the frigid rain causes him to shake. His furious partner is immersed in the muck trying to right himself.

"Butt first. Ease it out with two fingers. Slowly," I say keeping the weapon leveled at his center mass. "Toss it into the water."

He complies with my request. "Zip ties or cuffs?" I ask.

"Cuffs," he says.

"You know the drill. On your knees. Interlock your fingers over your head."

The second he's on his knees I whirl around, pointing the Glock at the man still thrashing in the water. We lock eyes. "Don't move." I thought about saying "freeze" but that would be cruel.

He struggles to his feet or knees, I can't tell how deep the water is, but nods his head before yelling, "Goddamnit!"

My eyes are back on the man in front of me.

I call over my shoulder without looking at the man in the water again. He's knee deep in silt, bird droppings, and mud. He's can't go anywhere fast. I steal a glimpse at Deac who's banging away on his phone. "Are you watching him, Congressman?"

He nods his head without looking up and continues to type.

"Ease your cuffs out," I instruct. "Slowly. Stay on your knees."

He eases his handcuffs out awkwardly.

"Cuff your right wrist and kiss the deck face-first. Quickly, please."

I hop on top of him driving my knee between his shoulder blades and cuffing his wrist to the other one, leaving him face-down on the wooden planks. I pat him down for a backup piece, but he's clean.

The Congressman walks past me, stepping over the handcuffed man. "We don't have much time," he says. "I see you still possess a flair for the dramatic, Mizz Walker."

I face the muddy pond and eject the magazine and bullet in the chamber and tomahawk the gun high in the air, watching it land in the water. The splash disturbs a mallard couple that had been on the opposite shore enjoying the show. I watch the concentric rings ripple in the pond. I'm unable to suppress a smile. I flipped a man into the pond, cuffed his partner on the footbridge, and the Congressman couldn't be troubled to look up from his phone. I don't know what the hell his game is, but he's a cool customer.

"We're about to be picked up," he says smoothly. "I'm going to implicate you as my mole. Any thoughts on that?"

"I'll deny it down the line of course. But we need to make one thing clear, Deac."

"I'm all ears."

"Why the hell should I believe you? Why should I believe anything you say to me?" I say looking him straight in the eye.

"I would be sue-preemly disappointed if you did," he says.

"If you cross me on this, hurt Speaker Vasquez, or use me as a tool for this friggin' revolt against the American people, you'll be the trailer park. I'll be the tornado. And nothing will stop me. They'll find your ass facedown in this pond."

We lock eyes for a long moment and then a small smile creases his features.

"That's exactly why you're the person for the job, Cora Walker," he says simply. "You need some background before we're picked up."

"I don't understand."

"Did you see the body cams on the men you were dancing with?" he asks.

I shake my head no.

"Well, you just introduced yourself to the President and his people as a press secretary with maybe a little something extra in the tank," he says. "I created a file on you two months ago, identifying you as someone I've been covertly working with."

Two months? That was before the election. I didn't even agree to meet this man until two weeks ago.

"I've been working on various versions of a plan since the summer," he says. "Plans to subvert the election were already underway. The idea that my party would be willing to ignore the voting process for a second time and select their own president shook me to my core."

"I haven't actually agreed to work with you at all," I say, stupidly realizing that I already work for him, whether I decide to trust him or not.

"Any *real-world* communication between us," he says, continuing on as if I hadn't spoken, "cannot be communicated electronically—no emails, no texts unless we're trying to lead someone astray. Everything is burn after reading. But for now, we're about to be taken away. I'm sorry. I know I've put you in an impossible situation, but we live in a police state now. A second revolution is coming to the Capitol, whether we like it or not."

He leads me through the muddy grass toward Constitution Avenue where three black government Suburbans sit idling on the sidewalk waiting for us. Six men pour out of the vehicle shuffling the Congressman and me into two different vehicles.

Twenty minutes later I'm sitting in an ornate conference room with a towel and a cup of coffee. I use the towel to pat down my hair but ignore the cup of coffee. I won't ingest anything I didn't see them make. I'm not interested in drugging myself.

The door opens and an attractive woman enters. She has long flowing blonde hair and is sporting an expensive long cream-colored dress with a solid black triangle that starts at her right hip and expands all the way down to the hem. I recognize her instantly as the President's Chief of Staff and stepdaughter. And if you believe the D.C. rumor mill, she's intimately involved with the Commander and Chief. I don't bother getting up.

"Cora Walker, I'm Cecilia Danforth," she says brightly. "I see you haven't touched your coffee. Can I offer you something else? You must be freezing."

"I'm fine, ma'am, thank you for your concern," I say evenly.

"Cecilia, please," she says, appraising me carefully.

I say nothing, studying her with great interest.

"I thought we should finally meet," she says after a moment of silence. She's obviously around men all day that can't or won't shut up.

"How long have you known Congressman Lobdell?" she asks, cutting ahead past any further attempt at pleasantries.

"I'm not at liberty to say," I answer.

She nods her head, staring at me with open curiosity.

"Were you or have you ever been a government operative?"

I remain silent.

"Involved in covert intelligence and counterintelligence operations overseas? Afghanistan? Libya? Iraq?"

I stare back.

"Were you or were you not with Congressman Deacon Lobdell in 2012 in the city of Benghazi, Libya?"

"I am unaware of any such activity or operation that you are referring to," I say looking directly into her eyes.

"You're the Press Secretary for the Speaker of the House and you're not aware of Congressman Lobdell's contributions in Benghazi in 2012?" she says mockingly.

I'll give her credit. She doesn't seem even mildly put out by my shutdown. Despite my intense dislike for everything she represents, I find myself warming to her. Which is a problem. She's very likable and many times more dangerous than someone pointing a gun in my face.

"Where did you receive your training?" she asks, changing the subject with ease.

"Ma'am?" I ask.

"Well," she says pausing dramatically, like a defense attorney readying for the kill. "You disarmed two government agents in a local park and threw them into a duck pond." She's unable to suppress a chuckle.

"Ma'am, I do recall one gentleman losing his footing and falling into a pond," I say seriously. "I believe the Congressman tried to assist him."

"Mizz Walker, you are in a unique situation where I can either help you or hurt you. I'd really prefer to help you."

"Ma'am. Am I being held by the state or am I free to go?" I ask.

"You appear to be a stunningly resourceful woman, but a really lousy conversationalist," she says shaking her head. "I need to know what you discussed with the Congressman before you were approached by the agents."

We hold each other's eyes for a long moment.

"I'm afraid you'll have to ask him," I say.

At this point, most men would either be pulling their hair out or trying to yank out my fingernails or both. This woman is smooth and unperturbed. And above all other virtues, I appreciate calm in the face of fire.

"I believe myself to be a gifted student in the nuances of human behavior," she says. "But you? Honestly, I'm not sure where to begin. Two men cornered you on a footbridge. I watched you. You wrinkled your nose, walked up to the closest man, and tossed him into the water like you were turning over the laundry."

Now there's a fascinating stereotype. Women and laundry.

"So, what gives you the confidence to walk up to a pair of government operatives and confront them the way you did?" Pressing this line of questioning, she continues, "I guess what I'm trying to say, is you don't really fit the mold of any press secretary I've ever heard of."

"Don't I?"

"Guess what I did find in your service jacket?" she asks with a gleam in her eye. "Aren't you a little curious?"

She's certainly dying to share this nugget with me.

"It appears that you're the only female to ever win the Interservice Pistol Championship. Eighty-five entrants from all the branches of the armed services." She pauses for effect. "You were the only female and you swept the field."

She looks at me expectantly. "I'm sorry, was there a question in that statement?" I say.

She shows me a photo I've never seen before. Interesting that it's stamped "classified." I look at the smile on my face from 2008. Jesus, I'm so young. I think about my belief systems from that time period and wonder how the last twenty years and the current political landscape has changed me.

"Why are you working with Representative Lobdell?" she asks. "I need to know."

"I can't help you," I say.

"You can't or you won't?" she asks.

"May I ask you a question, Miss Danforth?" I ask.

Her poker face shows a mini crack in the armor but lasts for less than a second before she nods congenially.

"Your pedigree and education are beyond reproach," I say, searching for the right words. "I obviously can't ignore the fact that your stepdad is the President, but how do you align yourself with a party that throws immigrants into labor camps, allows teens to carry AR-15s, and demands complete control over a woman's body?"

She smiles broadly, and pauses before answering.

"Come ask me when *your* stepfather becomes the most powerful man in the world."

CHAPTER 16

December 21, 2028
Capitol Hill, Washington, D.C.

A SERIES OF faraway vibrations yank me out of a dream as I snatch up the offending device.

"Walker?"

My brain tries to orient itself, but I know the voice. It's the Watch Commander of the Capitol Police Force, Reginald Devereux.

"Morning, Commander," I say trying to sound like I have a pulse.

"You never logged out of the complex last night. Is the Speaker's Press Secretary pulling another all-nighter?"

"Still at my desk, playing online poker with a six-pack of PBR," I say. Jesus, it's almost four in the morning. I was still going strong with this stack of intelligence briefings at two thirty. I must be getting old.

"You never had a beer in your life," he says, laughing out loud. "Could be why you're wound so tight."

I almost ignore the jibe. "What can I say, I'm a free spirit and apparently so are you. Calling a girl at three forty-four in the morning might get people talking."

"Can you be out back in ten? Thought we could grab some breakfast," he says.

"Make it fifteen," I say ending the connection.

I look in the mirror, less than impressed with the woman staring back at me. I've aged five years in the past two weeks. I need to
finish my Christmas shopping, convince the federal government
to defend the United States Capitol, and wrap up three press
releases to email out before noon. Piece of cake!

I peel off my blouse, giving it a sniff. That can be burned. I grab
deodorant from my desk drawer and workout clothes from the
filing cabinet. I pin my hair back into a tight bun, put on a little
makeup, and pull on a Broncos baseball cap. I check the mirror
one last time—that's as good as it's going to get this morning.

I bound down the Capitol steps where a Dodge Charger flashes
its lights across the street. I hop in the car and it's moving before
the door is fully closed. I laugh out loud. "Hello, are you sixteen
years old?"

"Life offers only a few pleasures, and one of mine is driving the
beast," he says flipping an illegal U-turn and racing toward 395
South.

"Virginia?" I ask.

"Bob and Edith's on Columbia Pike in L.A. I made it there
once in seven minutes," he says, smiling.

"*L.A.*?" I ask.

"Lower Arlington. I grew up there," he says.

We are Virginia Tech graduates from two different eras. He was
a Hokie linebacker in the 1980s with hopes of playing in the NFL.
But a leg injury pushed him toward a career in the military. We
talk a little Hokies football and basketball, but we both have more
pressing matters on our minds. We roll up just a few minutes later
and the diner has at least four tables occupied. That's a booming
business for four in the morning.

"I've been coming here since the early seventies. Biscuits and gravy
and a huge plate of scrapple," he says smiling. "It's the simple things."

As soon as we place our orders, he gets down to business.

"What are you hearing about the Keep the Peace March?" he asks, rotating his plate.

"Jesus, Dev, what am I not hearing? Ask me a direct question; I'll give you a direct answer. I've been up to my eyeballs in this nightmare for weeks. I've had three briefings with HSEMA in the past five days and I'll tell you this—Fusion Centers are saying the revolutionaries are going to get it right this time. In twenty years, they've never seen such a tide of evidence that points to a specific time and a specific place for a riot. In less than two weeks, the worst humanity has to offer plans to seize the Capitol Building and hold everyone inside captive. This isn't an insurrection; it's an occupation."

He nods his head and temples his fingers.

"Fifteen hundred confirmed reports of various people descending on D.C. and promising violence and a forced occupation," I add. "All courtesy of the Commander and Chief himself."

"Since it's the president and his den of serpents, I assume that we'll be on our own?" he asks.

I spread my hands. "The Speaker has been working diligently to enlist help from the FBI, the federal DHS, the Joint Chiefs of Staff, and even the Pentagon. We have the head of the DHS coming in to see the Speaker this afternoon, but no one except the local authorities seems very concerned. Especially the FBI."

"How so?"

"It's the FBI leadership," I say disgustedly. "The President has them under his thumb, and they would rather kiss the ring than rock the boat. Even if it means a stack of body bags rolling down the Capitol steps while the world is watching."

A massive western omelette appears in front of my face with rye toast, but our discussion has turned my hunger back into fatigue.

I use my fork to slide a chunk of yellow pepper back into the fold of the eggs.

We sit in silence for a moment, staring at our plates of food. He eyes his home fries that are under assault from the gravy pooling off of the biscuits on his plate.

"That's not our only problem," he says just above a whisper.

I look at him, curiosity blooming inside of me. "Come again?"

"Congressmen are giving guided tours of the Capitol again, but this time they're not bothering to hide it. I got veterans with more than ten years on the job. They know what's coming and they don't want a repeat of 2021. More than thirty have quit and more than a hundred have requested emergency time off for the first week in January," he says.

"So who's touring the building?" I ask.

"Bad people. Paramilitary, ex-military, ex-police, God knows who else. For all I know, they're using mercs," he says forking a generous portion of greasy potatoes into his mouth.

"*Mercs?*" Two people barge into the restaurant laughing loudly, but they're just college kids.

"One of their key focal points is your boss's office and the other is the Vice President's chambers. Speaker Sarah Vasquez can definitely expect condition red when this goes down. I'm trying to authorize the use of deadly force this time."

I nod my head. Gets better and better.

"I'm not one to tell a press secretary or anyone else how to do their job, but you shouldn't be within miles of this place when the hordes arrive," he says sawing a biscuit in half and shoving it into mouth.

"Kind of puts a damper on the holidays," I say trying to mask my swirling emotions as my temper gnaws its way deep inside of me.

"President Terry and his minions are pulling the plug. Grab your little girl, grab your granny, and get the hell outta here, Walker. Get as far from D.C. as you can. Go back to Blacksburg. Anywhere, just go."

I feel dumbstruck and numb. Two words that were never part of who I was before. This is the third person that's tried to run me out of the Capitol and leave the Speaker to fend for herself. I have a pretty amazing life. I'm set financially. Why throw away everything I've worked so hard for? Of course, I already know the answer. Doing the right thing is a bitch, always has been.

"You know the old saying about what to do when your boat is surrounded by alligators?" I say, suddenly smiling at the Commander.

"Shoot the alligator closest to the boat?" he says.

"Bingo. I'm a modern-day Don Quixote," I say out loud. "Ready to battle the windmills of sickness and disinformation that's infected every pore of our floundering country."

"You're an optimist," he says shaking his head. "It'll be a miracle if either one of us gets out of that building alive."

"I'll tell you this, I'll take more than a few with me."

Dev's revelation cements the gathering disorder of my life. I live in a crumbling wall of hope, content to meander in the delusion that justice might actually prevail. But this is no time for an internal civics debate. People are counting on me. Besides, nothing is set in stone.

The feds, the military, or maybe the National Guard could actually decide that America and our principles are worth fighting for now. No one wants a repeat of January 6th except the President. Maybe someone will poison Locke in his sleep and end this dystopian disaster.

I sneak into the Speaker's Chambers ninety minutes later, hoping I had beaten the Speaker back to the office, but the smell of grapefruit bathes my senses as soon as I open the door. The Speaker must have just applied her Halfeti perfume. It's a fragrance I could never pull off, but I find the citrusy cocktail exhilarating.

I worry about coming into the office with my inappropriate workout outfit. The Democratic Speaker of the House, Sarah Vasquez, gives me a wide smile as I try to skirt past her office decked out in my workout clothes. My Lululemons are skintight. I give the Speaker the same guilty look Abby gives me when she's up to no good.

"Cora," she calls out pleasantly. "We're expecting the head of the Department of Homeland Security sometime around seven this morning."

I make an immediate U-turn and stick my head into her office.

"Good morning," I say feeling my cheeks color. "If you can arrange it, I really need to speak to you before you meet with the DHS."

She answers my question with a question. "Did you stay here all night?"

"Ahhhh," I stammer.

"After I ordered you to go home and be with your daughter?"

"I'm sorry, ma'am," I say honestly. "It won't happen again."

"Don't you *ma'am* me, Cora Walker." She fixes me with a hard motherly stare. "Christmas is Monday, and if you're in this office past four this evening, I'll have you escorted out of the office in chains. Questions?"

"Understood," I say. "There's something else. I have critical intelligence I need to share with you as soon as possible."

She looks at me pointedly, but then her features soften. "How long do you need, Cora?"

"I'm not sure, but this information can't wait," I say feeling my nerves coming apart.

"Is this about your cloak and dagger meeting with the Hero of Benghazi?" she asks knowingly. Nothing gets past this woman. Mind like a steel trap. She waves me in asking that I close the door behind her. I spend the next twenty minutes briefing her on my meeting with Lobdell yesterday afternoon.

She listens patiently and takes a few notes while I give her my full assessment. I leave nothing out.

She gives me quick recap to make sure she has the story straight so far.

"You took the Congressman to the Signer's Memorial, tossed two of the President's men into a duck pond, and then you were taken into custody to meet with the President's Chief of Staff, Cecilia Danforth?"

"Yes, ma'am," I say. "Actually, I only threw one of them in the water."

She shakes her head with an *of course you did* smile. "You fought side by side with Lobdell in Benghazi, didn't you?"

I nod my head.

"Do you trust him?"

"No, ma'am, not yet. Maybe never."

"Do you know what he wants from you?" she asks.

"Not exactly," I admit. "He says the President's people plan to take over the building and hold it. No government agency is coming to the rescue. The President made sure of that."

"I thought the Congressman wanted to help you stop the insurrection?" she says.

"No, he wants my direct help—only if the occupation is successful and Congress fails to certify the election results," I say. "If the attackers fail and Congress is able to certify President-elect Hayden, we will have no further business or contact on the matter."

"But Lobdell is a staunch conservative from Texas and an ardent supporter of the President. What would be his motivation to block the President from seizing power for a second term?" she asks.

We sit in silence for a long moment.

"My gut tells me that he is a deeply moral man who bears true faith and allegiance to the Constitution," I say, choking up a bit. "But I've been fooled before."

"I'm inclined to trust your instincts, Cora," she says, standing up and walking over to her window. "Once again, no one in any leadership position has shown the courage to defy the President and do his or her job. Any agency head that dares to uphold their oath and defend the Constitution might end up before a firing squad."

CHAPTER 17

December 21, 2028
Capitol Hill, Washington, D.C.

"AS YOU ARE well aware, I have spent a great deal of time and effort trying to educate you on the finer points of subtlety. You're a brilliant woman and a formidable strategist, but your greatest strength is also your greatest weakness—you do not suffer fools. Despite your wealth of attributes, let's just say you're not a top-flight poker player. However, I think I've been mistaken," she says pointedly.

I hold my breath wondering what I did this time. My mind scrolls through my interactions during the past week and I come up empty, but I don't sit up at night thinking about the delicate lilies that might have wilted under my glare.

"Just for this morning's meeting with the FBI and only for this morning's meeting, I'm going to let you break free from the chains of society," she says looking at me mischievously.

"Madame Speaker?" I have zero idea what she's talking about.

"Have a go at Deputy Director Carolina Stokes. Tell the FBI what you really think. They've collected reams of evidence about the Capitol takeover and they're not going to lift a finger. I've tried everything I can to get them to do their job and protect the integrity of our nation. All of my pleas have fallen on deaf ears."

"Wait," I ask, warming to the suggestion, and then I shake my head. "Honestly, Madame Speaker, how far do you want me to go?"

"Shoot for the stars and stick to the facts," she says, appraising me carefully.

"Is this a good cop, bad cop routine?" I ask.

"I don't give a damn to be honest. If we don't make it out of this building on January 6th, so be it. But if we don't come out, I want the world to know the FBI had all the information they needed and did *nothing* with it."

"You're going to record the meeting, aren't you?" I ask.

She smiles at me in approval.

"Cora, contrary to what Clinton Sinclair and the boy's club over there at the FBI Headquarters believe, the agency was never meant to be an extension of the executive branch. Their job has never been to do the President's bidding. If they let this insurrection play out like they obviously did in 2021, the world should know how they failed the American people when they needed them the most."

Fifteen minutes later, Deputy Director Carolina Stokes and her staff stride into the conference room like conquering heroes. Letting me off the leash is probably an unforced error on the Speaker's part, but I live by the edict, "let the bridges I burn light my way!"

Carolina Stokes is obviously OCD. She spends almost an entire minute arranging pens, her iPad, and an ominous black binder emblazoned with the FBI logo. I'm surprised she doesn't use a level and compass to make sure everything is perfectly synchronized and pointing due north.

"Speaker Vasquez, thank you for having us," says Stokes after the introductions are made and adding a few corrections to her personal space.

"The pleasure is all mine, Deputy Director," she says warmly.

Stokes does a brief summation of the threats the FBI has received over the past week. She downplays every plausible threat and lies right to our faces, but that's to be expected inside the Beltway. HSEMA and a deeply placed FBI analyst have been feeding me intel since the election and it paints an apocalyptic picture of a second Capitol Revolt, not this whitewashed Keep the Peace compost Stokes is force-feeding us.

"Excuse me, Deputy Director," I say respectfully. "I've been collaborating with our nationwide network of Fusion Centers and their findings do not quite align with what you're telling us. As a matter of fact, according to HSEMA, FBI field agents and informants have submitted no less than 250 pieces of evidence suggesting that right-wing extremist groups are smuggling weapons into Washington D.C. for what some are calling the 'occupation' on January 6th, which, as I'm sure you know, is a little more than one week from today.

"I have a reference guide to help each one of us before I turn your attention to the screen behind me," I say, standing up with a little stack of red books. I make my way through the room and lay a little red book down to the right of each one of them.

"Do I get one, Miss Walker?" asks the Deputy Director of the FBI.

"Oh, sorry, ma'am. Here you go." I rush the last little red book over to her.

She scans the title and looks back at me quizzically.

"It's just a pocket copy of the Constitution of the United States of America," I say with a wink and a smile. "It should come in handy while we watch the following presentation. Jimmy, can you dim the lights?"

The room goes dark, and before Stokes can raise any objections, I dive right in. "This post was submitted by the FBI Washington field office the day after Christmas. I believe you personally shared it with the D.C. Police Department but somehow forgot to share it with us here at the Capitol Building this morning.

"Let me read it to you: '*The time is now, Patriots. Get yourself armed and be there on January 6th. Let's remind Congress who they work for.*'"

I click the projector again and another image appears: "'*If you're going to D.C., record everything so the media can't spread their evil lies. LOCKE AND LOAD! FOUR MORE YEARS!*'"

I click again. "'*We still have the power! Our President is challenging you to answer the call. Time to take hostages! Time to set things RIGHT! Stop the goddamn STEAL!!!!*'"

And this one is really my favorite.

"'*Drop a couple cops into the blender and watch the piggies scatter. We're coming for you, Sarah. How does JAN 6 SOUND!!!!*'"

I click through twenty more at a high rate of speed, just long enough for them to read each slide.

"Lights, Jimmy. I can go on and on and on and on. I have 124 slides if you'd care to review them. But heck, you've seen them all already because the information was gathered by your agency. Your field agents and informants from all over the country collected this data in just the last week. I assume you're in communication with your field offices in St. Louis, Columbia, Toledo, Tallahassee, and Scranton, Pennsylvania?"

When she doesn't answer, I press on.

"So, Deputy Director, perhaps you want to share with us why the FBI is ignoring the fact that those of us who work at the Capitol can expect to be attacked, overrun, and possibly executed next week to celebrate the Election Certification?"

"Well, you see—" says Stokes when Speaker Vasquez cuts her off.

"I see fine, Deputy Director Stokes," says Vasquez, freezing the room with the ice in her voice. "It's obviously your agency that can't *see*. Answer the question: *Why* is the Bureau ignoring all of this evidence? *Why* are you pushing this *Keep the Peace* gibberish? Your own people gathered this evidence. *What's* the problem?"

"The First Amendment," blurts out Stokes. "This has to do with Freedom of Speech!"

I let out a large artificial cough. It's all I can do to stop myself from picking up this bureaucrat and bouncing her down the Capitol steps.

"I'm sorry," I say composing myself. "Please, Deputy Director, you were saying something about Freedom of Speech? Please enlighten us."

"I don't like your tone," she snaps at me.

"Oh, I'm terribly sorry. *Freedom of Speech?* Is that what you said?" I ask with a condescending smile.

"It's complicated," Stokes says looking me straight in the eye.

"Threatening violence is *not* protected under the First Amendment. Are you familiar with *Dennis v. the United States*, Ms. Stokes?" I ask, my temper simmering just beneath the surface.

She looks away and says, "Of course."

"Fantastic. Let me refresh your memory anyway. In 1951, the Supreme Court ruled that the First Amendment does not protect the speech of any person or persons plotting to overthrow the government."

She and her half-wits sit there in silence. Maybe her next excuse for leaving the nation's Capitol unprotected against an imminent attack is buried somewhere in the Articles of Confederation.

"We're all on the same side, aren't we, Deputy Director?" asks Speaker Vasquez.

It takes Stokes almost fifteen full seconds to nod her head and say, "Yes."

"Then why is the intelligence community remaining silent on a clear and present danger to everyone who works in this building?" asks the Speaker.

"As I said, Freedom of Speech—"

This time it was me who cut her off and I was done pulling punches. The Speaker told me *shoot for the stars*. I hope she doesn't regret her decision.

"It doesn't matter if it's negligence or ineptitude that's keeping you happy folks over there at the J. Edgar Hoover Building warm in your beds at night. The Bureau ignored the same tide of evidence in 2020 and you let the attack play out. And two weeks from now, when they start hauling bodies out of the Capitol, I'll make sure every news outlet knows that the Federal Bureau of Impotence sat around with your thumbs up and locked while Rome burned. You people better pray that the President and his revolt are a smashing success, or I'll make sure everyone one of you paper-pushers ends up sharing pudding with Aldrich Ames at the Federal Correctional Institution in Terre Haute."

It was as if the air had been sucked out of the room and everyone inside was struck dumb by the harsh truth ringing in their ears. The silence was deafening and every eye was still on me.

"Someone has to say what everyone in this room already knows. You don't work for the President; you work for the American people. You swore an oath to the Constitution of the United States, not President Locke. So conjure up any last remnants of that infamous 'fidelity,' 'bravery,' and 'integrity' and stop licking at the boots of an unelected autocrat."

I stand up and take two steps toward the door and spin around on all of them. "Your agency and your outgoing president think you can run democracy out of this building? Not on my watch."

CHAPTER 18

December 21, 2028
Northern Virginia

THE BRIGHT AFTERNOON sun punishes my sleep-deprived eyes through sunglasses as I work my way in and out of traffic on Route 66 West. I have a fifty-fifty shot to get home in time to walk Abbs home from school. There's a mountain of work spilling across my desk back on Capitol Hill, but the Speaker kicked me out and told me not to come back until I spent some quality time with my daughter.

I admit that I was worried after I eviscerated the Deputy Director of the FBI a few hours ago, but my anxiety was unfounded. Speaker Vasquez had her Chief of Staff shuffle them out of the conference room and out of the building, and hustled me into her office.

She motioned me into a seat, sat down at her desk, and fixed me with a hard gaze asking me what I had to say for myself.

I sat there fidgeting. I obviously went too far this time and probably had about two to four weeks to find a new job. And then something unexpected happened. The Speaker came out from behind her desk, hugged me, and sat down in the chair next to me.

"Good Lord, Cora Walker—Glad you're on my side," Vasquez says shaking her head and breaking into a fit of laughter. "Twenty-eight years I waited for a moment like this on Capitol

Hill and you fulfilled my wildest fantasies in ten minutes. Did you see the looks on their faces? You just set the Federal Bureau of Investigation back forty years with that diatribe."

"You're not angry with me?" I ask, not sure if I might be hallucinating.

"Angry? I mean, maybe we should send them flowers or a bereavement wreath because you shoved them in a wood chipper, spit them out, and went back for more," she says smiling broadly. "It looks like President Locke has issued some hush-hush executive order ordering any and all federal agencies not to interfere with his personal coup."

She scooted me out of the office and sent me home. The stars aligned and, more importantly, so did the traffic lights when I got to Route 50. I made it home just in time to throw on some clothes and run out to the school to pick up Abby.

"Hi, Gertie," I call, running up the stairs and practically tearing off my blouse.

"Cora!" she calls, hustling out of her bedroom to greet me at the top of the stairs. "I was about to pick up Abby from school."

"I got her. I'm gonna run over there so we can walk home together," I say lacing up my running shoes.

"She will just be over the moon," says Gertie.

"I think I'm gonna take her out to dinner tonight, if that's OK?" I ask.

"That's a great idea, dear. You lovely ladies could certainly use a little alone time together."

I know Gertie didn't mean anything at all by that comment, but a wave of guilt crashes over my inner jetty and threatens to wash me out to sea. I'm such a jerk—I didn't even come home last night.

"Are you OK, dear?" asks Gertie with genuine concern.

"Sorry, I haven't slept much the last couple days."

"Two things before ya'll scoot," she says, still not able to drop the worry out of her voice. "I don't want to be dramatic, but I think there's been a big black car spending a lot of time in our neighborhood."

I freeze in my tracks. "Yes, ma'am?"

"Well, it's a big black truck," she says quietly.

"Truck, like a pickup truck or more like an SUV?" I ask, alarm bells pounding in my temple.

"Yes." She nods. "I suppose it's an SUV. I've seen it at least twice for sure, maybe more times than that."

"What drew your attention?" I ask.

"Well, the tinted glass reflects just like a mirror, and I don't see too many of those in our neighborhood," she says, thinking hard. "It's lurking around, if you know what I mean."

"I'm sure it's nothing, but I'll check it out," I tell her. "You said there were two things. What's the other item on tap?"

"I don't really recall," she says.

I give her a kiss on the cheek and tell her I'll be back with the Chicklette. My hand grabs the door when she blurts out, "I remember now. Ya'll got a special delivery about two hours ago."

"Special delivery?" I ask.

"It was a Federal Express envelope," she says. "It's on the kitchen counter."

I chuckle to myself. FedEx hasn't been Federal Express since the nineties. I tear open the package revealing a little blue Nokia flip phone. Congressman Lobdell said he would contact me *off the grid* by the end of the day. I guess this is from him.

I slip the phone into my desk and bound out the front door, sprinting by the time I hit the driveway. My body mistakenly thought it could go soft because I missed my morning run. I race across the neighborhood, working my legs and trying to beat the school bell. I can see the school in the distance when I hear the final bell ring. I slow down to a light jog to make sure I don't spook the soccer moms who are already dutifully lined up at their designated dismissal points.

Abby spots me right away and comes ripping out of the door, while a teacher behind her yells, "WALK!" She launches herself and I catch her in midair, wrapping my arms around her.

"You're home!" she yells burying her face into my chest.

We begin our walk home, holding hands as Abby recounts her day in school and announces her intention to email a revised wish list to Santa for Christmas. That's when I notice a big black Suburban with blacked-out windows turning around in a cul-de-sac about a hundred yards up on the right. It definitely wasn't there when I ran by about ten minutes ago. Gertie was right and the fact it didn't show up until school let out was no coincidence.

My blood runs cold as I grip Abby's hand a little tighter and pick up the pace.

The SUV rolls out of the cul-de-sac and parks on the street behind us, positioned to watch us walk up the street. I try to call up the calm that slows me down before a combat situation, but walking in the middle of the street with my daughter leaves me feeling naked, vulnerable, and ready to kill. Maybe Deacon was right.

I dial my phone. Gertie picks up on the first ring. "Hi, Gertie, can you get a snack ready for Abbs? I have to run out and take care of something."

"Awwww," Abby protests loudly. "Where are you going, Mom? Can't I come with you?"

"Mommy is just going to finish her run, baby, and then I'm spending the rest of the day with you," I say, looking at a pickup truck parked about ten feet up on our right. It belongs to the Andersons.

"As a matter of fact, if my hair looks OK, we should go out to dinner!"

"What? We're going to dinner. Tonight? You and me?" she says gleefully. "Can we go to Wendy's?"

"Why, do they have ice cream?" I ask.

"Let me check my hair in the reflection up here," I say, trying to keep my voice neutral.

Abby is temporarily baffled by my sudden concern with my hair as I take a close, but rapid-fire look into the back windshield so I can see the reflection behind me. The black Suburban hasn't moved. I wonder if they have cameras set up. If I yank some government goon out of a car and inflict some real damage, it would be satisfying, but counterproductive. Maybe there's a better way to handle this.

I hustle Abby inside and look out the window. Sure enough, the black Suburban is now parked at the curb across the street from my house. This is a wooded area, so they might be hard pressed to have video surveillance set up facing the back of the house. And who the hell are these guys and what do they want?

I remember the phone that came in the FedEx package while I was at work. I retrieve the burner phone from my desk and use my personal phone to call Jimmy Larsen, the tech guy in my office.

"Jimmy Larsen," he answers.

"Jimmy, Cora," I say.

"Um, hi, Cora. Um, what's going on?" he stammers.

"Jimmy, I need a favor."

"Sure thing," he says sounding relieved. What did he think I was going to ask him?

"I need you to call a congressman's office, using your personal phone. Can you do that for me?"

"Umm, is this legal?" he asks.

Jesus help me. "Jimmy, are you asking me if it's legal to call a congressman on a cell phone?"

"Ha," he laughs. "I guess not. Which congressmen?"

"Please call Congressman Deacon Lobdell's office and tell the person taking the message that one of the Broncos is trying to reach him. Can you do that for me?" I ask.

"Umm, is this like a fantasy football thing? Like a practical joke?" he asks.

"You nailed it, Jimmy. Don't ad-lib. Just call the number, talk to his secretary, and tell her what?"

"That the Denver Broncos are trying to reach him," he says. "You know I play fantasy football too."

"That's great, Jimmy, but this is a private league," I say patiently. "And let's keep this little joke between the two of us, OK?"

I walk over to Abby at the kitchen table and snag an apple slice off of her plate.

"Heyyy," she protests with a big smile. "Want another?"

"Don't mind if I do." I pilfer another slice when the burner begins to vibrate. "I need to take this; back in a flash."

I run upstairs, taking them two at a time until I reach my bedroom.

"Walker," I say.

"Mizz Walker, I—" says the Congressman before I cut him off.

"Wanna tell me why some government jackoffs have been following my child to school every day in a black Suburban? Any line on that, Congressman?" Rage permeates every word.

He doesn't miss a beat. "I can not be absolutely sure, but I can only guess this is some form of intimidation designed to provoke a response from you, but I suggest—"

I cut him off again, my voice straining to remain under control. "I'll deal with them on my end; you deal with it on your end."

"Understood," he says. "But you and I need to meet tomorrow on a separate, rather pressing matter."

"Take care of this first—your top friggin' priority—then we'll talk," I say, breaking the connection.

I return to Abbs at the table. "I'm running and gunning and then we're going to the mall—how's that sound?"

"What's the matter, Mom? You look flustered," says Abby.

"Flustered? Good word, baby girl. Something at work is bothering me, but I'm fine now," I lie.

She rolls her eyes and let's out an exaggerated, "If you say so."

Scary, she sounds just like me.

"I know what you're really going outside for. It's the black car out front."

"Well, I'll be back in a few minutes since you seem to have it all figured out." Oh my God, this kid needs to spend more time in front of a television or something. She's far too observant. I don't know what else to say, so I peck her on the top of the head and call out to Gertie, "This shouldn't take too long."

"Be careful, Cora," Gertie says just before I slip out the door.

I walk up to the SUV and knock respectfully on the glass.

The driver's-side window comes down about five inches, and I walk right up, taking in everything I can see with a mental snapshot.

These idiots are trying to blend into my neighborhood by dressing like golfers.

"Is there something I can help you with? You gentlemen seem lost?" I ask innocently.

"We're good, thanks. We're just waiting for someone," he says cordially.

"OK, have a nice day now," I say walking back toward the school. I pick up my government-issued personal phone with a blocked number and call 9-1-1.

"9-1-1 Operator 362. What's your emergency?"

"Oh my God," I say breathlessly. "This is Leslie from the Brighton School in Chantilly. There are some perverts or something taking pictures of little kids coming out of the elementary school. Oh m'God. They followed a little boy, rolled down the window, and started talking to him. Oh m'God, help me. I ran over and grabbed him away from them. I got a look inside. One guy had a camera, maybe a gun, and one of them had their thing out. Help me, Lord. They drove away, and I called you guys right away."

"OK, ma'am, slow down," says the operator. "Did you get a plate number?"

"They had Virginia plates, the first three numbers were 424, I think. Four-two something. Wait, it's a black Suburban. They're coming back. We need help!" I break the connection and walk back home past their vehicle. This is an affluent community and sex offenders of this nature are rare, but I imagine my call will trigger a formidable response from the local authorities.

Abby and I pull out of the garage twelve minutes later to the sounds of a wailing siren. We notice some kind of commotion going on about three blocks up to our right. Two men in golf shirts are out of their SUV and surrounded by Fairfax County Police Officers and a Virginia State Trooper with his hand on his sidearm. Fantastic response time, gentlemen. Perverts in Chantilly. What is the world coming to?

CHAPTER 19

December 23, 2028
Capitol Hill, Washington, D.C.

I GAG FOR a third time as a rancid cocktail of rotten mystery meat, spoiled milk, and lemony disinfectant assails my nostrils in an effort to purge the contents of my stomach. The hum of hidden generators all around me reminds me that I'm not in a dump, but a massive tunnel underneath the Capitol Building. The powers that be put a lot of thought into this one, naming it the "Garbage Tunnel"—which also happens to be a classified location.

The outline in the darkness gives me the feeling of wandering around a massive airport hangar. I guess to conserve money they keep all the lights out at night. I wonder what else goes on down here in the bowels of the Capitol Building. I've been doing a great deal of exploring lately to familiarize myself with all the forgotten hiding spaces housed here on the grounds. I've found at least twelve unoccupied safe rooms in this maze and at least two tunnels where someone might be able to hide or escape from the Capitol if it was overrun again like it was in 2021.

Of course, it's hard to keep pace with the low-life Congressmen who have suddenly become happy tour guides for groups of white nationalists and mercenaries during the past few weeks. Representatives from North Carolina, Ohio, Georgia, and Arizona are taking a cue from their counterparts from 2021. Why they haven't been detained, interrogated, and sent to a federal prison facility will have to remain one of life's great mysteries. I could break any one of them in under an hour.

I've worked here for two years and had no idea what lay beneath me until I started digging into classified records a few weeks ago. I've been meaning to check this garbage tunnel out for a while now, but never took the initiative. But this morning I didn't have much of a choice. A series of encrypted text messages from the Congressman pulled me away from my desk and led me down here.

04:16 GARBAGE TUNNEL NOT ON MAP
FIND 2814B DOOR BY THE COMM OF APPROP
   OFFICE
ACCESS CODE 4C71F2JCAB*
STAIRS ACCESS CODE – 7VV#VP2
ELEVATOR CODE – PV#T#19191
TAKE LEFT STAIRWAY MARKED AWAY STATION

04:16 FIND RED DUMPSTER WITH HAZMAT LOGO
4TH ROLL OFF BIN YOUR LEFT
GET THERE BEFORE 5:45, THAT'S WHEN LIGHTS
   COME ON
04:17 GO TO RIGHT HAND CORNER. REACH FAR
   UNDERNEATH
CAN YOU MAKE IT?

I want to text back:

WHY IS THE CONGRESSMAN PLAYING SPY?

Instead, I text back:

Copy

But I wonder if my text got through at all. There's no phone signal down here—it's a dead area. I switch off my phone before entering the tunnel to ensure total radio silence on my end. I don't want to give away my position with a vibrating phone. It's very dark down here, but I've always been at home in the blackness. Probably says something about my personality. Even when I was a child playing in unexplored caves in western Colorado, I always felt at peace with the absence of light. If the Congressman is setting me up for some sort of ambush, this would be the place to do it.

I work my way past the dumpsters, silently listening for any signs that someone else might be down here wandering around in the dark. Each garbage bin is about eight feet tall and forty yards long. I come up on the fourth dumpster as instructed. This might be the red HAZMAT bin I'm looking for, but it's too dark to see what color it is. I go to the right corner and crouch down, running my hands underneath. I come into contact with what feels like some kind of binder. I lift it up, not wanting to slide it out and risk making any noise. I'm easing it into my bag when I hear noise that I can't attribute to the rats that are enjoying a hearty morning breakfast. I'm not alone.

I take two steps forward, stop, and slip deeper into the darkness. I close my eyes and listen, controlling my breathing. Whoever is down here with me has stopped moving. Humans make very definitive noises when they're trying to hide and stay quiet. I glide fifty yards away and quickly double back to my original spot. Old tactics are still the best tactics unless your adversary is enjoying the advantage of night vision technology.

The stalker creeps back, having no idea where I am, but obviously searching. He moves quickly past the glow of a red exit sign. I circle back into the darkness and silently move in behind him.

"Trick or treat," I say.

The Congressman jumps a foot in the air swearing, "Goddamnit." His outburst shatters the silence of the garbage tunnel startling a few hidden rodents. "Goddamn woman! What are you? A ghost! It ain't Halloween and Christmas Eve is tomorrow!"

"Keep it down," I hiss at him. "It's not my fault you're sloppy." I can hear his heavy breathing and fight myself not to laugh out loud. I scared the crap out of him. "Why are you playing hide-and-seek with me?"

"I didn't know it was you, damnit. I didn't even know if you were coming in today at all," he says. "I heard the trash elevator right after I dropped off your package and had to duck out of sight. I had no idea you were already on the grounds and I didn't know who was joining me down here. You scared the shit out of me."

I chuckle softly. "Did I?"

"We're dead if we get caught dancing down here with those materials. Burn every scrap when you're done." His voice is deadly serious.

"Why trust me with it?" I ask.

"Hell if I know, Walker," he says and then stares into the darkness for a long uncomfortable minute. "Since you got down here so quickly, I can only assume you've been scoping out various extraction points and hiding places for a while now."

"I have been."

"Smart," he says clearly grappling with an important decision. Should he, can he trust me? Can I trust him? I wonder if he can see me at all.

"I have something else for you this morning," he says clicking on a penlight and leading us deeper into the tunnel. "An early Christmas gift."

"I heard you encountered a couple perverts in your neighborhood yesterday afternoon," he says, laughing out loud.

"You heard about that?" I say smiling broadly into the darkness.

"What size shoe do you wear?" he asks.

"Why?" I ask. What kind of question is that?

"Because we have to find some way to get your shoe out of that lead agent's ass," he says, laughing at his joke. "I made some calls; they won't be back."

"I won't be so gentle next time," I say, but then I start laughing too. "Who are they? Presidential operatives again? And why are they following my kid?"

"Officially, the gentlemen who are seeking your attention are former USPP," he says. "The President and his inner circle have been using them for their so-called special projects since the incident at the Lincoln Memorial."

"You mean the Lincoln Memorial massacre a couple years back?" I say in disgust.

"Same people," he says.

"The U.S. Park Police?" I ask. "I know they were censured for murder at the Lincoln Memorial. Twelve dead and almost thirty more who suffered from gunshot wounds. They used tear gas and clubbed their way through moms and civilians before opening fire."

"I can tell you that while they were publicly chastised, the President not only approved of their overzealousness in dealing with the public, he promoted many of them to his ever-growing protection detail."

"Every tyrant lives in fear of the people he oppresses," I say. "But why are they following my daughter?"

"They're testing you. Gauging your reactions. Seeing what your capabilities are," he says.

"For what purpose?" I ask.

"They're screening you in case you decide to switch sides and come work for me," he says.

"Stop," I say in a deadly whisper. "You're having these people harass me and my family?"

"Absolutely not," he says, anger flashing through his voice. "I had to announce my intentions to bring you on to my staff, and apparently, the President has issued a new universal screening process before any of his inner circle brings on a new employee."

"But I'm not coming to work for you," I say.

"One thing at a time, Mizz Walker," he says.

What makes him think I'm coming to work for him? We creep deeper into the tunnel, but surprisingly the smell of garbage is breaking up and the air is actually circulating better.

The Congressman is obviously looking for something and I'm getting anxious.

"Look here," he says shining the light about ten feet up the wall. See the House of Representatives Eagle with the number four on top?"

"I do." It's a Roman numeral four, but not worth mentioning.

"Look straight down in a straight line. See this electrical outlet?"

"I do."

"It's not an electrical outlet. It's a card scanner. This is a false wall—actually it's a door. It leads you into a safe room and freedom if you're on the run."

"Did you people snag this idea from a James Bond movie?" I say shaking my head.

"Here's the key card to access this escape tunnel. Actually, it will access just about any security door in the building. This is your break glass in case of emergency card only," he says. "It's a last resort. Don't use it unless it's life and death."

"Who does the card belong to?" I ask, wondering who might get in trouble if I use it.

"That's not something you need concern yourself with," he says, ending the subject.

"Need to know?" I ask.

"If the revolt fails, our cloak and dagger act will have run its course," he says. "We will go our separate ways. Maybe grab a lunch someday. But . . ."

He's clearly struggling with this.

"If President Locke is successful and brings down Congress, which is the more likely scenario, I'm going to bring you on to my staff immediately. All the paperwork is done and the order has been signed and predated. That's why people are following you."

"What order? What are you talking about?" I ask incredulously.

"What else do you need to know at this point? If Congress falls, the Republic has fallen. The President will want to get himself sworn for his second term as soon as possible. I have a plan to prevent that, but it's a nuclear option."

We stand in silence for a long time.

"You're going to overthrow a president who's just toppled our democracy?" I ask, lost in the sickness and chaos of the topic. For the fiftieth time this week, I think: *This can't be happening. This is piss poor fiction because it's so wildly unrealistic. And yet, here we are.*

"If the President is able to derail the election certification on January 6th, his next course of action will be to declare martial law. It's not conjecture—it's fact—and not an *alternative* fact. The plans are in motion. You, obviously if you're still alive, make sure you show up to work at my office on Monday, January 7th, because I can't do this without you."

"Do what? What's the nuclear option?" I ask, feeling the need to lash out at the man standing in front of me.

"Cora Walker, I swear to God. I pray every morning that I will never have to tell you."

CHAPTER 20

January 3, 2029
Capitol Hill, Washington, D.C.

I RANG IN the New Year with Abby and Gertie and accomplished my New Year's resolution of turning off my phone and stuffing it into a drawer for the entire day. Being unplugged was an odd and surprisingly liberating sensation. But it's been nonstop and all hands on deck since I returned to work yesterday. I walk into the Speaker's office with a backpack of items the watch commander helped me smuggle past security.

Beth Fleming, the Speaker's secretary, stops whatever she's doing and rushes over to me.

"Cora," whispers Fleming urgently, "the Speaker needs to see you ASAP."

"Why didn't you call me?" I ask with a gentle smile suppressing my annoyance.

"She said not to bother you until you actually walked through the door," she says.

I hold my breath to avoid blowing it out in a long sigh. I walk over to the Speaker's door to knock, but Beth throws it open in front of me before retreating.

The Speaker is talking on her office landline. She waves me in silently and gestures for me to close the door behind me.

I sit down in front of her desk. "Unless they're off property or putting out a fire, I need you, Dickie Graves, and Reggie Devereux in my office at the top of the hour."

I can't hear what the person on the other end of the phone is saying, but the Speaker intones, "Then that gives you sixteen minutes. Make them count."

She breaks the connection and looks at me.

"You've been a busy little bee," she says, smiling at me broadly. "I can only assume you pulled another all-nighter?"

"Why would you say that?" I ask, knowing that the Speaker doesn't make a statement like that unless she already knows the answer to the question.

"It could have something to do with the roughly three hundred pages you have tacked up to the wall in your office," she says holding my gaze. "Let me see, you're a warrior, a mother, and John Nash in your spare time."

"John Nash?" I ask.

"The American mathematician who was the father of mathematic game theory?" she says.

I give her a confused look.

"I've never seen anything quite like it, Cora. It's really stunning. You should have been a prosecutor. How did you gather all of that information in such a short time?"

"I started at eight last night and I finished around four thirty this morning," I say.

"Well, you can show your board to the *powers that be*. They should all be here in about ten minutes," she says. "I have the Sergeant of Arms for the Senate, Dickie Graves; the Chief of the Capitol Police, Kevin Almagro; and of course Emmet Burdick, the Sergeant of Arms for the House, coming up here to meet with us in your office."

"They don't need to look at the board in my office, Madame Speaker. I collated all the information and put it on a PowerPoint for you this morning. It should be in your inbox."

She laughs and hits the SPEAKER button. "Miss Fleming, please get the conference room ready—our visitors will be here any moment."

"Anything else, Madame Speaker?" she asks.

"Please find Monica Davies. Tell her I need her in my office," she says, punching the SPEAKER button off.

Monica is the Speaker's Chief of Staff. She always has some snark to share with me when the Speaker is looking the other way. Her late invitation to the meeting is sure to push her over the edge. It's the little things.

Twenty minutes later, all the players are in place in the conference room, including my friend Commander Devereux. The Speaker thanks them for joining us on such short notice and turns the meeting over to me.

"With the hard work of several FBI analysts and the national network of Fusion Centers who work under the Department of Homeland Security, I put together a threat matrix to give you a snapshot of what we can expect during the election certification and planned hostilities scheduled for January 6th, which is of course this Sunday."

I take a sip of water and rub my eyes before beginning.

"Let me just say, this is a first. Never before has our vast national network of intelligence agencies independently come to the same set of conclusions for a pending terror attack here in the United States or anywhere else on the planet. Apparently, there is widespread agreement that World War III is coming to the Capitol on January 6th. I looked up the background of the four analysts who used the term 'war.' Their track records are impeccable," I say, looking around the room to see if they're paying attention. All eyes are on me. Even Monica Davies is dialed in.

"Please forgive my slides, they are far from polished. This is a bare-bones PowerPoint presentation to give you a snapshot of the various threats that have been pouring into our intelligence networks from Guam to Seattle to Washington D.C.

"More than two thousand individuals and several extremist groups have made it clear. Their weapons are already stockpiled in Washington and the organizers are already in the city. They intend to overrun the Capitol and occupy it by employing the use of deadly force against members of Congress, including the Capitol Police Force.

"Let me reiterate, all of this information was gathered by our domestic intelligence community including the FBI and local branches of the Department of Homeland Security."

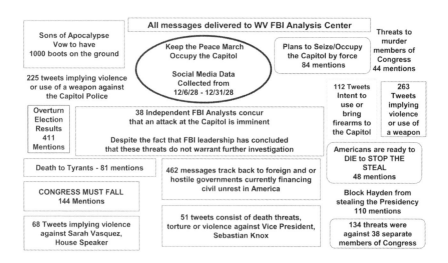

"All of these captured communications have been forwarded to the FBI Analysis Center in West Virginia. *Captured* meaning that these individuals posted these violent intentions on the internet.

All of the social media traffic on this slide has been collected during the past twenty days starting on Wednesday, December 6th."

Someone blurts out, "All of this? In just one month?"

"This slide represents more than 42,000 posts all referring to the *Keep the Peace March*, initiated by the President of the United States. This so-called peace march has been meticulously constructed by the Locke administration since it was determined that he lost the election to President-elect Drew Hayden in November.

"Besides the normal *blood and soil* and *Jews will not replace us* rhetoric, there are an inordinate number of threats against two specific individuals: Speaker Vasquez and Vice President Sebastian Knox. The Speaker is an obvious target because of her outspoken differences and clashes with President Locke. As I'm sure each one of you knows, several Congressmen have been touring the halls of the Capitol with some very dangerous people. I don't have a clue as to why these tours have been permitted by the very people sitting in this room. Only you gentlemen can answer those questions, but it's 2021 all over again except this time, the President isn't some blowhard pushover—he's the real deal."

The bitching and moaning spreads across the room like wildfire. I hold my hand up to stop the grumbling and finger-pointing by the Capitol leadership in the room.

"It doesn't matter why the tours are happening, gentlemen. They've already been permitted, so let me finish." I lock my glare onto Kevin Almagro, the Capitol Police Chief, who's still protesting a little too vehemently.

"Something to add, Chief?" My lack of respect for him chills the air in the room.

He shakes his head no and looks away. Smart man.

"The focal point of these tours has been the Speaker's office. Exactly where you are seated right now. But I'm sure these invaders mean no harm. Maybe next week after they storm the building, they intend to drop off some leftover baked goods."

There are a few stifled laughs. I'm tired and I need to get back on track quickly.

"As far as the fifty-one threats against Vice President Sebastian Knox, this is specifically the President's doing. He's putting pressure on Knox to throw out the vote and somehow reinstall him as President. This has been tried before and failed, but if Locke throws the Vice President in a cell, no one is sure what might happen next."

I pause, gauging the reaction of each man in the room.

"There is no legal way for Knox to throw out the election results, even if he really wanted to, but let's face facts, the current administration has been trashing and circumventing the rule of law since the President raised his hand and swore to uphold and defend the Constitution."

I stop and snatch up my water bottle and take a long drink while people scratch notes or type into their phones.

"Most of threats against the Vice President echo the President's words. *MAKE SURE Knox does the right thing or there will be consequences.* Signs and bumper stickers pushing that narrative are popping up all around the city. Besides Vasquez and Knox, thirty-eight individual members of Congress have been threatened with the violence that is to take place on January 6th. Forty-four tweets mention committing murder at the Capitol on January 6th. One hundred and twelve tweets revolve around smuggling firearms into the Capitol on January 6th. One extremist group, the Sons of the Apocalypse, vows to put a thousand boots on the Capitol grounds on January 6th. They are making long-term plans and the weapons stashes are all over Washington D.C. Forty-eight people say they are ready to lay down their lives to make sure Locke gets another four years or more. Jimmy—lights, please."

The room comes alive with heated conversation as soon as the lights come up. Everyone is talking at once and I let them go on. I have more critical information, but I'm going to let them chew on this for a while. After fifteen minutes and because I'm dying to get out of this room, I have Jimmy flash the lights. Sometimes I even find my rude behavior shocking. When the room falls silent, I continue.

"To make matters worse, our Russian friends scattered around Eastern Europe and the Balkans have been responsible for at least 462 violent posts relating to January 6th. So not only is the President of the United States waging war against us, but foreign governments are also actively engaged in operations to finance our civil unrest. And if the United States can't hold its democracy together, this gives the Russian empire, which now extends to Poland and China, a window to run wild and declare war against the rest of the world while Americans wage a civil war on the streets of Washington."

This sets off another round of comments, and I wait again for the uproar to subside.

"So you've heard all the evidence about what we can expect on Sunday, so let me brief you on what the federal response has been so far. Because the President of the United States and his administration are organizing this attack, all federal agencies are frozen in place. So far, the FBI, DHS, the Joint Chiefs, the Pentagon, and the National Guard have pledged to do absolutely nothing even though they've independently concluded that the attack is imminent.

"In other words, the feds are gonna let this all play out one more time. No one is coming to save us. If we were under a potential attack from the Black Lives Matter movement, there would be tanks lining the streets and attack helicopters hovering overhead, but that's not the case. Jimmy, lights please."

I pull up the same slide.

"Six of the FBI's top threat analysts concur that the Capitol will be attacked on January 6th and that they will target Congress and the Capitol Police Force. One person used the term *kill the palace guards and the rest will scatter*. But the FBI leadership is flatly ignoring the counsel of their best and brightest people. Obviously, the Director of the FBI, Clinton Sinclair, and his inner circle plan to ride the coattails of President Locke while the Capitol burns."

"You're out of line! That's quite an accusation, young lady!" blurts out Dickie Graves, the Sergeant of Arms for the United States Senate. *Young lady*?

"Is it Mr. Graves?" I ask pointedly. "Check the screen, sir. Front and center underneath the Keep the Peace March oval. Can you read it for me?"

He hesitates as all eyes fall upon him. His face drains of color. "Um, the FBI has concluded that these threats do no not warrant further investigation."

"And the line above it, please?"

"Even though thirty-eight FBI analysts concur that an attack is imminent," he says quietly.

"The politics don't matter to me. They shouldn't matter to any of you," I say, raising my voice. "This is about the future of our nation's democracy and a life and death struggle for every one of us in this room. These people are coming for us. You can't wish this coup away. The President is cheering them on and demanding results from his followers. January 6th, 2021, was just a warm-up. Make no mistake, there is no one out there to answer our distress signal. We're on our own."

CHAPTER 21

January 5, 2029
Capitol Hill, Washington, D.C.

THE SECURE LINE rings on my desk, and I expect to hear the Speaker's voice when I press the receiver into my ear.

"Yes, ma'am," I answer dutifully.

"Walker," comes the sonorous voice of Reggie Devereux.

"I guess you would know better than anyone that this line is secure and encrypted," I say.

"I don't know anything of the sort," he says with a hard edge to his voice. "Can you meet me at the racks?"

"When?" I say feeling the floor spinning underneath me. I need to get out of here; it's already past lunchtime. Tomorrow is insurrection day, and I'm damn well going to spend my last afternoon and evening with my baby girl.

"Ten minutes," he says breaking the connection.

During the late 1800s and early 1900s, the Capitol Crypt was used for informal storage and a place where people could park their bicycles. It's an anecdote Dev shared with me when I first started working at the Capitol. It was my third day on the job when he noticed the Virginia Tech Hokie on my key chain. He pulled me aside to talk Hokie football and we've been great friends ever since.

Twenty-two minutes later, I tentatively walk into the crypt looking over my shoulder. This is not an ideal meeting spot for privacy, but with the Visitor Center shut down, the crypt is empty.

The crypt is situated directly beneath the Capitol rotunda, and nobody is actually buried down here. When George Washington was buried at Mount Vernon in Virginia, I guess the men in charge decided never to bury anyone in the Capitol Crypt. I spot Dev standing by the Suffrage monument. He looks very jumpy. His head is on a swivel like someone might sneak up on us at any moment. He waves me over with a finger to his lips. He thrusts a very heavy and stylish woman's backpack into my arms and whispers into my ear, "From a friend."

I thank him with a nod, put on my new backpack, and rush back up to the Speaker's chambers. I lock myself in my office and inventory the contents of the backpack. Four flairs, eight flash bangs, a fourteen-inch bolt cutter, and a two-foot-long retractable baton. I've been stashing stuff for the big day tomorrow, but the flash bangs and baton are actually a godsend.

I buzz the Speaker's phone and she answers on the first ring. "I told you to be gone by one this afternoon and not to darken the doors of this office again until tomorrow morning."

"Yes, Madame Speaker, I need a word in private before I head out," I say.

"I need to speak to you as well. You have two minutes, starting now," she says breaking the connection.

I rush into her office, softly closing the door behind me. This is one of the most powerful women in the entire world, yet she always manages to grant me her full attention.

"One minute and forty seconds," she says firmly.

"Madame Speaker, regarding the election certification and the revolt tomorrow, I have a few additional requests," I say.

"You already had me pack two weeks' worth of clothes. Where are my suitcases?" she asks.

"They're long gone, Madame Speaker. Ma'am, I need you to bring your most comfortable workout shoes, oversized flannel shirts or hooded sweatshirts, a backpack, and a pair of black workout pants," I say quickly.

"I can do that, Mizz Walker," she says. "If you think of anything else, please call me from the road."

"Thank you, Madame Speaker," I say.

"Trying to alter my appearance to sneak me out of the Capitol tomorrow?" she says with a knowing smile.

"That's why you're the boss." I smile, turning around to leave.

"Cora," says the Speaker.

Jesus, I knew it. She's going to make one final push.

"Yes, ma'am." I say quietly.

"Take a seat, please," she says in almost a whisper.

I comply with her request.

"You've done an amazing job here." She stops, laughs, and shakes her head. "That's the understatement of the year. You've blown away every expectation and taken on the responsibility of five people."

I squirm in my seat.

"I believe in the concept of self-sacrifice. I really do. But I want you to ask yourself a question. Haven't you done enough?"

"Ma'am?" I say looking her in the eyes.

"I think you should stay home tomorrow. You don't need to be here," she says.

I nod my head.

"Ma'am. Are you ordering me to stay home or suggesting it?" I ask. My voice teeters on insubordination.

We eye each other carefully. I have followed every order this woman has ever given to me, more or less, and never said "no" to her.

"Let's forget that I'm your superior for one moment. Whether you like it or not, you've become more like a daughter to me." She stops, shaking with emotion.

I've never seen her like this before and she takes a moment to compose herself.

"I care about you and I know that if you're here when these knuckleheads swarm the Capitol tomorrow, you're going to do things that cannot be undone. I know what you did in Benghazi and I've seen your unredacted file. You and I both know that you will be forced to take lives tomorrow. Not in the cover of night, but in broad daylight in the halls of this building."

She gives me a moment to digest her statement.

"This isn't Benghazi," she says quietly.

"Excuse me, ma'am, but this is Benghazi," I say more forcefully than I intended. "This is Benghazi all over again, I promise you. Terrorists are terrorists, whether they're born in Libya or Ohio. I know these people have been abused by the system and manipulated by their government, but when they take up arms against the United States, they need to be put down."

Now she takes a moment to process what I just said.

"And if I'm going to spend the rest of my day with Abby, I really need to leave now. If that's still OK."

"You may leave," she says. "I knew I was never going to talk you out of standing tall for your country and standing up for me tomorrow, but I had to try. However, you and I are going to sit down in this office tomorrow morning before the insurrection and you can explain to me how 'this is Benghazi all over again.'"

I smile broadly, standing up. "That's a conversation I'm looking forward to, Madame Speaker."

Two hours later I'm at the swimming complex in Chantilly, Virginia, with Abby. I tried to get her to skip swim practice today and just swim with me, but she looked at me as if I had lost my mind.

I watch her long strides in the pool, hypnotized by the motion, seeing but not seeing. It feels like I've been dreading January 6th forever. I knew when the American people put Locke into power that he would do his best to tear down our democracy—and he's done just that. He's pardoned war criminals, jailed more than a million people, championed police brutality, tried to shut down the press, and now he wants to burn down the Capitol because he lost the election.

I feel another wave of rage bubbling inside of me, but it's instantly vaporized by a more powerful emotion. Guilt. Here I am spending a few precious hours with my daughter and I'm obsessing about work. That's how you really know what a really awful mother you are.

Abby has four laps to go. No one was more surprised than me when she wanted to join competitive swim when we moved to Northern Virginia. Why she is so driven is a mystery to me. She's improved so much in the last year and made many swim friends. She obviously knew what she needed more than I did. Again, no surprise there.

It's so cute—she catches my eye on every lap to make sure I'm dialed in and paying attention. That's my intense little girl. I wish I could get her to slow down. Twenty minutes later, we're in the parking lot.

*   *   *

"There's Nanna," I say looking at the Toyota Highlander parked up front.

"Ha," says Abby. "Nanna bought Big Blue."

"*Brought*," I say gently. "She didn't *buy* it, she *brought* it."

"Ha ha!" She laughs at me like an evil villain. "That's what I said!"

Once we're in the car, Abby explodes with her news of the day, details of her swimming practice, and her desire to work on some math problems.

Just before we pull up to the house, I make a suggestion for all the women in the car.

"Nanna, Abby, we have a pile of pictures in a box. I was thinking that after dinner the three of us could work on putting a photo album together."

"Whhhaaat?" squeals Abby. "Best idea ever, Mom. There's a picture with me and the snake you caught, pictures from sledding, when we went zip-lining, and Christmas, Fourth of July, and that kitty we kept for a while!"

Abby tosses off her seat belt and races out of the car before the garage is even fully open.

"Abby, you forgot your swim bag," I call after her, but she's long gone.

Gertie looks at me for a long moment and unbuckles her seat belt. She leans over and gives me a long hug before I lose all control. I grip her tightly as my chest heaves. Sobs and moans and regrets and rage puncture the dam in my black heart. I cry harder and more intensely than I ever have in my life. Gertie doesn't say a word. She just keeps patting me gently saying, "Shhhh."

I pull away. "You're all she has, Gertie," I say my voice unrecognizable, racked with tears and emotion. "I've screwed it all up."

"Cora, this is one of those times for listenin', not interrupting," she says with iron in her voice. "That little girl loves you with all her heart. You called yourself selfish and you were right, but not for the reasons ya think. Calling yourself a *pretend mom*—that's selfish and it's stupid—and you're not a stupid woman. So cut out all this *bad momma* routine before I really lose my cool."

I hold her again and this time it is all tears. No words and no more accusations. After five more minutes, my showered little dove is screaming at us from the garage: "Why are you guys still in the car?? It's cold and I'm starving!"

After an amazing dinner and a night of picturing, I send Abby upstairs to brush her hair and teeth. Gertie and I watch her disappear up the stairs.

"I'm going to lie down with Abby for a while, but I need to show you something first."

We walk into my office and I motion her over to the black briefcase on my desk.

"I know you don't want to hear this, but you and Cat are the co-executors or executrixes of my will," I say. "As you know, Cat has agreed to take on my role as a parent and raise Abby with you in case I'm no longer able to perform my duties."

I look at Gertie, waiting for a reaction. She's dialed in and listening.

"You really don't need the briefcase. Everything is filed electronically, but I know you prefer paper," I say with a little smile. "You already have access to my bank accounts. There are deeds to property and there is a sizable trust fund I've set up for Abby. She'll have access to some of the money when she's eighteen and the rest when she turns twenty-one. You know the estate attorney, Ellen Poist. She will help you with everything. She's smart, professional, and a very good woman—for an attorney."

"You trust her?" asks Gertie surprising me.

"Implicitly," I say without hesitation.

"Cora, I appreciate all of your mindfulness and preparation, but you're coming back to us tomorrow, and if not tomorrow, the day after," she says. "You have to believe it, Cora. Even if you don't, I know it in my heart of hearts. January 6th will be a horrible day for you and this twisted country. I'm sure it will be worse than the first one—I believe you. But I know you can turn away an army at the gates of hell. I know you'll do just that tomorrow."

Abby is sound asleep nestled deep into my arms and I feel a sense of peace trying to force its way through the twisted thoughts swarming inside my head. So many people who care about me told me to quit and leave town. Even the Speaker of the House wants me to sit this one out. I try to give my weary mind a break. If only it were that easy.

CHAPTER 22

January 6, 2029
Chantilly, Virginia

MY FOUR-MILE RUN turned into a grueling six miles of self-inflicted punishment in the frigid air. I dared my lungs to burst—no, I begged them. Today is January 6th. Today isn't the day to do this to my *body. Or* maybe it is? I sneak back into the house and shower, hoping to cuddle with Abigail one more time before I "Storm the Capitol!"

I laugh to myself and say it again: "Storm the Capitol." If I had it my way, I'd stack the attackers six feet high after I raked them with machine gun fire and use them as a bulwark to repel the invaders. That would play well on the evening news. Jesus, I'm salty this morning. What would the PTA moms think of such a proclamation of inappropriate behavior?

I try to wash the rage out of my soul and down the shower drain, but it only grows stronger, taking on a life of its own. I can feel it all around me. The killer is back, the monster I was before I became a mother. It's terrifying, knowing firsthand what evils you are capable of.

It's almost four in the morning, and I'm uncharacteristically impatient. I want to jump into the trenches and be done with it. I watch Abby sleep from her door, not daring to come any closer.

I'm afraid of my sickness, afraid that what I've morphed into overnight might infect her.

I hear whispers all around me: "Don't let the killer near the baby."

I look at Abby's wild curls and that perfect button nose. Here come the tears again? I want to stroke my baby's hair, kiss her face, pull the covers over us and block out the evil world around us. But the world brought this fight to me, so of course, forget your child and plunge headfirst into the maelstrom. How do you know when you're really an unfit parent? When you have the ability to prioritize your job over the welfare of your own child. Again and again.

*   *   *

Fifty-eight minutes later, I'm parked in a garage four blocks from the Capitol. I don't think I'll be returning to my vehicle any time soon.

I climb the steps of the United States Capitol Building two at a time trying to ward off the cold and the anxiety that's put a chokehold on the District of Columbia. White tendrils of breath curl around my face and fade like apparitions. The morning sun won't be up for hours. I'm searching for any additional security measures around the building and come up empty. By the end of the day, the country that I have served for much of my adult life may very well brand me as a murderer, traitor, and an enemy of the state. Maybe all of the above.

A stack of threat assessment reports waits patiently on my desk for my attention. I read every one of them at least three times. Government agents from the former Soviet Union are still banging away on their keyboards in Macedonian apartments trying to

fire up the huddled masses in America and get them to destroy
their own country from the inside out. Once again, social media
has brought my country to the brink.

The most revered building in the United States is in the crosshairs of President Terrance Locke, and every extremist group from
Texas to Virginia is here to die for the cause all over again. Flights
into Reagan National and Dulles have increased more than 40
percent in the last three days, and hotels are sold out all over D.C.,
Northern Virginia, and Maryland for the big event.

Today's lack of security is a red flag even during the most peaceful of times. I didn't exactly dress up this morning. I'm wearing a
hoodie, a camo running outfit, and black running shoes—not my
usual attire for my role as Communications Director for the
Speaker of the House. But if I thought this outfit might grab someone's attention on the dark steps of the Capitol, I was mistaken. No
National Guard, no barriers, no extra personnel, not even a bike
rack. Maybe the entire Capitol Police Force has the day off?

With the current void of security surrounding the Capitol this
morning, Abby and her elite team of safety patrollers could take
the building and have it secured before lunch. I have plenty of
time before I need to be in my office, so I make a beeline for the
White House. Before the insurrection, I think President Locke
promised refreshments at the White House Ellipse before his
white power rally.

I learned long ago in infantry training to approach your target
from the high ground. I settle on the rise of the Washington
Monument to get a bird's-eye view of the crowds flooding in for
President Locke's speech.

The time for campaign speeches has long since passed. Locke
got slaughtered in the general election. This is just another

alcohol-induced Presidential pep rally to rile up the herd. A tsunami of red LOCKE n' LOAD hats slowly wraps around the White House from every direction.

The crowds resemble a giant serpent coiling around the White House to choke out democracy once and for all.

From the earliest days of President Locke's campaign in 2023, MAGA hats all but disappeared in favor of a new wave of "Locke n' Load" hats. The words LOCKE n LOAD are stacked on top of each other in bold block white letters. Each "O" has been replaced with the crosshairs one would see when looking through a sniper scope. Not surprisingly, the logo was a slam-dunk for those who believed that their Second Amendment rights were in danger without President Locke in their corner.

Since I'm dressed for the occasion, I decide to join the crowd for a better look. I stride through the camouflage pajama party studying the frenzied faces of the President's rapidly expanding congregation.

There's a lot to take in: Pirates, tough guys, and comic book characters. What really grabs my attention are the guys with tactical vests and zip ties hanging out of their pockets. With the new gun laws in place, people are wearing sidearms on their hips like we're on the set of a bad Western.

The anxious looks and the rising pitch of conversations around me are often a precursor to violence. I'd seen the same looks as an operative on the streets of Kabul and as a journalist in Charlottesville, Virginia, during the Unite the Right March. More and more, groups of disenfranchised people abandon common sense and leave humanity at the doorstep to join the ruptured hornet's nest of mayhem and discontent. For the most part, people avoid eye contact with me. I wonder if they're secretly ashamed of themselves. A part of me feels sorry for them, a very small part. I've seen enough. It's going to be a busy day.

My decision to move on coincides with an outburst of chants that ripple through the frenzied crowd and echo down Constitution Avenue. "Locke and load! Locke and load! Locke and Load!" I shake my head, smiling under the cover of my mask. This whole *Lock and Load* movement has *zero* basis in reality. I've been around guns my whole life and you sure as hell have to *load* before you *lock*.

Judging by the size of the crowds this morning, I'm guessing at least 12,000 strong already. The Capitol will have no chance this afternoon. Locke's Loyalists will march two klicks to the east and the festivities will get underway.

I'm picking my way through the crowd when I spot a television cameraman and a female reporter being harassed by a group of Locke supporters. The cameraman has a bloody nose. My guess is that the news crew waded too far into the deep end looking for an exclusive. I really need to stay out of the fray here for professional reasons. I'm not a babysitter for wayward journalists.

The reporter looks terrified as a grizzly bear of a man beats their camera equipment with a flagpole. He's wearing a camo design baseball cap that says TAKE AMERICA BACK—2028. He's really getting into his work. Cameras and equipment are covered by insurance, so I see no reason to get involved in the fray. But when the man whips around and strikes the cameraman on the shoulder with the flagpole, I feel that sick burning feeling crawl up the back of my neck.

I read the back of the grizzly's shirt as I draw closer:

ROPE. TREE. JOURNALIST
SOME ASSEMBLY REQUIRED

My inner voice starts a chant that drowns out the noise around me. *Walk away! Walk away! Walk away*! This is sound advice, but playing by the rules has never been my best attribute.

Grizzly boy has drawn quite an audience, but no one seems the least bit interested in protecting the journalists who are now part of the story. I was a journalist myself before being sucked back into the black hole of government service.

I ease out my Toro, making sure to keep it out of sight down by my side. This Toro isn't a lawn mower, it's a beast. It's a next-gen stun gun that wreaks havoc on a victim's central nervous system. Its rubberized grip fits perfectly into my hand and the business end emits a nanosecond electrical pulse. One touch and it's lights out before anyone knows what hit him or her. It's powerful, compact, and certainly not available to the general public. The Toro is not supposed to be lethal, but new technology can be fickle.

It's a high-tech stun gun, not a Taser device, so I need to make physical contact with the guy to put him down. I slide up behind him and shove the live prongs into his lower back. His body goes completely rigid as an involuntary cough blows a buckshot of mucus and saliva out of his mouth, showering the people in front of him. I bet they wish he had taken the time to brush his teeth this morning.

The Toro is already tucked away deep into my pocket before he collapses back into my arms. Blood trickles down his chin. I panic for a moment wondering if something inside of him has ruptured until I see that he bit off a huge chunk off of his bottom lip. Serves him right.

With all the confusion and chaos around us, no one has any idea what is going on right in front of their eyes. I ease the man to the ground, checking for a pulse. He's heavier than a damn bear.

I scream out, "Clete? Cletus? Oh shit, it's his heart. It's his heart!"

I frantically wave my arms, drawing attention from all sides. "Somebody get us some help! Get a goddamn doctor!" I cry out as if I'm really concerned for this man or if I have any idea who he is. "Somebody, help us!"

Spectators crowd around us as a few mini seizures take hold of him. He's totally out of it and his breathing is labored. His neurological impulses are trying to right the ship, but for now, he's lost at sea. Could be out for ten minutes or forever if his heart quits.

"One of our brothers is down! We gotta get him some help!" I scream as I latch onto the young reporter, propelling her in front of me to part the crowd and get away from the commotion. The cameraman is right behind us as we force our way closer to the sidewalk and away from the growing crush of people.

I lead them close to the edge before breaking away from them and blending back into the crowd. I look back and the cameraman is staring at me. He waves to thank me and I turn around heading back to the office. My stomach grumbles, reminding me that I sacrificed my breakfast time to come play in the President's backyard.

McDonald's is too far from here, so my only chance for salvation this morning is the Cap cafeteria. If I double-time it, I have a fifty-fifty chance of arriving before they run out of eggs.

CHAPTER 23

January 6, 2029
The National Mall, Washington, D.C.

THE SUN IS still trapped behind the massive dome of the Capitol and shows little interest in pushing any higher as I quicken my pace up Madison Drive. I peer to my left looking through the naked trees at the rows of state flags hanging limply next to the south entrance of the National Museum of American History. I glance up at the Infinity Sculpture just as my internal radar starts pinging. The warning bells warn me far too late to do any good. A black SUV screeches to a stop twenty feet away. There's no viable exit point and no decent cover within fifty yards. Nothing to do but meet the threat head-on and try not to get shot.

I glance at the plates on the vehicle. Second time I had seen them this morning. I walk casually past the SUV like it's nothing more than a wayward pigeon. This forces the driver to recklessly swing his vehicle around so it's now facing the wrong way on Madison Drive. Madison is a westbound one-way street and this clown is now pointed due east toward the Capitol. The driver failed to anticipate that I would completely ignore his or her advances. The driver's-side window slides down and a pair of reflective glasses matching the vehicle's tinted glass mirrors my distorted reflection.

"Cora Walker," yells the driver. He has a smirk on his face.

I keep walking.

"I need a word with you."

"You've already used eight," I say.

"Eight what?"

"Eight words. Actually, you're up to ten now."

"We need to talk," he pursues.

"Talk."

"Get in the car," he barks.

I watch his hands, satisfied that they are still on the steering wheel. "I don't think so. You're going the wrong way."

A few cars come down the street blaring their horns at the wrong-way driver. There's no way to know how many are inside the vehicle or what they're carrying. Even if they come out with guns drawn, shooting me on the Mall isn't a realistic option. Too many cameras in D.C. My best bet is to take out the driver and reassess after that.

I'm just about to move when the back window eases down revealing the mysterious woman behind the curtain. I do a double take. Whoever might be stalking me in D.C., this was one of the last people I expected to see ever again. The President's stepdaughter—also his Chief of Staff—Cecilia Danforth—apparently wants a word with me.

I hate to admit that this is a welcome distraction. I wonder what the hell she wants. I should beat her ass after those goons harassed my family.

"Cora Walker, I need a few moments of your time," Danforth says flashing a wide grin.

"I realize this is an insane day," she says. "But can you spare a few precious moments of your time?" There seems to be an edge to her voice.

"I'll skip the ride," I say. "Why don't you hop out and join me for a stroll on the Mall? It's a lovely morning." Such a lie. It's not a lovely morning. It's cold, overcast, and muddy.

"I have heels on," she says.

"Jesus," I say, laughing. "Option two—lose the goons. I'll drive while you talk."

We lock eyes for a long moment. She knows that option two is her only choice if she wishes to have a discussion with me this morning.

"You heard the lady," the Chief of Staff snaps to her Secret Service detail inside the vehicle. "You're walking. Get out, please."

Someone in the seat next to her says something to her that I can't hear. She answers back curtly, "That's terrific. I certainly appreciate your concern. I've made my intentions quite clear, and your objection is both noted and irrelevant. Gather the team. Get out." She looks at the driver. "Leave the keys in the ignition, please."

Three men file out of the car. I shift my weight to the balls of my feet in case one or all of the agents have any intentions of forcing me into the SUV. They have sullen looks on their faces and are ready for a fight.

"Move to the back of the car away from Miss Walker—quickly, please," snaps Cecilia. They move immediately to the back as she jumps out of the car. "Satisfied?"

I nod my head.

"Get in. I'll drive." She hops into the driver's seat. "See you boys back at the ranch."

I jump in the passenger's side, and she's already revving the engine. She guns the SUV in reverse, scattering the agents behind the car, and backs up on the sidewalk before pointing the car in the right direction again and shooting down Madison Drive, going the right way.

I smile to myself, quickly fastening my seat belt—Cecilia Danforth is a total nutjob. Despite my disgust for everything she stands for, I can't help but like her.

"This is some strange twist of fate, you showing up on today of all days," I say. "I don't know if you've heard, but we're expecting a little trouble up on Capitol Hill this afternoon."

The clouds break free for a moment allowing the sun to cast a few pink flecks over Washington. I stop looking at the sky and stare at her.

"That's really out of my control, but that's one of the reasons I decided to track you down this morning," she replies.

"Let me guess," I say. "You believe I've done all I can for the Speaker and showing up to work today is nothing short of a suicide mission."

"It is," she says looking over at me and nearly taking the mirror off of a yellow cab as she swerves to avoid a pedestrian.

"Being in a car with you driving is one of the riskier things I can ever remember doing," I say, grabbing the handle above the driver's-side door.

She laughs out loud. "You're funny." She puts on the right turn signal and rifles the car into reverse to parallel park in front of a fire hydrant that sits in front of a local bagel joint. "You want to run in?"

"You had your enforcers primed and ready in the SUV to whisk me away with or without my permission this morning," I say as my stomach grumbles.

"You can't protect the Speaker from what's coming," Cecilia Danforth says.

"And what exactly is it that's *coming to our nation's capital*? It's *your capital* too, Miss Danforth," I ask, trying to force a flicker of truth from her lips.

"My name is Cecilia, and I think you and I both know what's coming," she says, smiling. "From what I hear, you bitch-slapped the Deputy Director of the FBI and called her a traitor?"

I, too, smile at the memory. That was a good day.

"You even gifted her a nice little copy of the Constitution. That was a nice touch." She shakes her head. "You saw the mob this morning. There are thousands. You gonna mow them all down and leave them dying on the steps of the Capitol?" she says, blowing out a long sigh.

"That's the plan," I answer. "I have a job to do."

"Does your job include assaulting civilians on the White House lawn?" she asks.

"Only when I can squeeze it in," I answer. She obviously saw me break up the assault on the journalists a few minutes ago. "You must be paying a lot of overtime to follow my actions so closely. What do they call that—enhanced surveillance? Or did you see the video? I know the Patriot Surveillance Act added another 10,000 cameras to the D.C. Metro area. Big Brother is working overtime for you people!"

She says nothing.

"I work for the American people, Cecilia. Maybe the pertinent question I should be asking is—who do you really work for?"

We get out of the car, walking toward the bagel place. I'm surprised it's so empty, but the city has a strange vibe this morning, as if everyone is waiting for something bad to happen. I remember that feeling when I was in Benghazi. Everyone was in on the secret except the Americans.

A jogger pads toward us on the sidewalk. I notice the metallic snake pattern on her white leggings, her blonde ponytail swishing back and forth in perfect time like a metronome.

For a fleeting moment, the smell of freshly baked bagels sweeps away all traces of my angst. We walk out of the shop five minutes later. My bacon, egg, and cheese bagel is already half gone while Cecilia Danforth delicately sips her bottled water and dabs at her lips.

"The protesters are armed and organized. Sanctioned at the highest levels," says the Chief of Staff as she seems to admire her parking job.

I'm having difficulty mustering the proper level of respect that the President's Chief of Staff should be entitled to.

"Maybe these *protesters* as you call them are planning a mass suicide on the Capitol steps to protest the election results. I suggested posting fifty-caliber machine guns around every entrance of the Capitol to gauge how badly they really want to come inside."

She says nothing as she fishes the keys out of her handbag. As soon as she pulls them out, I hold my hand out. "I've cheated death once already this morning," I say.

She flips them at me and I catch them in the air.

I stow the remainder of my bagel in the bag, pulling out a large orange juice and firing up the government SUV.

"Is there anything else on your mind this morning besides my continued well-being?" I ask.

"Where are we going?" Danforth asks as I flip an aggressive U-Turn in front of a line of approaching cars.

"Back to where you and your team intercepted me."

"So," she says. "This will sound crazy, but hear me out."

I see the yellow light ahead and punch the accelerator, sweeping through the intersection and making the turn before it turns red. She barely notices, and I feel her eyes appraising me.

"Go on," I say, feeling my anxiety rise.

"I have an egregious proposal for you," she says, choosing her words carefully.

"You want me to brush your hair and tell you all of my secrets?" She purses her lips.

"Come work for me," says Cecilia.

I don't say anything. I'm about to make a left toward the Capitol but change my mind at the last second, swinging back down Madison Drive.

"Cora?" she says.

We roll up in silence right back to where we started at the National Museum of American History.

"Walk with me," I say, pulling over on the sidewalk and hopping out of the vehicle.

We walk over to the smooth marble façade of the museum. I place my hands on the wall and rub my palms over the smooth stone as if I'm trying to comfort it. I close my eyes, welcoming the numbing cold into my fingers. It helps to remind me that this nightmare isn't a dream.

"Do you know what's on the other side of these walls?" I ask.

"The Batmobile?" she answers, throwing her hand up in exasperation.

"The Star-Spangled Banner," I say quietly. "The actual flag that flew over Fort McHenry on the morning of September 14th, 1814. You know the story. The British had just burned Washington, and the Royal Navy was sailing up the Patapsco River to lay waste to Baltimore. They bombarded Fort McHenry for twenty-four hours plus, stopping only to reload. A nonstop barrage of shelling in a driving rainstorm, but the flag was still there." *Quoting the National Anthem, Cora?* I shake my head at my own naïve child-like patriotism.

"The Brits never took Baltimore. Generations of Americans stood up for that flag and the potential it represents. Where are we two centuries later? Ten thousand Americans are going to attack the Capitol for the second time in a decade under orders from your stepdad?"

I feel her eyes on the back of my head. "You're gonna die up there today," she says, ignoring my history lesson.

I turn my head, staring at the dome of the Capitol through the trees. It looks gray and peaceful up there.

"You're going to orphan your daughter or end up rotting in a cell, Walker."

"Don't talk about my daughter," I say, a warning in my voice. "You got this whole thing mapped out, don't you?" I answer, clearing my head, steadying myself for whatever might lay ahead.

"Do you?" she asks. "Come work for me—you don't need to play *Captain America* today. If you die or end up in prison, how does that help you? How does that help your country or your cause?"

"Patton said that moral courage is the most valuable asset a person can possess, but it's also the most absent characteristic in all men," I say quietly.

"You're an idealist," she says. "Quoting Patton and Francis Scott Key. Fine. Go up there. If you survive, then you can come work for me. We can do great things together. I need your intellect. Your fearless insight and that all-consuming passion."

"Question," I ask. "Does the position come with a wardrobe allowance?"

"It's an open offer, Walker," she says, handing me a card after scribbling her number on the back.

She hugs me and says, "Good luck up there today. I'll do my best to bail you out if you end up on the wrong side of history. Don't be afraid to use the number or drop my name. You're gonna need all the help you can get."

CHAPTER 24

January 6, 2029
The National Mall, Washington, D.C.

MY STOMACH GRUMBLES again, but it was worth it. I'd just surrendered the other half of my breakfast bagel in front of the National Gallery of Art. I'd approached a homeless guy scrunched up against a trash can. I talked to him briefly and with a great deal of effort, he stood up. He was hunched over like a T-Rex, his upper frame far too heavy to keep him upright. His odd build and disheveled wiry red hair reminded me of Ronald McDonald. Except this Ronald was coming off of a weeklong bender and looked pretty hungry. I told him he could have the other half of my coveted breakfast if he let me read his bright red shirt.

"Of course," he said with a wink.

With great pomp and circumstance, he grabbed his shirt, pulling it down tight for me to read. It read: I'm NOT LAZY in bold black letters. And underneath it read, I JUST REALLY ENJOY DOING NOTHING. I laughed out loud and handed over my half of the sandwich.

Cecilia Danforth had an annoying habit of always leaving me with more questions than answers.

Sanctioned at the highest levels? What the hell does that mean? My life pivoted on those five words. What form of democracy would I be forced to fight for during the golden age of disinformation if the hordes managed to sidetrack the Election Certification and take up residence in the Capitol?

Approaching Capitol Square, I catch a glimpse of the weeping woman statue and it stops me in my tracks. I've seen the statue several times, but this morning, the woman of stone speaks to me.

The statue depicts two women dressed in flowing Roman robes perched near the top of the statue with the dome of the Capitol Building dominating the canvas behind them. One woman is studying a tablet while the other one weeps into her shoulder. Their frozen beauty commands my full attention. I snap two photos with my phone before Googling the statue for more information.

A moment later, I had my answer. The statue is called the *Peace Monument*. "They died that their country might live," was the hidden inscription on the tablet. I stare again at the women and wonder if they will mourn my passing.

The silence surrounding the grounds of the Capitol Building sets the stage like a Western town before the glorious gunfight at high noon. A piece of paper—or is it a tumbleweed—scampers past my feet as I wait for hidden enemies to yell, "Draw!"

The only problem is that there is no such thing as a *glorious* gunfight. Death is not grand. It's pitiless and final. I've been trapped inside my head watching the grains of sand fill up the bottom half of the hourglass. Time's up.

I step into the employee entrance to the Capitol, taken aback by the vacuum surrounding me. The giant dome is holding its breath, commanding absolute silence from all of those who dare to enter.

I make my way past the metal detector seeking out the watch commander, Reggie Devereux. His infectious smile and erect posture have been replaced overnight by a dour expression and sagging shoulders. His eternally crisp white shirt looks like he scraped it up off of the bathroom floor before getting dressed this morning. I've always known him as a consummate professional. Today he looks like an out-of-work pro wrestler.

"Commander Devererux, a moment, please?" I call to him.

His large bald head swings in my direction and motions me to follow. As soon as we are alone, he dives right in.

"I thought you were taking today off," he says sadly.

"Reggie, what's the plan this morning?"

My question causes an involuntarily wince.

Without giving him a chance to answer, I plunge ahead. "Tell me there's an Army infantry division prepping in the basement ready to defend this building for this afternoon's election certification. I just came from the White House, and we are condition red, sir, and expecting rain."

Devereux sighs heavily, plunging his fingers deep into his temples. He appears to be at a loss for words.

"Reggie?"

He kneads his temples and stares past me, possibly pondering life in an alternate reality.

"Jesus! You've been ordered to stand down!" I whisper harshly, putting a hand on the back of my neck and squeezing too hard. It was a statement, not a question.

He looks queasy for a moment, unsteady on his feet. I want to help steady him, but that was the kind of person I wanted to be, not who I really am.

"Be outta here by noon. *Don't* be here when this goes down," he says, punching the word *don't* for emphasis.

I blanch under the weight of his revelation. An attack on the United States Capitol Building not only had the green light, but the Capitol Police Force had been ordered to stand aside and let it happen.

"All of us may be out of work tomorrow," he says with a firm jaw. "But I'll be goddamned if any one of us stands down. This is our Capitol—no cowardly group of shit-kickers is gonna waltz in here and take it from us a second time."

I look at him. "I'm with you."

"Speaker Sarah Vasquez can definitely expect unwanted company this afternoon. Half the force called in sick this morning." He shakes his head. He says something else under his breath that I can't make out.

"So we're the last line of defense. You and me, Reggie. Not just for this building, but for democracy," I say.

He fishes the phone out of his pocket and reads to me. "'We have the weapons. We have the numbers. We're gonna build our gallows and we're gonna hang these fuckin' traitors on the fuckin' lawn. God Bless America!'"

He looks at me and stops reading. "This is what we're up against."

His words hang in the air, but he leaves me standing alone, *dumbstruck and numb.* Two words that have never been part of who I am. I feel the balloon slowly deflating.

Dev's revelation cements the gathering disorder of my life. I live in a wall of hope, content to meander in the delusion that justice will eventually prevail. But there's no time for an internal civics debate. People are counting on me. Besides, nothing is set in stone. Our nation survived George Wallace, Joe McCarthy, and even Tricky Dick—why can't we overcome this one?

My phone buzzes and I snatch it up. "Walker."

"Cora." It's the Speaker of the House. "Are you on the grounds yet?"

"Yes, ma'am," I answer.

"There's a new development," she says.

"I'll be there in five," I say, breaking the connection.

Time to get squared away and combat ready. My father imprinted one core principle into me as a child: *Hope for the best. Plan for the worst.* I think about the words spoken by Abraham Lincoln and echoed a hundred years later by JFK.

"I see a storm coming, but if he has a place for me, I am ready."

The problem was, I wasn't ready and neither was anyone else. Not even close.

CHAPTER 25

January 6, 2029
Capitol Hill, Washington, D.C.

SPEAKER OF THE HOUSE Sarah Vasquez sits transfixed by the television monitors in her office watching the massive crowd spill out onto Constitution Avenue because the fifty-two-acre Ellipse in front of the White House is already bloated with people. She knew, I knew, hell, everyone in Washington knew that after President Locke finished his hate speech, he'd escort the evil hordes two klicks east to take Capitol Hill.

I stand next to her desk. "Maybe Locke will dole out his usual dribble about a stolen election and leave it at that?"

The Speaker's eyes fill with tears, but not a single one falls from her eyes. After another minute she whispers, "You don't believe that."

"No, ma'am, I don't believe that at all," is all I could manage.

"Look at all of these poor, angry, misguided people. It's 7:43 in the morning and the Polyester Messiah isn't scheduled to take the podium and give them their marching orders until ten."

Poor people? "I'd sacrifice every last one of them in a heartbeat to preserve our democracy and protect you."

"I know you would, Cora, but you're a warrior not a diplomat. If our party had more warriors, and fewer college professors, we might actually get somewhere."

"I've been here before, you know," I say walking past her desk and staring out the window behind her.

She shuts off the television monitors and joins me looking out the window. We both lean on the ornate windowsill in front of us.

"Have you?" she asks quietly.

"I started to tell you yesterday, this is Benghazi all over again. I'm reliving September 11th, 2012. With one crippling exception."

"What's that?" she asks softly.

"Abby is at home and I love her more than anything else in this sorry world. And if I fail or die here today, she'll grow up without a mother," I say fighting back tears.

She moves closer to put an arm around me, but decides against it.

"The players have changed since Benghazi. There's a different political party running the show, but it's always the same. They overran the Capitol in 2021 and this time it will be infinitely worse. One political party wants to goose-step down Constitution Avenue while the other one wants to practice yoga while the world goes to hell. This is just another abject failure by the United States government to protect its people," I say wondering if our nation has always been this way.

"If you look at American history, our country is infamous for trying every other avenue before even considering the right path. Our leaders have no courage and are bereft of any semblance of decency. They will always pad their pockets and take the easy way out while pointing fingers at other politicians and agencies once the damage is already done," I say. "All the crazies in the streets are carrying guns just like they were in Benghazi."

"Explain that to me," she says.

"I was sent to Libya to gather information on a potential terrorist plot against the United States and give our country a heads-up before terrorists had a chance to inflict any catastrophic damage against American interests. I uncovered irrefutable intelligence and relayed it to Washington and the CIA Chief in Benghazi. The people back in D.C. verified my intelligence. They knew the attack was coming and that Ambassador J.T. Stevens was the target. The Libyans knew that if they could kidnap or kill him, the whole world would know and it would become a spectacle. We had the who, what, where, when, and the power to stop the attack and save the ambassador's life." I shake my head. "And how did that turn out?"

Her eyes radiate with sympathy.

"And here we are, the big day that's been lumbering toward us since the beginning of December and it's finally tracked us down and there's nowhere to hide. January 6th didn't sneak up on anyone and neither did Benghazi. And if the President's attack fails, what then? The FBI will bang their gongs and arrest the attackers while the men responsible including the President of the United States will lawyer up and scream to the heavens, 'It wasn't me! It wasn't me! Fake news!'"

The Speaker snorts. "That's not what will happen."

"It won't?" I ask dubiously.

"No. Locke and his sycophants will call the people arrested heroes. Just like they did in '21," she says. "These *heroes* will thrash the police, murder Congressmen, and take over the building. President Locke will call them patriots or turn them all into martyrs."

I shuffle to my office feeling worse than I did before. Contacts from various agencies confirm that at least three white supremacist militias including the Sons of the Apocalypse, Southern Exposure, and God's White Guardians will join the mob and hit the Capitol this afternoon.

If the Capitol is breached by hostiles, protecting Speaker Vasquez will require a level of violence on my part that's usually reserved for the battlefield or back alleys. If I'm forced to take lives in a public forum, this could become a serious problem for the people I love, especially my daughter.

I slept with Abby last night. The last act of a desperate mom who can't get out of her own way. I know this country isn't worth it. *I hope you can forgive me, Abby.*

We have one final meeting—the Capitol Police leadership at ten—but I have personal business to tend to first. Cat and I have to finalize plans to protect my family.

Cat's real name is Zoe Infante. She's an Army veteran, a warrior in every sense of the word whose career was cut short by an improvised explosive device in Sandland. She's my confidante and best friend. She's also my mentor and, perhaps most importantly, my daughter's godmother. Not only does she love Abby, but Cat guided and nurtured me when I was growing up with a vicious and abusive stepfather when I was a teenager living in Rocky Mount, Virginia. She gave me the tools I needed to overcome my early circumstances and make something of myself. Abbs loves her to death, and I trust her with my life.

I have six new burner phones charging on a power strip underneath my desk. I memorized the numbers when I purchased them two weeks ago. I've always had a thing for numbers. They live in my head. When I was a little girl, my dad always joked that someday I was going to run out of space.

I grab the first phone ending in 4645 and punch in the numbers for Cat, dialing star-six-seven to block the incoming number. After six long rings, the call goes to voicemail. I break the connection with the end button and hit redial.

"Answer the friggin phone, Cat!" I snarl at the phone.

This time she picks up.

"I can't wait!" she says, her voice dripping with snark. She obviously thinks this is a telemarketing sales call.

The sound of her voice sends waves of emotion crashing over my defenses.

"Hey," is all I can manage. My voice threatens to buckle under the weight of what I'm about to ask her.

"Snowflake?" Her tone shifts from annoyance to pure concern. *Snowflake*, the nickname she came up with for me a lifetime ago, long before it was turned into something nasty.

"Hey," I say again. *Get your act together, Walker. That's an order.*

"You callin' me from a burner?" she asks.

"I am. No names, OK?" I feel tears taking shape in my eyes again. I'm a wreck.

The connection falls silent as she waits for me to compose myself.

"Where are you?" I ask.

"Bethesda. Jesus, what's wrong, kid?"

"Bethesda? Thank God. You're close. I need you to execute that exfil plan we discussed," meaning I need her to collect my family and get them out of Dodge.

The phone falls silent again, this time for a full thirty seconds.

"I'm on my way," she says.

"It's probably nothing or maybe this afternoon will morph into a full-fledged bloodbath? I really don't know." My half-assed response disappoints me.

"The news on the radio says the crowds at the White House are out of control and the President isn't due to speak for another two hours. They keep showing clips from 2021. It's déjà vu all over again."

I don't answer.

"Are you sure you want to go all the way with this one?" Cat asks.

"I don't know what I'm going to do yet. We never know what evils we're capable of when we wake up each morning, do we?"

"Whoa, you are steeped in some heavy philosophy this morning," she says. "Slow down, girl."

"The attack has been in the works for weeks. It's been green-lit by the jerk-off in the White House. They're coming. Period. There's no way to stop them."

"What about the FBI or the National Guard?" she asks.

"No one is coming, Cat. There are rumors that the National Guard may run point on the attack. The National Guard is now the President's Parliamentary Guard."

"Well goddamn, girl. So don't do anything. Get the hell out of there. You have a good life. Whatever it is, it ain't worth this shit. This country has changed so much since 2020. Don't piss it away playing *Captain America*."

That's the second time someone's called me *Captain America* today. What a joke. I'm anything but a hero. A rogue tear escapes down my face and I swat it away.

"I know this is a huge ask, Cat. I need you to collect my assets"—*meaning my family*—"and get on the road and disappear. You know where to take them. Ping me on this number when you have them. I have six burner phones and I'm only using each one of them five to six times. You are my first call. Big Brother is always listening."

"Don't do this." Cat is angry now.

I blurt out, "I don't have time, OK?"

"This is bullshit," she says.

"First, no electronics," I say. "Second, use my emergency account and grab twenty large. Third, buy a used car or steal one. See if you can get something made before 2005, so there's no GPS."

"Anything else?" she asks, dripping with snark.

"I set up a pair of accounts. After the attack, let's stay in contact using the terrorist comm system," I say. "I don't want anybody pinging a cell tower giving away your position."

"On the happy network?" she asks. Happy of course translates into Yahoo. It's not that hard to figure out, but Cat won't make it easy for anyone who may be monitoring our transmission.

"Yes, ma'am," I say feeling some glimmer of hope. She has that effect on me. When we weren't training and shooting together when I lived with her as a teenager, we were always playing word and number games trying to one-up each other. She couldn't match me with a gun in my hand, but everything else I learned from her.

"The usernames are the same for each account. The username is that band you hate. The one that sings the funny song that Abby sings to you. At the end of each username, tack on two digits from that place's address where we stored those items after the incident."

There's a long pause. "You mean the things, from the ones who did the bad thing?"

"That's exactly what I mean. You got the usernames?"

I imagine her furrowing her brow before putting the usernames together in her head: wallofvoodo24 and wallofvoodo13.

"I do," she says.

"You got the subsequent digits?"

"I got the whole enchilada, lady," she says. "What about the passwords, little Miss WindTalker?"

A smile at her reference. WindTalkers were Native American undercover operatives in World War II who used Navajo code words to communicate in the Solomon Islands so that the Japanese

Imperial Army couldn't decode their messages. She taught me that when I was a teenager.

"The password is where we first engaged in hand-to-hand combat along with my age at the time. I've already left the other password in a folder for you to find along with some other relevant information."

"Hold on," Cat says. "I'm not like you, Rain Man. I have to write down this shit before committing it to memory. You love this cloak and dagger stuff," she says with grudging respect.

"Get your own burners, I know you have plenty. Ping me once you have the packages. What time do you anticipate liftoff?" I ask.

"Fourteen hundred hours, give or take," she says. "Is your mind made up on this?"

"There's no good outcome for me with today's events. I'll do what needs to be done. I'm going to war with a water pistol against thousands of white nationalists and inbreds with AR-15s. I'm gonna take a chunk out of them, and when the dust clears, I'll either be dead or wanted for murder."

She laughs into the phone. "Goddamn, girl, I might have taught you too well."

"Remember the procedure. Nothing sent. Nothing received," I say. "I may very well be considered a domestic terrorist when all of this is over."

"You're not already?" she asks. "What else do you need from me?"

"Remember the Alamo," I say.

"Benghazi was the Alamo, Cora. And you came out of that with flying colors."

"Yup, but this time, I'm not supposed to shoot back," I say breaking the connection.

CHAPTER 26

January 6, 2029
Capitol Hill, Washington, D.C.

MONICA DAVIES, the Chief of Staff for Sarah Vasquez, looks up from her phone eyeing me warily as I approach the table where she's sitting in the Capitol Café. As the Speaker's Chief of Staff, she's technically my boss, although the Speaker crushed that illusion during my first month on the job. The smell of baking cookies coming from the kitchen soothes my soul.

"Cora," she says, grimly looking down at her half-eaten cup of yogurt.

We are the only two people in the cafeteria and my patience for this woman crashed and burned yesterday when she blew me off for another morning meeting. With Locke and his people coming, I have no time for egos or hurt feelings. I shove a chair back and plop down next to her.

"Monica," I say making no attempt to suppress my aggression. "You've been avoiding me for two days and missed two meetings in a row. But it's real now. I need you squared away and dialed in to every word I say, because your survival and the Speaker's survival depend on it."

A look of sickness whitens her face.

"I'm going to force you to do things that aren't in your job description today, and you're gonna do them, or I'm gonna get medieval with you. You feel me?" I say very quietly with a maniacal smile.

"Jesus, Cora. You're certifiable," she says, her voice cracking in fear.

"Sweetheart, you have no idea what I am capable of," I say. The chair screeches on the floor as I stand up, towering over her.

"Bad people, with bad intentions, are gonna run down these halls in a few hours and the rules of civilized society will evaporate in the carnage. They're coming for the Speaker. Are you gonna stand by and let them take her?" I ask.

"What? N . . . No." She coughs.

"I need to know if I can count on you, Monica. You're smart and confident, but like everyone else in this cesspool of a city, you've been sidetracked by your ego. That's fine and dandy in the civilized world of bureaucracy, but that ain't gonna work today when the dogs of war bust through the doors and want a little taste."

"What do you want me to do?" she asks hesitantly.

"Can you shoot?" I ask.

"A gun?" she stammers.

I look at her quizzically.

"I have never fired a gun before," she says.

She shakes her head no.

"That's OK; it's not that hard. You point at the center mass and pull the trigger," I say.

She nods her head but says nothing.

"If we can get out in one piece this afternoon, I may need you to drive," I say.

She nods her head again.

"Do you know where Havre de Grace, Maryland, is?"

"What?"

"Havre de Grace. Do you know where it is?" I ask.

"Sort of," she says.

"It's simple. Just get on 95 and head north, OK?"

"But what if—"

I cut her off in mid-sentence. "As you can tell, I'm wound a little tight this morning." I'm trying to bring her down after my initial approach. "We have a long, terrifying day in front of us. But if we work together, we can get the Speaker out of this death trap when the mob comes calling. I have every confidence in you and your abilities, but today, you stow the personal hostility and work with me. Can you do that?"

She nods her head slowly.

"I need to hear you say it," I say.

"We can work together," she says, looking like her yogurt might be coming back up.

"C'mon, then. Let's go see the Speaker."

A few minutes later I'm back in the Speaker's office standing side by side with Monica Davies. The Speaker has already changed her outfit. She's squared away and looks like she's just walked out of a photo shoot. Her vibrant red blazer is flawless and her choice of color draws me in.

"Back so soon?" asks the Speaker.

"I apologize, Madame Speaker," I say. "I love your outfit, by the way, especially that shade of red."

Speaker Vasquez stops writing, appraising me with a smile.

"The color red isn't just for President Locke and Load and his silly baseball caps or the MAGA hats that came first," she says with a mischievous smile. "I decided that on such a historic day, it was time to reclaim this color from the forces of chaos and disinformation."

She slowly closes her computer, giving us both her full attention.

"Good morning, Monica. Somehow, I don't think you two came in here to compliment me on my outfit."

"Can we take a walk outside of the office?" I ask.

The Speaker looks down at her buzzing cell phone, mountain of paperwork, and the phone ringing on her desk and then back up at me with a smile. "Why not?"

I lead Speaker Vasquez and Monica out in the hall and past the House Chambers to a series of storage rooms. I stop them at room 12866b. I unlock the door with a key and let them step past me into the darkness. I close the door behind me before hitting the light switch to my right.

We walk down five stairs. There's a door marked BOILER ROOM on the left and a nondescript fuse box on the right. I open the small metal door of the fuse box and flip fuse numbers 1, 13, 28, and 5 in rapid succession. I stand back and with a small click, the fuse panel releases and swings open revealing a combination dial. I enter the four-digit combination and the boiler room door makes a series of metallic unlocking noises before popping open next to us. I gently shut the panel to the combination dial and click the faux fuse box back into place before motioning to the open door.

"After you, ladies," I say.

Motion detectors activate a series of bulbs, bathing the room in soft white light. They walk into a lavishly furnished area with ornate couches, two large conference tables, and monitors on the walls. I follow them closely as the door behind seals behind us with a whooshing sound just before another series of metallic pops indicates that we are bolted in. I can feel the pressure change as my ears pop.

"It's like the door to a safe," says Monica with wide eyes.

"It's a bunker," says the Speaker. "A nuclear bunker?"

"It is, Madame Speaker," I say. "If you want me to collect some items, I can bring them here before the certification begins. I may need to relocate you to this location later depending on what happens during the election certification process. I have access to two more safe rooms, but this one is the closest to your office and the Senate Chambers."

"How did you find all of this, Cora?" asks Monica.

"Friends in low places," I say smiling at her, trying to break through her mask of stoicism.

She nods with a grimace, or was that a smile?

"If we have to flee the Capitol, I want to give you an idea of what to expect," I say.

"Cora, I can't leave until the certification process is complete," the Speaker says resolutely.

"Madame Speaker, permission to speak freely?"

"I suspect you're going to anyway, but please," she says, glancing toward Monica with a knowing smile.

"I'll make you a promise. If there's any way the certification process can continue and the protesters are kept out of the building, then, of course, I would never dream of taking you away from your duties. But if people wielding pitchforks and brandishing firearms are swarming through the halls, I have to protect you the only way I know how. That means leaving this building before it becomes your final resting place."

The three of us sit in silence for a long moment.

"Probably 95 percent of them will be nothing more than drones sent to chant, vandalize, and batter the police like they did the first time. But the plan to grab hostages is real, and you're at the top of their priority list. Your office has been a very popular destination during some of your fellow Congressmen's illicit tours of the Capitol."

"Options?" she asks.

"Madame Speaker," I say firmly, "you shouldn't be within a ten-mile radius of this building right now. The Capitol Police are undermanned and outgunned. In their current state, they cannot begin to adequately defend this building. You are in clear and present danger."

"I appreciate the gravity of our current situation. But you also know I will not abandon today's election certification process. That leaves our country to the wolves and that is not a viable option," says the Speaker. Her voice is as calm as a summer breeze in the face of a Cat-5 hurricane. "What's option two?"

"Madame Speaker, option two is keep me glued to you. I will do everything in my power to protect you if the walls come down. I can't and I won't pretend that I can guarantee your safety, but you'll have no chance without Monica and me by your side if Locke's forces seize the building."

Monica's shoulders puff up a little bit and she stands a little bit taller.

"If we have to exit the building, you ladies are going to work with a man I trust my life with. I'll keep you close to Washington so you can return quickly, but not too close."

"Who is this man?" asks the Speaker.

"For operational security, I can't share his name. He's off the grid, no social media, no email, no nothing. He's a trained operator. Works only for himself. I've fought side by side with him. His morals are above reproach and he would do anything for me. He's not hard on the eyes either," I say with a twinkle in my eye. "For an older guy."

"So how do we contact him?" asks the Speaker.

"Monica and I will have burner phones," I say looking at Monica. "All you have to do is hit redial—it's the only number on the phone. He will only talk to the Speaker, Monica, or myself. If you have to call him, identify yourselves only by the first four digits of your Social Security number before speaking."

"You need our Social Security numbers?" asks the Speaker and Monica at the same time.

"No, I have them already," I say.

"That's more than a little creepy," says Monica.

"You get used to it," says the Speaker, shaking her head at Cora.

"This is a fluid situation," I say. "All of my best-laid plans will go up in smoke in the first hour—that's just the nature of war. But according to numerous intelligence community assessments, my strongest trait has always been ruthless adaptation, whatever the hell that means. So strap your boots on tight."

The women look at me and then look at each other like they're sharing a secret. Then the Speaker gives us her own update.

"The President's lapdogs on the other side of the aisle have spent the last three days trying to assure me that any rumors about a second attack on the Capitol is nothing more than a wild conspiracy theory concocted by the media. They insist that the *Keep the Peace March* is just that," says the Speaker.

"One newbie from the great state of Georgia pulled me aside this morning and insisted that President Locke is just blowing smoke. She says there is zero chance that Locke is planning any action against Capitol Hill with the whole world watching. Of course, with the way that woman lies, she all but assured me that an attack is imminent."

"Madame Speaker, there is one more thing. Both of you must understand that my methods can be unconventional—" I pause searching for the right words, feeling uncomfortable for the first time.

"Please continue," the Speaker says, nodding for me to finish.

"I can't represent the dead. I don't speak for them. The people who have crossed me made their final choice and I'm forever burdened with their state of unrest." I lock eyes with the Speaker, "I want you to understand that I will be forced to terminate any threat I perceive against you."

"*Terminate?*" she asks.

"*With extreme prejudice,*" I explain.

"Martin Sheen from *Apocalypse Now?*" she asks.

"*The horror,*" I reply, quoting Marlon Brando from the same movie.

PART THREE

THE MOB IS THE MOTHER OF TYRANTS

Diogenes

CHAPTER 27

January 6, 2029
Rose Garden, White House, Washington, D.C.

"*Locke n' Load, Locke n Load, Locke n Load.*"

The chants grow in intensity while President Terrance B. Locke bobs his head up and down in mock approval.

"Listen to them," he says doing the same little tap dance he used to do on his talk show years ago right before someone got hit with a chair or punched in the face. He laughs, turning to his step-daughter and Chief of Staff, Cecilia Danforth. "They're fired up and ready to go this morning."

They are set up under a tent in the Rose Garden of the White House with about thirty of the President's closest supporters and Secret Service staff. They give the President and his stepdaughter the space you would expect when a monarch is holding court. The two of them stare at the giant flat-screen television broadcasting the video feed from the crowd gathered at the Ellipse. The President points to a man in a pirate outfit and shakes his head. "What the fuck is that guy supposed to be? Do they think this is a Comicon convention?"

"You're going to make history today. I can feel it, Mr. President," Cecilia interjects quickly, trying to distract the President and keep him positive. "These people—your people—won't let the politicians take away your presidency."

"The traitors up there on Capitol Hill will never know what hit them. I have a special surprise that will shock the world. Especially that boney-assed bitch Sarah Vasquez," says the President just a bit too loudly. "Has anybody heard from the VEEP?"

"Not yet, Mr. President," says Cecilia. "We're still trying to locate him."

"Sebastian Knox better damn well do the right thing by me or these folks might tear his ass apart," he says, laughing at his own amazing wit. "Knox will have one last chance to fulfill his duty. If he refuses, we're going to take that chess piece off the board."

"How will that work?" Cecilia asks.

"Don't worry, Daddy's thought of everything," says the President feeling the dull ache for a proper drink.

Cecilia turns her head like a model flashing a grin at him, her gorgeous long blonde hair cascading around her sculpted shoulders and settling perfectly on her eight-thousand-dollar white Versace dress. He puts his hands on her shoulders and squeezes them in a non-fatherly way. When it comes down to it, she's the only person he can really trust in the swamp. And if he was honest with himself, even if she was his stepdaughter, he knew that all women craved a powerful man and there was no one more powerful than him.

The President's son, Artie Locke, cautiously approaches them from the back, sidestepping a stone-faced Secret Service agent. "Look at them," he says sweeping his hand toward the screen. "True patriots who are fed up with the bullshit." Cecilia gives him a caustic look that would melt steel.

"You're right, Son," says the President, making no effort to hide the fact that he did not appreciate being interrupted. "They're gonna fight like hell for us today. I can feel it."

"Good luck, Mr. President," says his son, seeking the slightest hint of his father's approval.

The president's derisive snort signals Artie that it's time to walk away. The chants of the crowd grow more frenzied as Locke senses that it is nearly time to raise the curtain and make his grand entrance. He gives a slight nod to one of his people who appears a moment later with a capped presidential Locke and Load travel mug. He takes a long, generous pull and walks over to the mirror. He smiles at himself, very impressed with the man staring back at him.

"You look perfect today, Daddy. You're the only leader in American history who ever had the courage to take what's rightfully yours." Endless flattery was the only path to her stepfather's heart and Cecelia had mastered that art form when she was ten years old. She noticed his little pull of presidential courage, but now was not the time to risk distracting him. A little buzz would be fine as long as some of his liquor had some coffee mixed in with it.

"Let's keep them waiting for another few minutes. I want them screaming for blood this morning," says the President. Locke loves to keep his worshippers waiting and today he would whip them up into a fever pitch before sending them to occupy Capitol Hill.

"Great idea, Daddy," Cecelia agrees. "I can actually hear the love in their chants. You're their savior." She hopes she didn't pour it on a little too thick with that last comment, but it appears to have pleased him.

"I am, aren't I? I really am. The savior." Locke shakes his head, but his thoughts are interrupted as the opening notes of "Right Now" by Van Halen erupt out of the speakers blaring across the National Mall. He nods his head, singing the song to himself. "I'm ready to grab this country by the balls. And I'm ready to do it, 'Right Now.'"

"Please welcome the President of the United States of America, President Terrance B. Locke!"

President Locke jogs four feet onto the stage and starts clasping his fists above his head like he just knocked out the heavyweight champion of the world. The crowd erupts into bedlam watching their champion shadowbox onstage.

He takes his time, soaking up every drop of the undiluted adulation echoing up and down the National Mall in Washington, D.C. He stops every few steps pointing at people and pumping his fists like a drunken boxer. Repeating the gestures again and again as he makes the fifty-foot walk to the podium.

The Van Halen song plays even louder as the President approaches the lectern. The hidden DJ expertly silences the music right after the line "Turn this thing around!"

"Turn this thing around!" yells the President of the United States enthusiastically. "Isn't that what they said? Turn this thing around?"

The crowd breaks into wild applause that lasts another ninety seconds. This is pure presidential palooza.

"So I have a question for you," the President says seriously, causing the crowd to grow eerily silent. "You heard the song, right? So when are we going *to turn this thing around?* When, America? When are we going to turn this thing around?"

He pauses, looking at their confused faces.

"Right now!" he bellows to the crowd. "Right here. Right now!"

"Right Now, right now, right now," chants the crowd dutifully.

"Today we make history!" he yells, sending the crowd into complete pandemonium. It takes almost six minutes to bring the crowd back under control. Locke is their shepherd and he moves his flock with absolute precision. He wants them on the edge of insanity today.

"We've accomplished so much in the last four years. I couldn't be more proud of every one of you. I see my 'Labor Equals Freedom' caucus who helped us root out the evil immigrants and force them into an honest day's work for the American people," he says gesturing to a large group of men in brown shirts with American Flag armbands.

The crowd cheers them on enthusiastically, and the President presses on.

"And let's not forget my proudest achievement. The children, the children that made America great again! Our amazing America First Youth Informant Council—AFYIC. My God, you kids are amazing. The AFYIC helped our great country root out the people who were not loyal to the stars and stripes of America. You played the starring role in my Rejection of Evil Literature initiative that led to the arrest of more than five hundred subversive writers and professors and teachers. The same people who hate our great country."

This recognition of the youth informant council pumps pride into the frenetic crowd as the junior informants jump up and down waving their customized black Locke and Load hats in celebration.

"Look at you! Hundreds of thousands of patriots here today for me! But the lying media won't show that to anybody, will they? Nooo . . ." he says sending throngs of people into a long chorus of booos punctuated by chants of: "Fuck the Press, Fuck the Press!"

When the chants run out of steam, the maestro picks right up where he left off.

"Make no mistake, we're in a battle to save the soul of America, and you know what? We're winning!" he roars, sending the crowd into another riotous frenzy.

"You know the leaders from the opposition party. We know them, don't we?" says the President in a conspiratorial stage whisper.

"They are the Satan worshippers who promote the sexual exploitation of your children in our public schools. They promote the sexual mutilation of innocent and unsuspecting children. They teach anti-white racism while the press tries to sweep their dirty secrets under the rug," says Locke as his throngs of supporters gasp and shake their heads in disgust.

"We all know about the media, don't we? We all know what their game is. Don't we? They're part of the plot to destroy America. To destroy the America we love. Just like the Democrats. They want the immigrants to steal your jobs. Rape your women. Steal our children. Let the environmentalists force you to live in a cave and eat grass like a goddamned animal. I say no more!"

Hundreds of sycophants wave their Locke n Load flags back and forth trying to conjure up a magical storm of hate and outrage.

The President's speech continues for twenty minutes, hitting every one of his cherished fear talking points. He lashes out at minorities, immigrants, political opponents, and any other enemies, real or perceived. The mob hangs on every word and you can smell the fury billowing up from the crowd. They are past the breaking point. His true believers know that this is their last chance to save their America. Any enemy of Locke is their sworn enemy as well.

"We got a lot of work to do today, folks, am I right? Keeping the Peace ain't easy. We got a lot of work to do," he says. "You know what people are saying? Do you? People, all kinds of people, coming up to me, all day long saying, 'Mr. President, you pulled our nation together. Four years ago we were in the dark ages. You saved the country, Mr. President.' You're goddamned right I did!"

Locke and Load chants begin, but the President waves for them to quiet down.

"Wanna know who else has a lot of work to do today? I mean, we got a guy here who can save us a hell of a lot of trouble, don't we? The Vice President, Sebastian Knox. This guy better do what's right when he gets up there on Capitol Hill this afternoon, you know what I'm sayin'?" He pauses for effect.

"Let me let you in on a little secret."

The crowd falls completely silent waiting to be clued in.

"Knox might need a little kick in the ass? You know what I mean?" The president flicks out a little kick to show what he means.

The crowd breaks into uproarious fits of laughter. What could be more funny than kicking the Vice President of the United States of America right in the ass?

"I'm only kidding. *Or am I?* I don't know, folks. He needs to get his head on straight. He needs your help to save what we've built together! I've seen the numbers, you know. I saw them. I sure did. I love the law and I love this country. The VEEP, Sebastian Knox, needs your help. You have to help him do what's right, don't you?"

When the crowd doesn't answer right away, he snaps at them.

"He's up there on Capitol Hill right now. You're gonna help him, right?"

The mob is uncontrollable as more than half of them start pushing their way out of the crowd fighting their way toward Capitol Hill.

"So let's walk up Pennsylvania Avenue. Let's Keep the Peace! You know what to do? I'll be right there with you. Keep the Peace by helping Congress follow the letter of the law!"

The rabid chants of "Law and Order" echo across the National Mall for a full minute before allowing the President to speak again.

"You set Vice President Sebastian Knox straight. Give Sebastian the goddamn courage he needs to fight for us. And while you're up there, why don't you pay 'Stupid Sarah,' a little visit. You teach the Speaker a lesson for the history books. I'm counting on you. So are your children and so are your Christian brothers and sisters. In the precious name of our Lord and Savior who died on the cross for your sins! March up to Capitol Hill and let nothing and no one stand in your way!"

CHAPTER 28

January 6, 2029
Capitol Hill, Washington, D.C.

THE LIVE VIDEO feed coming through my phone spells disaster for those of us trapped inside the walls of the United States Capitol Building. There's a surreal quality to it as I'm watching a mob of mindless zombies slam into the marble walls of the Capitol Building as if they intend to eat their way inside. Handguns, compact automatic weapons, stones, and bricks appear out of backpacks as the siege takes shape on network television for the world to see.

The Capitol Police are hopelessly outnumbered. They already lost the battle of the bike racks. They're being sprayed, beaten, and worse by Locke's Loyalists. Members of the mob are using bike racks as battering rams trying to smash their way into the Capitol. I watch in horror as another Capitol Policeman in riot gear is dragged away into the maelstrom of hate. Sporadic gunshots cause everyone on both sides of the line to stop, flinch, and look around before resuming their roles in the riot.

Watch Commander Reggie Devereux is texting update after update as his people are swept away like shells disappearing off a sandy beach. I'm sitting inside the Capitol in the Senate Chambers ignoring the pro-Locke politicians grandstanding in an effort to subvert the election certification process. God bless those Capitol Policemen. They're displaying uncommon valor against overwhelming odds all over again. Some have been shot, punched, stabbed, and sprayed with chemicals, and as far as I'm concerned, their level of restraint is far past anything I could achieve in ten lifetimes.

The coverage on my video feed switches to a different camera showing rioters scaling the walls between two dead policemen. These are the same people I encountered early this morning when I was at the White House. They attended Locke's rally before he sent them to march on Capitol Hill. The camera pans in for a closer shot of the building just in time to watch a man hurl a cinder block at one of the reinforced windows. The large block ricochets straight back into the man's face, knocking him out of the picture. Too bad it didn't take off his head. There's no stopping this tsunami of rage—the mob will be inside in a matter of minutes. I need to get the Speaker the hell out of this rattrap. To the right I see several puffs of smoke and realize that the rioters have opened fire on the police.

My sources tell me that thousands of National Guardsmen are all over the city, but apparently, they're too busy directing traffic and monitoring the Metro stations to be bothered with defending the Capitol Building.

I'm transfixed looking at my phone while a senator from Colorado is trying to explain why the majority vote in his state should be thrown out in favor of installing President Locke into power for another four years. My phone buzzes again and my blood thickens to ice. The text message is in all caps: THEY'RE IN!!!

He must have copied and pasted the message because the same message flashes on my phone four more times in rapid succession. I thought we had at least another ten minutes. I was wrong! Time to get the Speaker out of here before the rioters join us in the Senate Chambers.

I ease up to her slowly causing several heads to turn in our direction at the audacity of my intrusion.

"Madame Speaker," I whisper to her. "You have a personal emergency."

"This isn't the time," says the Speaker so softly only I could hear her.

"Madame Speaker, we are leav—"

A giant boom cuts me off in mid-sentence, rocking the building and causing several people to cry out in fear. A chorus of angry voices joins the sound of breaking glass as the rioters crash into the doors surrounding the chambers.

I blew it. Missed our escape window.

Mass confusion ensues inside the Chamber as several members of Congress scurry around like frightened rabbits. Security people draw their sidearms and aim them at the front chamber doors where people are now pounding away on the other side.

"Barricade the doors, goddamnit!" screams a Georgia Congressman.

Gunshots ring out from somewhere in the building, causing further panic inside the chamber.

"Take off your Congressional pins so they can't identify us," someone else yells.

"Take off your shoes," I say to the Speaker hustling her over to one of the back exits, "and put these on." I hand her her workout shoes.

The Speaker seems unfazed by the events unfolding around us. It's like we do this every day. We get to the back exit where three security people have taken position in front of the door.

"Make a hole, boys. Move your asses!" I bark at them like a Marine Corps drill sergeant. They're startled at first, but clear a path for us.

I look back at the Speaker, going through three possible routes to her office in my mind. A deafening roar of chants and yells echoes through the corridors emanating from Statuary Hall: "OUR HOUSE—OUR HOUSE—OUR HOUSE!"

"Let's go," says the Speaker with otherworldly aplomb.

I smile to myself. The only thing more impressive than the Speaker's intelligence is her calm under fire. I snatch her arm, hustling her up the stairway on the left.

We take the steps two at a time. The seventy-five-year-old Speaker is remarkably spry for her age. Our luck runs out halfway up the stairs when we come face-to-face with two stone-faced intruders.

The man on the right is wearing the infamous red Locke and Load baseball cap, but it's his black t-shirt that staggers my mind. The words sear themselves into my soul:

LOCKE AND LOAD
CIVIL WAR
JANUARY 6TH, 2029

I have no time to worry about this sickening evidence of premeditation on the part of the federal government, but I will remember this moment forever. The man on the left is sporting a sloppy beard and is pushing at least two hundred and fifty pounds. He's dressed in tactical gear and goggles with a holstered Glock and zip ties in his right hand. He drops the zip ties, reaches for his holster, and leans forward—a fatal miscalculation that would be the last conscious decision he would ever make because at the same moment, the blade of my forearm shoots out and strikes the man in the throat.

His slight forward motion coupled with the force of my blow fatally crushes his windpipe. He falls to his knees, goggles cock-eyed, half on and half off his head as I seize the second man by the testicles. I twist and crush them violently feeling one of them burst under the pressure of my grip. I lock my leg behind his leg and hammer my elbow into his sternum. His upper body shoots back-ward and gravity finishes the job. His head cracks like an egg on the marble stair while his hat lands a foot behind him. Two tan-goes down. An entire army to go.

I scoop up the man's cap before the slow puddle of crimson spreading from the back of his head reaches it. I place the cap on my head and rotate it backwards like a baseball catcher. He has a thigh rig with a K-Bar knife and shoulder holster for his Glock. I confiscate both including his Glock and turn to his partner with the jacked-up goggles who's hopelessly grasping at his throat for air. He's come to the desperate realization that these are his last breaths. I relieve him of his tactical belt, sidearm, and zip ties. He won't need them anymore.

"I've never seen a human being move like that before," the Speaker whispers to me while we hustle toward her office.

"I'm not sure I understand," I answer, stopping her with a gentle tug on the arm and listening to the sounds echo off of the hallway around us.

"You hit the man so fast that I only saw your hand coming back—I never saw the actual strike. And when I turned to look at you, the other man shot backwards like he'd been hit by a bus," she says.

I wonder if she realizes that the first man will be dead by the time we get to her office. She never saw my hand hit his throat because it was my forearm.

"You move at the speed of thought, without the burden of self-doubt or hesitation," she says more to herself than me.

"You mean without mercy? He moved slightly forward at the wrong time. It was just bad luck for him," I say trying to justify the violence of my actions.

"I'm not judging; you did your duty. No shame in that," she says.

I need to keep her talking to distract her from the carnage she's just witnessed. I'm afraid it might soak in any minute.

"It's years of MMA training, boxing, and close-quarter fighting practice. My dad had me sparring before I was ten years old," I answer with a quiet shrug.

"Are they dead?" asks the Speaker suddenly. "Both of them?"

"I'm afraid so," I say.

"Are you OK?" she asks me with concern in her voice.

"I will be, ma'am, thank you for asking."

I'm shocked that the Speaker is taking all of this chaos in stride. We pass the waist-high heavy wooden sign that reads: OFFICIAL BUSINESS ONLY. Above our heads, a single bright beam lights up the entrance to the office with the sign underneath proclaiming:

SPEAKER OF THE HOUSE
SARAH VASQUEZ

No one coming down the hall could miss that sign assuming they can read, but for now, there's no immediate threat. I lock the door behind me and place the thigh rig and the tactical belt onto a plush velvet chair. Vasquez studies me very closely. It's one thing to read about someone's propensity for violence, but seeing it up close and personal must be unnerving, even for her. I wonder if she thinks I'm a monster.

"Madame Speaker, I know you're not a fan, but I need you in the safe room until I can establish a viable escape route," I say, hopping up onto a chair and punching in a code on the hidden keypad behind an elevated light sconce. The door, which looks like a bookcase, swings open with a slow hiss.

"Grab your change of clothes first, please strip off anything that looks formal, and I'll be back shortly," I say.

"How long?" she asks, cutting to the point.

"If we don't leave in the next fifteen minutes, we won't be leaving at all."

She looks curiously at the *Locke n Load* hat still perched on my head from one of the men we encountered on the stairs before making direct eye contact with me. "I assume you're going out to collect some more gear from our visitors?"

I smile mischievously. "I prefer to call it a scavenger hunt."

She nods at me. "We probably have at least three staffers who have locked themselves in the conference room. Please get them some appropriate gear too. And, Cora."

I turn around. "Yes, ma'am."

"Thank you," she says quietly.

I have no idea what she's thanking me for, but I quickly reply, "Yes, ma'am."

The safe room was a huge point of contention between us when I first joined the Speaker. We went back and forth on the project. Speaker Vasquez was absolutely opposed to what she called "a bunch of James Bond BS and a monumental waste of taxpayer money."

I think we're both relieved she finally gave in to my demands. I was stubborn and made it a condition of my continued employment. The safe room was constructed in secret during the dead of the night when the office was empty. Everyone who noticed a difference just assumed the Speaker had done a bit of remodeling.

Speaker Vasquez grabs a small bag with her clothes, laptop, and handful of documents off of her desk. She walks into the bunker without another word. I enter the code, sealing her inside. I set my watch knowing all too well that time is a formidable adversary.

"Cora, what should we do?" asks someone on the verge of tears, peeking out from the conference room. Her question leads to an exodus from the office comprised of three people: Monica Davies, the Speaker's Chief of Staff; Jimmy, the audio guy; and the Speaker's secretary, Beth Fleming.

"The best course of action is for all of you to stay put right now." My heart aches for them. They look so terrified.

"You want me to sit here on my ass while they burn the Capitol down around us?" asks Jimmy nervously.

I ignore him and address the group.

"Listen, friends." I find the same tone of voice I use with Abby after she scrapes her knee. "We have to be here for one another right now. It's us against them. We're a team and a team that's not just better than the mob, we're stronger than them too."

I make eye contact with them trying to instill a sliver of hope and maybe a little bit of confidence.

"We need to trust each other. You have every right to be pissed off, but we can't get emotional right now because we can't afford mistakes," I say in a gentle whisper. "I can get us out of here—it's what I do. But we have to work together and you have to trust me."

My motherly tone has the desired effect. It casts a protective net over the room. I can tell by the look on their faces.

"Are you going to stay here with us?" asks Monica Davies.

"I'll be back soon," I say, running into my office with the items I borrowed from the men outside the Senate Chambers. I snag my duffle out of the filing cabinet and literally rip the lavender dress off of my body while kicking my flats off across the room. I throw on thick black jeans, thick socks, a long Dri-FIT t-shirt, black with long sleeves, along with a tactical vest including a .38 Special.

I sit on the couch and shove my feet into black combat boots and lace them up in seconds. No one gets dressed more efficiently than the military. I strap the thigh rig on my left leg and slide the K-Bar knife into it. Then I grab my double-edged diving knife out of the bag and slide it deep into the sheath on my tactical belt. I quickly inspect the weapons I took from the men on the stairs—one's a Glock 19 and the other is a Glock 17. I stuff the 19 into the back of my black jeans and secure the other one to my new shoulder holster. Nice holster, that guy must have paid a fortune for it.

The .38 is a six-shot revolver that's easy to conceal and that goes into my right boot. The .38 is a throwaway gun with no serial number so, theoretically, it can't be traced back to me.

I come out of my office and the Speaker's staff stares at me like I'm Spider-Man and just dropped out of a comic book.

"Being anxious right now is totally normal," I say with a gentle laugh that washes over them.

"*Anxious?*" says Jimmy. "We're scared shitless!"

"We have to be brave right now, not just for ourselves, but for the Speaker and for our country."

Each one of them straightens up a little bit and a few nod their heads.

"Anybody have workout clothes with them?" I ask hopefully. "Monica, I know you do."

She nods her head.

The secretary says she has a pair of jeans in her bag, too.

"Please change as quickly as possible. We need to move out as soon as I return," I say, checking my reflection in the mirror. I see a ridiculous female soldier of fortune staring back at me. I arrange my Locke and Load hat and pull my thick hair through the back. I hope the previous owner of this cap didn't have lice. I can blend in with these people for now, and they'll learn soon enough, I'm not trapped in here with them—they're trapped in here with me.

Speaker Vasquez has already been in lockdown for six minutes, far too long for the storm raging down the hall.

CHAPTER 29

January 6, 2029
Capitol Hill, Washington, D.C.

I BREAK OUT into the hallway turning left. I need to try and keep the Speaker's office in my line of sight while scavenging for outfits. I've been so focused on Speaker Vasquez in the days leading up to this event, I failed to properly prepare all the people in our office.

A series of gunshots echoes across the halls of the Capitol. I take out the Glock I took from the man on the stairs and fire a single shot, shattering the bright beam illuminating the SPEAKER OF THE HOUSE sign. I walk down the hall to the second stairwell and see two men coming up the steps.

"SARRRAHHHH?" calls one of the men.

One of them is dressed in desert camos with a nasty unkempt ZZ Top beard.

"Here piggie, piggie," laughs the man coming up behind him. He's wearing flannel pajama bottoms with a stars and stripes pullover and a baseball cap with an AK-47 that says, COME AND TAKE IT. His comrade has a STOP THE STEAL 2028 ball cap turned backward.

"Ten HUTTTT!" says the man as he catches sight of me at the top of the stairs.

"Jesus, what's a fine-lookin' gal like you doing up here all by your lonesome?" he says in a husky voice.

"Sarah Vasquez. I think her office is over here to the right," I say pointing in the opposite direction of her office just as the men reach the top of the stairs.

"Who are you?" asks Duck Dynasty as his eyes grope my breasts.

"Me? I'm the friggin' tooth fairy," I say in my best trailer park accent.

"OK, tooth fairy," says the other man. "You say you know where Simple Sarah's office is at?"

"Right here, boys," I say breathlessly pointing at an office away from the Speaker's location. "We reached the promised land, ya'll!"

"But the door says SITTING ROOM," says pajama man with a stupid look on his face.

"The sitting room for Sarah Vasquez, genius!" I say, bursting with feigned excitement.

"Any you boys got a gun?"

"No," they answer together as I step back, draw my weapon smoothly, and point it at them.

"On your knees, Duck Dynasty. You too," I order.

He's in the process of squatting down when he launches himself straight up at me, displaying suicide breakneck speed. I'm caught completely off guard as the round from the Glock punches a dime-size hole in his left cheekbone, killing him before he hits the floor. I aim my weapon at the second man, but he's off to the races, running down the long hall screaming. Probably a little more reality than he bargained for during this adventure.

My ears ring with the fury of the discharge of my weapon, and I wonder if the gunshot will bring people to the area or send charging off in the opposite direction.

What the hell was that guy thinking? Did he have a death wish? You have an adversary seven feet away with a gun leveled at your center mass. Maybe it was the fact that I'm a woman? I suppose cemeteries are stacked with men who underestimated a woman holding a handgun.

All of my plans just went to hell—I didn't expect to start mowing down people only five steps into the hallway. At least there doesn't appear to be any witnesses. I better drag ZZ into the sitting room. I grab his legs. He's very heavy but the frictionless surface of the hall makes the task infinitely easier. I dump him in the sitting room and close the door behind me. I'm losing time at an alarming rate and I can hear more and more voices bouncing off the walls of the Capitol.

I can't keep running up and down hallways mowing down everyone I come into contact with. And what about the squirrel that just scampered away from me. Was he going for help or fleeing the scene?

"Stop," I hear a man's broken voice pleading somewhere on the stairwell. "Don't come any closer!"

I look down over the banister above the stairwell spotting a beleaguered Capitol Policeman staggering backwards up the stairs with his gun drawn. I don't know him. His forehead is bleeding freely and it looks like he's been shot in the shoulder. He's being cautiously stalked by a hungry group of protestors advancing slowly toward him up the stairs.

The officer comes around the bend and staggers up the last ten steps, pawing at the blood pouring down his hairline. He gets to the top of the stairs and topples backward into my outstretched arms. I think he's lost consciousness. I drag him back five feet and try to prop him up against the wall; I don't want him drowning in his own blood.

I slide the officer's Glock into my fanny pack and return to the top of the stairwell. Suddenly I'm a walking gun locker. I level the Glock at the men coming up the stairs. I can drop them all without having to reload. That's far from a best-case scenario, but with the way ZZ Top just attacked me, it may come down to that.

I know from previous encounters that bravery and false courage instantly evaporate in small groups when the first person in a group gets shot, especially behind closed doors where even a small-caliber handgun booms like a cannon.

I'm pretty much a dead shot within seventy-five to eighty yards, but at this range, I would be shooting fish in a bucket.

"Gentlemen, you are trespassing on federal property. Turn around and exit the premises or I will open fire. This is not a drill."

"Who the fuck are you?" asks the man farthest away wearing a military uniform with a green mask and a pullover knit cap with a Jolly Roger's symbol that reads DREAD PIRATE ROBERTS.

"That Capitol Policeman you just about beat to death had orders not to fire on you people. I'm more of a party girl, and I take orders from my lord and savior, Smith and Wesson," I say. "In other words, one step closer, and I'll shoot the man closest to me. At this range, I could drop you with my eyes closed."

"Ohhh really—Is that watchoo gonna do with that gun, sweet thang?" one of them laughs.

"One way to find out," I say conversationally.

"She can't shoot us all," says a man wearing welder's goggles and a black and tan CAMP AUSCHWITZ hoodie featuring a skull and crossbones.

The masked man one step up from his fellow rioters is wearing combat fatigues stamped with an American flag emblem that has the cartoon skull of a character called *The Punisher* in the middle.

He licks his lips nervously and laughs again. "How bout I fuck you with that gun?"

He smiles at his friends, taking the next step up.

"See?" he says a split second before his right kneecap explodes spraying shards of bone and cartilage all over the welder's goggles of the man wearing the Camp Auschwitz sweatshirt. The gunshot victim spins through the air with a scream almost as loud as the retort of the gun. He lands four steps down staring stupidly at his knee and writhing in pain. The reverberation of the shot echoes through the hallowed halls of the United States Capitol Building.

Camp Auschwitz rips the welder's goggles off and throws them away in disgust, making labored wheezing sounds. As anticipated, the remaining men drop to the ground cowering while smoke eases up from the weapon, still rock steady in my hand.

"Who's got next? How 'bout you, Camp Auschwitz?"

He writhes on the ground whimpering as his bladder releases. Urine trickles down the step. Some tough guy.

"All right, ladies, take off your shirts and your hats," I order. "Now!" I say pointing the gun at the right eyeball of Camp Auschwitz.

They stare at me in disbelief.

"Toss them up to me and not into the puddle your nutty-buddy just made on the stairs." I turn my attention to the man with the faulty bladder. "You, collect their shirts and hats or I'm gonna shoot you in the kneecap too," I say calmly. "Double-time, boys— before this damn gun goes off again. You know how nervous we little woman can get. Jackets—backpacks—hats."

With the gunshot still screaming in their ears, they start untucking and yanking clothes off.

"Make a pile on the step right here below me," I say matter-of-factly to my new helper. My calm demeanor after shooting a fellow human being in front of them sends pulses of terror rippling through the invaders.

I ease the zip ties out of my utility belt and toss them to the man that gathered the clothing.

"Zip-tie your girlfriends, pervert," I say calmly. "I'm sure it's not the first time. Boys like you love the rough stuff."

"You're fucking crazy," says one of the men.

Camp Auschwitz grabs the zip ties.

"Behind the back. Tight, real tight, and double-cuff them," I instruct. "Tighter. I want all of you sucking marble facedown."

Three men now have their hands bound behind their backs facedown on the marble floor. The man with the gunshot wound to the knee is crying softly at the turn midway down the stairs.

"Now what?" he asks.

"On your knees, boy."

"Please," he begs sinking to his knees. "You don't have to do this."

"Ease the compact knife out of your belt and toss it away," I command.

The knife makes a surprisingly loud noise as it clatters onto the floor and skids about twelve feet away.

I slam the man face-first into the marble, plant my knee on the back of his neck, and zip-tie his hands behind him. The scavenger hunt is over. I collect all of their gear and sprint back to the office looking like a bandit who just robbed the Salvation Army bin. The clock is working against me, but I still might be able to get the Speaker out in one piece.

CHAPTER 30

January 6, 2029
Capitol Hill, Washington, D.C.

I FUMBLE INTO the Speaker's Office weighed down by an assortment of confiscated hate-wear including hats, jackets, hoodies, and shirts. The door locks behind me as another volley of gunfire erupts at the end of the hall. The situation is untenable. Too many people with bad intentions roaming the halls.

I plop the clothes and hats on the marble floor of the Speaker's office and free Speaker Vasquez from her safe room. The rest of her staff is on the verge of a mental breakdown.

"Madame Speaker, we have five minutes tops," I say. "Remember, you can't bring anything. No one can bring anything. No laptops, no phones, zero electronics."

The Speaker and three staffers eye the pile of clothes sitting in the middle of the floor with distaste.

"Gang, we're gone in three. Dress up fast. Let's put on a hell of a show," I say. "Madame Speaker, please, let me help you with your outfit."

"You want us to walk out into that? They're gonna chew us to bits!" says Jimmy, shaking his head. "You got a plan for all of this?"

I speak while I work on the Speaker's outfit. "S.E.R.E. coupled with deception," I say.

"Sear, like something really hot?" he asks.

"S.E.R.E. Survival, evasion, resistance, escape coupled with a healthy dose of misdirection. We're gonna put on these ridiculous clothes and cast a spell over the rioters making them *believe* that we are insurrectionists just like them. If all goes well, we march right out of the front entrance with a smile on our face."

"Do you think this charade will really work?" asks Monica.

I laugh to myself giving us no more than a one-in-three chance of success. But that's not something you share with a group of hyperventilating civilians.

"Since the first groups of human beings picked up clubs and sharpened sticks, one group has always tried to fool their adversaries to gain the upper hand and achieve victory," I say. "The old ways are still the best ways."

I help the Speaker pull on the CAMP AUSCHWITZ sweatshirt over her head.

"This thing stinks to high heaven, Cora," she protests. "Are you kidding me?"

I don't tell her that the previous owner might have soiled it a bit when he accidentally urinated on himself during my festivities on the stairwell.

I hand her a GODS, GUNS, AND LOCKE baseball cap along with a black mask.

"I'm sorry, ma'am, wear this and put on this face mask. It will help with smell," I say.

Her face sours as she looks at the words FUCK YOUR FEELINGS! on her new face mask.

"Cell phones, please. All of you, now. No time for debate. C'mon, let's go."

They look at me in horror. You'd think I just asked every one of them for a kidney.

"Drop your phones in the bag! Move it!"

I'm trying to stay patient, but these people are in slow motion.

"Guys, two things. One, I'm leaving the office with the Speaker now. Come or don't come, but I'm walking out of this door with her in sixty seconds! Two, if you need to address the Speaker for any reason, you will call her 'Chief.'" Do not use the word 'Speaker' or 'Vasquez' for any reason. Better yet, don't say anything. Questions?"

No one speaks up.

"We have two chants we will use out there: 'Locke and Load' or '17-76.' When I start chanting, you parrot me."

I smile broadly at the Speaker. She looks like an old broken-down cracker fresh from a cross burning, just the look I was going for.

"This is Acting 101. It's your time to shine. Get your head on straight right now. We'd die for the president. Terrance B. Locke is our personal Jesus. If you can't adopt this line of thinking for the next hour, that mob will do exactly what Jimmy said—they will chew us up and spit us out. If we're gonna walk out of here together, I need you to strut. We're pissed and we're drunk. If we can't stay in character, this will be our final resting place."

Monica Davies lets out a stifled sob.

"No time for tears. Everybody play your part. You're rioters, goddamnit, so act like it. We have one shot at this. Don't speak, don't stop, don't stare. Monica and I are up front. Chief, you're in the middle of the sandwich. Loop your hand through my tac belt and don't let go unless I say so. Jimmy and Beth, you're in the rear. Crowd the Speaker, I mean the *Chief*, from behind. Stay tight. *Do nothing* unless I tell you to. Got it?"

No one says a word. I slip two burner phones out of my fanny pack and hand one to Monica. "You remember what to do with this?"

"I do," she answers.

"Don't lose it!"

I flip my burner phone open and hit speed dial.

"R-E-M—Need a prom date—Party of five."

"P-U Charlie Whiskey Tango —SIX ZERO?" says the voice on the other line.

"Reservation confirmed."

I flip the phone shut. Jesus, who doesn't love a flip phone?

"Masks up, nothing but the brights of your eyes, we're headed for the Appropriations Committee Offices in the back." Heads nod. "Let's roll."

Things are deteriorating far faster than I imagined. People are lying in the hall bleeding, smoke is rising from the front stairwell. I turn around and look at the group. "Last stairwell. Stay tight on me. Stay to the left! Move."

The sound of automatic weapon fire sends a jolt of sickness through my body. Is the military here too? The last stairway is our only option now, unless we are willing to climb over the half-naked men I was partying with a few minutes ago in the second stairwell. I never did thank them for their clothes.

I scrutinize our disheveled pro-Locke costumes as we hustle down the hall into a glut of insurrectionists. I conduct a rapid 360 recon of our surroundings. As far as I can tell, we are invisible, a group of chameleons hiding in plain sight.

"No, *goddamnit*," yells a man next to us. "Sarah Vasquez."

That's not good! We're dead! The Speaker and I exchange unhappy looks.

Everyone in our group stops and stares at the man. I have the Glock in my right hand with two in reserve and the .38 in my boot, but even a former pistol champion knows when she's outgunned. I have zero chance of repelling eighty-plus people in close quarters. I can probably put down fifteen to twenty of them. But it won't be enough—not even close—but I'll get an "A" for effort.

Then the man yells again, "I told you, Sarah Vasquez! Her office is down this hall. Let's go get 'er," he says, moving a group of ten men, two of them leading the way with AR-15s toward the Speaker's Chambers.

I can breathe again. Oh my God, that was close. I stop and look at my terrified group. "Locke and Load," I yell at the group, bobbing my head up and down like a moron. "Right now. All of you, let's hear it!"

I join them as we sing out loud marching down the hall, "Locke and Load, Locke and Load, Locke and Load!" I figure this is a good way to burn off some nervous energy for all of us.

In a matter of moments, our chant catches on like we're at a football game, and as we reach the last stairwell, hundreds of people are chanting right along with us: "Locke and Load, Locke and Load, Locke and Load!"

I look at the bizarre collection of humanity all around us. Dipsticks waving Confederate flags, carrying selfie-sticks all dressed up like soldiers and cowboys. Someday, someone is going to stage a January 6th themed fashion show collection. I'll probably skip that one. The artery in front of the stairs is now choked with this collection of misfit toys, but it's our only viable path to freedom.

"Huddle up, team," I yell to my collection of frightened actors. All faces join up close enough for a group kiss. "I'm going to let off a pair of very loud explosives called flash-bangs. Very, very loud and they produce a blinding flash. They are not designed to kill so don't panic. When I roll them into the crowd around the stairs behind me, open your mouths wide, it will equalize the pressure from the possible shock wave. Do not look at the flash, it will temporarily blind you. As soon as the explosion goes off, I'm going to club a path to freedom, follow me through the hole I make. We get one shot at this."

Two of them look like they might faint, but I swear the Speaker looks like she's enjoying the action. I shove them all against the far wall. "Wait for me!" I stuff in earplugs, take three steps into crowd, and toss a pair of flash-bangs onto the floor. I move away instantly turning my head and closing my eyes with my mouth wide open.

Boom! Boom! Two enormous explosions rock the stairwell causing sheer pandemonium and widespread panic. Screaming people drop to the ground holding their ears, and several are accidentally shoved down the stairs in the initial panic. I look at my group and see instantly that we've lost one. I run up to them and scream to be heard above the chaos. "Where's Jimmy?"

Beth screams back, "He took off down the hall."

"OK, ladies, it's just us now," I yell above the pandemonium. "Follow me and make sure you don't get hit by my baton."

I remove my expandable ASP Friction Loc Baton and snap it open. Twenty-one inches of black, chrome-plated steel with a vinyl grip. It's basically indestructible, and you don't ever want someone to hit you with one. I raise the bar in front of my face like a weight-lifter that can't quite get the bar over her head and move forward followed carefully by the three women behind me.

I use short forward thrusts, battering the people in front of me with the steel pole. One woman with an I'M A LOCKE MOM shirt takes a shot to the face losing several teeth while another man drops to the floor after my bar connects with the back of his head. I reach the top of the stairs ready to strike anyone else barring my path as a man comes rushing at me from the right side. I instantly bunch my hands together and complete a perfect backhand arc of the baton. The man gets his arms up just in time but the steel buckles both of his forearms with a sickening crunch. I risk a look behind me and all three women are right there waiting for me with eyes wide open in terror. The stairs are as clear as they're going to get, and I can see metaphorical daylight at the bottom of the stairwell.

Six minutes later and much to everyone's relief, we suddenly find ourselves alone. There are no attackers fumbling around back here by the Committee of Appropriations Office. It takes a moment, but I finally locate office number 2814B. I go through the same steps Congressman Lobdell led me through a week ago. Was that only a week ago? Longest 168 hours of my life.

The four of us pile onto the freight elevator leading to the Capitol Garbage Tunnel.

"You women did an amazing job," I yell, making everyone jump a foot in the air. Oh God, I realize I'm yelling. "Sorry," I say lowering my voice. "My earplugs are still in."

"When did you find those?" asks the Speaker.

"I always have a pair close by. I stuffed them into my ears before setting off those party favors back at the stairwell."

They stare at me blankly. My attempt to lighten the mood obviously fell flat. What's the saying about people who can't take a joke?

"As you can no doubt tell from the smell," I say as the elevator reaches level G5 and the doors swish open, "this is the infamous secret Capitol Garbage Tunnel."

This is the first time I've seen it all lit up and I suddenly feel vulnerable. I was really hoping for the cover of darkness. With the soft lighting, the cavernous tunnel has a lunar quality to it coupled with the smell of rotting takeout doing battle with some kind of Lysol disinfectant chemical.

"Let's go—we don't have much time," I say, walking my party between the giant sets of dumpsters.

"Where does the tunnel lead, Cora?" asks the Speaker. She sounds exhausted and I can't blame her.

"The tunnel runs underneath Constitution Avenue. We need to walk a half a mile or so and then we need to start looking for the House of Representatives Eagle. It sits on the wall about ten feet high."

"There's the eagle right here," says Monica looking up the wall about ten feet high.

Sure enough, there's the eagle, but it has a number 8 at the top of the symbol. The last time I was down here, the lights were off and it was very dark.

"Great eyes, Monica," I say, feeling like a complete idiot. *How did I miss that?*

"Right symbol, wrong number. We're looking for the same symbol with the number 4 at the top." I can feel my face coloring with embarrassment.

We arrive at the proper eagle, and I take out the red "get out of jail free" card that Congressman Lobdell gifted to me. He called it the "break glass in case of emergency" card.

I walk over to the protected electrical outlet and lift up the black cover. It looks like a normal outlet to me. I press the card against the outlet and nothing happens. I press the card against it again and again. Sweat instantly coats my forehead. Lobdell must have betrayed me. That Texas Longhorn better pray I never get out of this friggin' tunnel.

I step back staring at the outlet, as I recalculate our next course of action.

"May I try?" asks Monica, holding out her hand.

"Be my guest," I say handing her the red card.

She walks right up to the outlet and slides the card into a thin slit at the bottom of the outlet. The outlet flashes blue, sucks in the card, and promptly returns it like an ATM machine.

Then a recorded voice declares, "Access granted. Please step back."

We follow the instructions as an eight-by-eight section of walls slides back revealing a long pedestrian tunnel.

I laugh out loud and clap Monica on the back, nearly knocking her over. "You're a genius, girl!"

The pedestrian hall dead-ends into a set of stairs going up. We climb five flights of stairs coming face-to-face with what looks like a standard hotel door with a key card pad. I wave the card in front of the circular black plate and the door unlocks.

I look back at Monica. "Did I get it right this time?"

She smiles for the first time. We file into an unattended, but nicely furnished guardhouse. I peek out the window and know instantly where we are and where we need to be for pickup. We're on New Jersey Avenue—that's the Taft Carillion right across the street from us.

I flip my phone open and punch redial.

"R-E-M—Change of venue—Party of four. What's your 20?"

"Walmart Super Center, H and N-Jay Ave," comes the reply.

With that kind of proximity, I drop any pretense of code words.

Finally, a piece of good luck. "ASAP, ASAP. Far side past the Taft Memorial Carillon, just past Louisiana."

In military parlance, ASAP means immediately.

"Reservation confirmed," barks Austin J. Barton, breaking the connection.

I snap the phone shut and turn to the group.

"Wheels up. Four minutes. Ladies, you did it!"

The small space erupts into cheers. I'm so happy for them, but for me, the escape from the Capitol was probably the easy part of my journey.

We step out of the guard shack still surrounded by the roar of invaders back at the Capitol Building. Check that, they aren't inside the Capitol, so technically, those outside of the building could be labeled as rioters. My stomach lurches thinking about those savages bludgeoning the Capitol Police Force and shooting them down like dogs.

I hear an approaching vehicle above the crowd noise about a block and a half away. I move the Speaker behind me, feeling the comfort of the Glock in my hand. An unmarked ambulance pulls up alongside the curb. My weapon is already trained at the passenger-side window

"I come in peace," says the grizzly bear behind the wheel. "Ghost Rider, party of four?"

I lower my weapon as the side doors fly open. I help the Speaker into the vehicle as the other two women pile in behind her. The doors slam shut and the ambulance hurtles forward.

"Where'd you find an ambulance?" I ask with a chuckle. "Never mind. Just get us the hell out of here!"

CHAPTER 31

January 6, 2029
Near Capitol Hill, Washington, D.C.

OUR RUNAWAY AMBULANCE bounces up onto the sidewalk
to avoid a row of police cars blocking Constitution Avenue while
the new occupants in the back fumble desperately to fasten their
seat belts. I stare at another group of protestors on Constitution
Avenue standing under a banner with the American Flag flying
next to an image of Jesus Christ with the caption:

JESUS IS MY SAVIOR
LOCKE IS MY PRESIDENT

A Nazi flag flutters side by side with the stars and bars of the
Confederacy. The promise of a 1,000-year Reich whispering to the
myth of the lost cause. Both empires crumbled to dust leaving
behind an enduring legacy of hate.

The cab of the ambulance is eerily silent. We watch the rioters
from a distance. I see three columns of National Guard Troops
funneling up the stairs of the Capitol in combat mode and wonder if they are there to protect the Capitol or seize it for the
Commander and Chief?

The sun is already slipping from the sky, giving a lover's gentle kiss to the very tip of the Washington Monument. No one says a word as we break free from the evil confines of Washington D.C. onto the 14th Street Bridge, heading toward the promise of Virginia.

Once we're across the Potomac I pipe up, "Ladies, this is Sam. I trust him with my life. He's one of the most capable people I've ever met, even though he's not a woman. We have to make a quick vehicle change in Pentagon City and we will be on our way."

They all greet Sam warmly, but everyone is trapped inside their own thoughts. Of course, Sam isn't Sam, he's Austin J. Barton, Sherriff Bart from my brief stint in Benghazi. He's the only one I really kept in touch with all of these years until Deacon Lobdell barged his way back into my life. But thank God for Lobdell—he was the key to our freedom.

Eleven minutes after our D.C. pickup, we enter the parking garage at the newly renovated Fashion Centre Mall in Pentagon City, Virginia. The place is a complete zoo, overwhelmed by weekend shoppers cashing in holiday gift cards.

The traffic going in and out of the garage is a total disaster. They either don't know or don't care that Locke and his loyalists are shooting up Capitol Hill just across the Potomac River. The driver and I exchange knowing smiles. This beehive of human activity is the perfect cover for us.

Perfect because we can ditch the ambulance. Perfect because the vehicle waiting for us inside is nondescript. Perfect because whatever agencies are going to try and track the Speaker down may not be able to untangle the web we've woven for several days even with all the surveillance cameras that have popped up all over the United States in the past four years.

"You need to return some Christmas gifts before we head out of town, Cora?" deadpans the Speaker, breaking out of her stupor.

I turn around to look her. "I thought we could all grab a late lunch together at the Ritz to ring in the New Year."

Eight minutes later, we're cued up in a row of eight cars waiting to pay and exit the Pentagon City parking garage. We're in a faded red older model Jeep Cherokee with a special touch dominating the back windshield. The back window features the image of the Gadsden Flag that displays the ready-to-strike rattlesnake over the infamous words: DON'T TREAD ON ME.

The Speaker's secretary, Beth Fleming, is at the wheel, her hair tucked into an old-school Baltimore Orioles baseball cap. Poor Sam is crammed in the very back like luggage with a cowboy hat obscuring his face. It feels like everyone is holding their breath despite the stench of deadly car fumes filling the cab of the vehicle and increasing the intensity of my punishing headache.

I guide Beth to a nearby abandoned recreation park just off of Columbia Pike in Arlington where the playground's been overrun by weeds and neglect. Once an up-and-coming area, crime and violence have infected most of the suburbs around here. There's no one here, no cameras, and a chance for everyone to catch their breath.

"We're gonna regroup here," I announce to the group. "I have a variety of essentials in the trunk. Everyone hop out, grab a drink and a PowerBar, and stretch your legs. Don't touch the Speaker's Evian water, please. Once we're on the road, we can talk business."

*   *   *

After a twenty-minute strategy session and some fancy driving, we're heading north on I-95 listening to D.C.'s 24-hour news station. However bad I thought the news might be, it's infinitely worse.

"Thanks, Geoffrey, we continue our live and exclusive Siege at the Capitol *coverage. President Terrance Locke dispatched the National Guard to Capitol Hill a little more than two hours ago. After a short, but intense firefight, the National Guard surrounded the crowds and forced them out of the Capitol at gunpoint. Two groups of rioters fought back and the troops opened fire into the crowd killing and wounding scores of people. More than two thousand rioters are being held in makeshift pens between Constitution Gardens and the Vietnam Veterans Memorial under armed guard. We also have confirmed reports that several high-ranking Democratic senators and congressmen have been arrested in connection with the riot."*

The radio host interrupts the live report.

"Sondra, just to clarify. Did you just say that the National Guard is arresting members of the Senate and Congress?"

"That's correct, Chris. A spokeswoman for the National Guard says they are charging certain members of Congress with seditious conspiracy. *This criminal statute became mainstream back in 2022 when people were charged after the first Capitol Riot. But this time, the Justice Department is using the same law to arrest members of Congress. Seditious conspiracy bars the use of force 'to prevent, hinder, or delay the execution of any law of the United States.' The charge carries a maximum prison sentence of twenty years.*

"The President released a statement from the Oval Office alleging that the Capitol invaders were acting under direct orders from the Speaker of the House, Sarah Vasquez, and other prominent members of the Democratic Leadership to discredit President Locke and seize the American government. A warrant has been issued for her arrest, and from what we understand, an arrest warrant has also been issued for the Vice President, Drew Hayden."

There's a moment of shocked silence. The anchor on the main desk isn't sure he heard her correctly.

"An arrest warrant has been issued for the Vice President," he says, repeating her. *"Ah, what charges have been leveled against the Vice President, Sondra?"*

"The same charge facing the Speaker of the House, Ted. Seditious conspiracy."

"Thank you for that live report. That was Sondra Larsen reporting and, uh. OK. OK. We're going to go live now to the Oval Office where the President is addressing the nation regarding today's violence at the Capitol Building."

Everyone in the ambulance falls silent as the President's voice takes over the radio.

"Today, the enemies inside of our great country hatched a plot to overthrow the government, and hundreds of innocent people paid the ultimate price. Our thoughts and prayers go out to those people who lost their lives today during what began as a peaceful demonstration today at the United States Capitol Building. The Keep the Peace March *was all about unity and healing our nation. This peaceful demonstration was hijacked and taken over by some very bad people who attacked our brave Capitol Police Officers.*

"Along with my Justice Department, we are swearing out arrest warrants for members of the lower house of Congress who have betrayed our country and incited this riot against our sacred democracy. Speaker Sarah Vasquez is still at large but has freely admitted to being the mastermind of this terrible attack on Capitol Hill in her efforts to bring down my presidency and she will be brought to justice."

Listening to his slightly slurred speech and semi-coherent rambling, the President obviously sucked up some extra liquid courage before addressing the nation this evening.

"Rather than waste taxpayer money with what has been a long-drawn-out effort to further challenge this year's presidential

election results, I have decided, and the people have decided, that in the face of this terrible crisis, I am forced to extend my term as your faithfully elected president for the next four years.

"During these uncertain times, this unprecedented measure has been insisted upon at the highest levels of government to bring stability back to our nation. Several senators approached me and said, 'Mr. President, you're the only one who can save our country now.' Congressional leadership has rallied around me and insisted this is our only path forward. I'm extending my term not only to save our country from the usurpers, but to unify the American people before it's too late," says the president as the cheers of the crowd crackle through the radio.

Like an evil sorcerer, even half drunk, the president knows just how long to pause before continuing his mythical speech.

"As you know, I was a celebrated attorney for many years. We can't coddle the judges who ignore the rule of election law any longer. They will rule in our favor or they will rot in prison cells right next to Stupid Sarah *who was looking down on us from her throne up there on Capitol Hill. The law of the land must be upheld and I have been chosen by God to do just that."*

Speaker Vasquez flinches again at the mention of the nickname the President gave her when he first began his presidential campaign.

"Simple Sarah, are you listening? You have been exposed. Your reign of terror has come to an end. When they find your body in the rubble of the Capitol tonight, we will stick your head on the top of the Washington Monument because your treachery has finally been exposed."

He pauses for the chants of *"Lock her up."*

"We're going to do a hell of a lot more than lock her up, I tell you . . ." says the President, laughing with the crowd.

"In addition, I signed an executive order this afternoon, which empowers Jeff Talbert, the acting Secretary of Defense, to 'seize, collect, and destroy all Peninsula Voting machines in the states of Georgia, Michigan, Arizona, Wisconsin, and Pennsylvania.

"Experts have determined that these Peninsula Voting Systems are owned and have been controlled by foreign agents, countries, and interests. Forensic experts from the Justice Department found that the Peninsula Voting System is intentionally and purposefully designed with built-in errors to create systemic fraud to manipulate the election results.

"This proves my earlier assertions that these machines are being controlled by secret groups of people who are determined to bring our county to its knees. If you look at the results in those states—Georgia, Michigan, Wisconsin, and Arizona—you know that I won every last one of them by a substantial margin."

The President pauses again, waiting for the cheers to subside.

"I will also be drafting new legislation that will further limit the reach and power of the inflammatory media. It took me four short years to turn our country around. Now—just imagine what I can do with four more years as your chosen supreme leader. Chosen by God. Chosen by you, the true patriots of our mighty nation."

"Turn it off," snaps the Speaker, staring out the windshield but not really seeing.

We drive in silence for about fifteen minutes, but I have to get the Speaker up to speed before I leave her.

"Madame Speaker, I have to return to Washington," I say quietly. "I have this flip phone for you. You can contact me at any hour, day or night. I will never be more than ninety minutes from you unless I am taken into custody. We have to seriously consider that possibility. If I am taken, I will send a 9-1-1 distress to Sam, or if I go dark for more than six hours, Sam will know that I'm likely lost forever. If that happens, please consider Sam your new and improved Cora," I say looking into her eyes and trying to keep my emotions in check.

This is no time for tears; it's time for strength. The Speaker needs me to be ten feet tall and bulletproof so pull it together, Walker. I take another moment before continuing.

"I have a new email address set up for you that Monica and Sam can guide you through. No messages in and no messages out; all communication must be done through the draft folder. I cannot stress how important it is that you NEVER HIT *SEND*! Type your message and when you're done, save the draft. Since no email has been sent, there is nothing out there for anyone to track. I can go straight to the draft folder and read whatever you typed. I already have a message waiting for you in the draft folder with further instructions."

"White Marsh Mall, ETA six minutes," Sam announces from the driver's seat.

"Copy that, Sam," I say smiling sweetly at him in the rearview mirror.

"Sam has a network of safe houses and they are all off the grid. Better yet, I have no idea where any of them are, so if I'm captured, drugged, or tortured, I can't tell them where you are," I say.

"*Tortured?*" says the Speaker, acting like I just smacked her in the face. "This is still the United States of America, Cora."

"With all due respect, ma'am," I say with my voice teetering on the verge of insubordination, "Terry Locke just declared himself the Supreme Leader of the United States, not the President. So we are playing by an entirely new set of rules."

"So you're sending us to live in a cave with Sam?" asks the Speaker.

I can't tell if she's kidding so I fumble on. "None of you will be cut off from the internet or cut off from the world, but you can't leave any kind of digital stamp. No tracks in the digital snow. No interaction, no contact with anyone until further notice. You are all MIA now and you need to stay that way. Let Sam guide you. Locke and his people will scour the ends of the earth to find the Speaker and they will likely try to use me to achieve those ends."

"My God, Cora," says the Speaker, suddenly in a total panic. "What about your family?"

"They are off the grid and safe. Thank you for asking. They are in hiding just like you and they will not resurface until I've achieved my mission or fail to come home," I say.

"I still don't know exactly what your mission is, Cora," says the Speaker.

"I'm not sure I do either." What space can I occupy in the new world order when the democracy that I served faithfully for most of my adult life becomes something sinister?

She looks at me, her eyes pushing me to finish my thought.

"I served my country in every way I know how. But she is no longer my master. I've been set free. Our democracy has failed us, or perhaps, we failed our democracy. What I do know is that it no longer belongs to the people. So sadly, my mission in life is to bring this new form of government to its knees before it has a chance to take off."

CHAPTER 32

January 6, 2029
White Marsh Mall, Baltimore, Maryland

I WATCH THE Jeep Cherokee turn the corner on its way to wherever the hell Sheriff Bart is taking them as my stomach growls to life. The Speaker is safe and I need to execute a rapid-fire shopping spree before heading back to the swamp.

Thirty minutes later, I feel like I've actually accomplished something. My giant cooler is packed with fruit, water, Gatorade, Power-Bars, and a foot-long sub. I sip my three-shot Starbucks drink and pop three ibuprofen.

I have four burner phones now, one for Abby and Cat, Bart, Congressman Lobdell, and the Speaker. I've programmed them with different ring tones to know who is who, but calling out maybe more of a challenge than I anticipated. I'll have to take care of that and mark them tonight.

But first things first, I need to make contact. I dial but the phone just rings and rings. I'm pissed, but I know Cat may have shabby phone service wherever she took Abby and Gertie.

The phone rings in my hand.

"Pizza Hut," I answer.

"Hiii, Momma, I love you!" comes the voice of my baby girl.

My throat tightens and the breath catches in my throat. I wasn't ready for Abby's voice.

"Hello, my angel, what are you doing?" I ask with a tide of my emotions pulsing though the cab of the Nissan Rogue.

"Aunt Cat came and got me out of school this morning with Nanna. She said we were gonna be toughin' it up in the mountains this week," says Abby in a conspiratorial whisper.

"*Toughin' it* or *roughin' it*?" I ask unable to squelch a delighted giggle.

Abby takes a serious tone and says, "I told her we would be *roughin' it* and she said we would be *toughin' it*. And then I asked her if we could stop for ice cream, and she said that's not what you do when you're roughin' it. But we stopped anyway and guess what?"

"What, my love?" I ask.

"Guess where we stopped?" she says. I don't have to see her to know she's rolling her eyes at me.

"Don't roll your eyes at your mother," I answer.

"Nope, we didn't stop there. Sorry, Mom!" she says.

"Ohhh, you think you're sooo funny!"

"Dairy Queen!" she yells.

"You met the fairy queen?" I gasp.

"Mom, you might be being a little bit too crazy, you know that?"

"I'm not the one who saw the fairy queen," I say seriously.

"Oooo . . . OK, Cat, I love you, Mom. Aunt Cat says she needs to talk to you for a second," yells Abby. "Um wait, when are you gonna get here?"

I pause for too long and baby girl nails me like a German shepherd sniffing out a bag of coke at the airport.

"It OK, Mommy," she says dejectedly. "I love you. Here's Aunt Cat."

"I love y—" I say but she's already handed the phone over to Cat.

"Cora," begins Cat.

"Cat, damnit, put Abby back on the phone for a moment, please," I snap.

"Hold on," she says.

A long forty seconds passes and Cat comes back on the line.

"Well . . ." stammers Cat.

I finish her thought for her. "Abbs is upset and won't come to the phone."

"I'm sorry," says Cat quietly. "She's fine, I promise. You know that little knucklehead will bounce back in two minutes."

Silence drags on for too long as Cat gives me a moment to compose myself.

"Not to change the subject, but how in the hell did you get out of that place? What about the package? Are you hurt? What the hell is going on?" Cat says, firing questions like an AK.

"Jesus, you're worse than Abby. All is well. No one is hurt. The package is safe," I say.

"What about this Capitol Marauder dude?" she asks.

"I have no idea who you're referring to," I say.

"The news is saying some psycho was in the Capitol before the National Guard rolled in and started executing people in the hallways," she says seriously.

"That sounds awful," I say. And it wasn't an execution—technically it was an assisted suicide. You don't lunge at someone pointing a gun at your chest. "Any suspects?"

"Just some random guy running around in a hoodie. They say he shot a couple of people, made them strip off their clothes, and they think he might have set off some explosives near the Speaker's Chambers. Apparently, the ATF has been called in to search the area for evidence," says Cat.

"Sounds like someone had a worse day at the office than I did," I say, still trying to shake off the dread of upsetting my daughter. "Glad I didn't cross paths with that guy. Anyway, sounds like you have everything under control."

"Under control my ass," says Cat. "You hear the mouth on your daughter? She's got a lot to say, just like someone else I know!"

I can hear Abby in the background, taunting her Aunt Cat. "Bad word, Aunt Cat. Bad word! We don't speak like that in this house. Please say sorry! Bad Word Alert!"

"You're right," I say.

"I know she's in great hands. Tell Abby and Gertie I love them and I love you too, Cat." Then I say quietly, "No one is on me yet, but I'm sure they're looking for me. If I don't check in after twelve hours, you need to relocate."

"Roger that, kid. For Christ sakes be careful. And email me—I mean draft me. Tonight—with real details. Do not wait until tomorrow morning," she yells, breaking the connection.

I decide to take the long way to Virginia. Instead of cutting through Washington D.C., I bypass the city altogether and enter Virginia by crossing the Woodrow Wilson Bridge and driving up the Potomac River through Alexandria. I stare out across the river and watch searchlights crisscrossing the dome of the Capitol as I drive past the Pentagon.

Fifteen minutes later, I'm parking the SUV in the monthly spot belonging to Leonard Black deep in the nest of the Ballston Commons Parking Garage in Arlington, Virginia. Although Leonard is a fictional character, he's known as an outstanding customer in this garage. He always pays six days early and always pays in cash with a little extra to sweeten the deal and avoid any questions. I don't know how I conjured up the name and it doesn't matter. Contactless parking is a godsend.

I've changed clothes so many times in a small car that this SUV feels like an oversized dressing room. I slip on a short denim miniskirt and a skintight tank top that I have to really stuff my boobs into. I top it off with a heavy and surprisingly warm denim jacket. I check myself in the mirror and adjust my wig, making sure the long blonde curly hair is mostly in my face. I pull on an oversized knit cap to complete the disguise. "Good as it's gonna get," I say out loud. I'm sure the search grid for me is already up and running, but the darkness, hat, and hair in my face should defeat any facial recognition software.

I count three cameras on the platform. I keep my head down and walk slowly toward a gap in the camera coverage. I can take the Orange or Silver Line to Rosslyn. It's only an eight-minute ride and I should be in my hotel room in less than fifteen minutes. Looking up at the endless array of square honeycomb patterns dominating the underground Metro tunnel reminds me that I just kicked over a massive hornets' nest with no visible escape plan. The Orange Line train arrives right on cue. There are plenty of passengers boarding the train and I do my best to blend in with them.

Forty minutes later, in a steaming tub full of soapy bubbles, I pick up the burner phone marked "D" for Deac. The Congressman answers after three long rings.

"Long day?" asks the Congressman in place of a greeting.

I try to portray a sense of calm I do not feel.

"Walk in the park," I say, blowing some soapy bubbles off of my arm and wiggling further down into the tub.

"So, I assume I can expect you at work tomorrow?" he says cautiously.

"I don't know. We never discussed PTO," I shoot back.

"Well, I'm sure something can be worked out," he says, pausing. "Ahhh, any chance we could meet this evening to go over your new duties."

I laugh out loud, nearly dropping the phone into the tub.

"All right," he says. "I'll expect you in the office at, hmm, let's say five thirty tomorrow morning?"

"Got a title for me?" I ask.

"How about Director of Information Services?" he says.

"How trite," I say. "So I'm wondering about this clandestine five thirty in the morning meeting. Are you gonna have a hit team waiting for me? Who's looking for me right now?"

"Where's the trust?" he asks.

I break the connection. I was probably on the phone for too long. It won't do much good, but I yank out the phone battery and drop it on the towel next to the tub.

I've built up a long list of enemies over the past month in the FBI, the DHS, and let's be honest, the entire Justice Department. And my only two *friends*—and that's stretching the very limit of the word *friends*—are the Congressman and Cecilia Danforth or Cecilia Locke or whatever her name is, the President's stepdaughter. Both of them have offered me jobs in the "New Order" where democracy has been choked out in favor of authoritarianism. This is a mess for the ages and tomorrow is a total crapshoot.

I'll either be plotting against the new government of the United States or I'll be getting my fingernails yanked out with a pair of pliers while evil men try to persuade me to give up the location of my family, the Speaker of the House, or both. Thank God I have no idea where the hell they are.

CHAPTER 33

January 7, 2029
Castle Gatehouse, Washington, D.C., Aqueduct

MY FACE BURNS under the assault of the frigid January air. Only an idiot would jog to a castle at four in the morning when the sun won't be up for another three and a half hours, but such is my lot in life. The Georgetown Reservoir Castle is exactly two miles from my hotel and I'm beyond excited to turn around because I've been running face-first into a stiff artic wind along the Potomac for the last twenty-five minutes. Any hack runner will tell you, running with the wind at your back is infinitely more comfortable than running into it.

The castle has always been a favorite landmark of mine. I was so excited the first time I saw it, a castle right in the middle of Washington, D.C. It took some of the shine off when I learned that it's just an aqueduct water pumping station for the District of Columbia. The run back to the hotel is a quick one, and I savor my quick journey across the Potomac. There's something magical about the Francis Scott Key Bridge, even in the darkness of the early morning.

I have to be dressed and on the first train out of here or I'll be late for my first day on the job. The D.C. Metro system doesn't fire up until five a.m. The trip to Capitol South takes seventeen minutes, and I'm supposed to be at work at five thirty. But maybe, in the "New World Order," I can add being late to my long line of less-than-desirable traits.

The Metro left three minutes late, so I'm looking at a five twenty arrival at the station. I dial Austin J. Barton who's off somewhere in the rolling hills of Maryland, Delaware, or maybe even in West Virginia.

"How's the first day of work?" Barton says in place of a greeting.

"Good morning to you too," I say. "How's the Speaker holding up?"

"She worked through the night and she's been making some noise about letting them take her into custody so she can fight the charges," he says quietly.

"Terrific," I say, quietly adding this new issue to a long list of my current problems. "Is this saber-rattling or is she set on a path?"

"If she could figure out a way to do it without burning the rest of us, she might. But she'll stay put for now," he says.

"OK. I'm headed into the lion's den this morning. I'll update you or they'll be hanging me upside down into a bucket of water until I spill all of your secrets," I say.

"Let me state for the record, one last time," he says. "You know better than anyone, you can't kill a bear with one shot. Maybe you need to take a step back and reassess the situation."

One of my phones starts buzzing.

I laugh gently. "Thanks for the tip. Gotta go—work's calling."

I find the burner marked with the lowercase "d."

"You comin' to work today, Mizz Walker?" he asks.

"Thinking about it," I say cautiously.

"Change of venue. You up for a little word game?" he asks.

"Always."

"Close, I mean, real close where the sun rises with the coffee, sprinkled with a dose of poetry and some light reading. Call me back when you get it," he says cutting off the call.

My mind spins. A civilian playing coding games with a former analyst is pretty annoying. I close my eyes—the train is still eight minutes from the Capitol South Metro Station. My brain organizes the Capitol map in my head into concentric rings. I got nothing. Real close? Coffee first, poetry second, and reading third? I laugh out loud. Not too bad, Deac. Damn redneck is smarter than he looks. I call him right back.

"Nine minutes," I say into the phone and hang up.

I give the Capitol Building a wide berth to the south before heading back north toward the Folger Shakespeare Library. Folger (coffee) Shakespeare (poetry) Library (reading). I call his number again. "Head south on second. Coffee Park."

He pulls up in a jet-black vintage Mustang GT. I climb into the passenger's side and he guns the engine, the forward momentum pushing me back into the seat. He and the Watch Commander of the Capitol Police Force have an awful lot in common.

"Can't men exercise any modicum of self-restraint?" I ask wearily. "Why don't you mount loudspeakers on the top of your ride and announce, 'Look at me!'"

"Wind resistance," he quips back.

Damn. Good answer.

"Where are we going?" I ask.

"We have a meetup this morning. Some bad people, scum of the earth actually," he says.

"Perfect," is the only comment that comes to mind.

"Do you know Brandywine Bay?" he asks.

"Not personally," I quip back.

"It's at the end of the Occoquan River. I'm not sure if it's in the town of Woodbridge or Occoquan. It really doesn't matter. We're picking up a few packages that may or may not get us killed. Are you carrying?" he asks.

"No."

"Did you get rid of that Glock?" he asks innocently.

I hold my breath, but my expression remains smoothly inscrutable.

"What are you talking about?" I ask without a trace of interest.

"The one you used to shoot that man in the face yesterday at the Capitol," he says peering over at me.

"Deac, God bless you," I say with a charming smile. "You got a vivid imagination, but I lost you." I feel my heart trying to punch its way out of my rib cage and hurl itself out the friggin' window.

"Those two men you encountered on the stairs were mine," he says looking me in the eyes. "Sons of the Apocalypse, you know, God's Messengers?"

I sit there in the passenger's seat, knowing to keep my mouth shut. I'm in way over my head. I'm not sure yet, but I'm pretty sure I made a huge mistake linking up with the congressman. The only way out now is to kill him. And if I'm not mistaken, he's figured that out as well.

"So before you do anything rash to the man driving ninety miles per hour down I-95 South, I think we should clear some things up," he says looking over at me. "If you kill me now, you'll probably end up just killing both of us. I know you don't fear death, but I also know you have a little girl you want to see grow up. So keep your six-shooter in your holster, cowgirl."

"I don't need a weapon to kill you, Congressman, and if 'ya'll,' as you like to say, don't have a gun pointed at me, you're a dead man driving," I say, continuing our discussion in a civil manner.

"Be that as it may, I sent those two men to capture Sarah Vasquez and detain her for me. You encountered them first, you executed one, and the other fled the scene," he says. "It's not a question. I'm just stating facts. However, I am a little confused as to why you shot him in the face. I'm not judging, but I am most curious."

He keeps his eyes on the road, and I decide the truth will have to set me free.

"If you want the truth, he did it to himself," I say.

The Congressman nods his head but says nothing.

"I put him and his partner on their knees. He was seven feet away, but out of nowhere, he lunged at me. His forward momentum couldn't have carried him more than six inches before the bullet struck somewhere near his cheekbone. Open and shut case. That's called an assisted suicide."

"He was excitable," he says, nodding his head again in understanding.

"Sons of the Apocalypse? You, Congressman? You're part of God's White Militia? You keep friends in low places, I'll give you that," I say. "But I'm also not shocked. Weren't you the one who championed the bill to rename slavery? Thanks to you, schoolchildren across the country are learning about the gentle institution of *involuntary relocation instead of slavery*."

He has no answer and keeps his eyes on the road.

"You sent two men to abduct the Speaker of the House and what? You think that's not a problem for me?" I ask. Now I'm the one who's curious.

"I didn't send two men to grab Vasquez. I sent eight. Four two-man teams. But you found a way to get the Speaker out before my men could locate her. I still have no idea how the hell you managed that. Damn impressive if you ask me. The radio is calling you the 'Capitol Marauder,' a serial killer hired by the Democrats, who came in with the rioters."

Now I'm the one staring ahead silently.

"My teams had explicit orders to bring the Speaker to me unharmed. When I found out that the President was calling in the National Guard to arrest members of the House Leadership, including your boss and the Vice President, I had to act fast. I couldn't let that happen," he says. "If they were arrested and detained in federal custody, I would have no access to them and we need them if we're going depose the sitting President and reestablish order to our Democracy."

"Depose? Depose the President of the United States?" I ask. "Are we going to ask him nicely?"

"I already have the Vice President. Sebastian Knox is safe and sound and tucked away where nobody will ever find him until he can be sworn in as our next President," he says. "He will take the oath of office tonight and peacefully transfer power eleven days from now on January 20th to the democratically elected President, Drew Hayden."

"So your plan was to capture Vasquez and VP Knox so you could protect them?" I ask, the ramifications of his terrible plan coming together in my mind.

He doesn't answer me.

"Don't keep me in suspense," I say.

"I finalized my plan during the first week of December. I had to make absolutely sure that Speaker Vasquez and Sebastian Knox were ready to reassume power if some *accident* were to befall the President of the United States. That something has to happen tonight, because if President Terrance B. Locke administers the oath of office tomorrow and is sworn in for another four years, we will never be able to undo the damage. Don't you see what I'm trying to say? We have a tiny window. If we don't act today, we'll never get another chance."

"And exactly how do you plan on removing the sitting President?" I ask, choking on the sickness of my implication. Deep down, I worried that this might have always been the Congressman's ultimate goal if Locke seized control of the government. "What in the hell makes you think I would help you or anyone assassinate the President of the United States?"

"I have no intention of assassinating the President of the United States. I plan on executing an unelected autocrat before he can take over the country!"

I look at him in horror.

"C'mon, Walker. Don't get squeamish on me now. If Locke dies today, the Vice President will be sworn in tonight as the President of the United States. I know the Vice President. His character is beyond reproach."

"*Beyond reproach?*" I ask. "How do you know Knox will transfer power and step down once he's had a taste of it?"

"Sebastian Knox is not remotely interested in the presidency and he's not capable of ignoring the Constitution or ignoring the will of the people. He is a man of honor and will stand tall when the country needs him the most," insists the Congressman. "He knows—hell, everyone knows—that President-elect Drew Hayden thumped Locke in the general election. And although Knox has served Locke loyally for four miserable years, he knows that the President's reign of terror must come to an end because the law of the land demands it."

"So he knows your plan to take out the President of the United States? Yes or no? Who else knows, Deac?"

"No one knows," he says. "You and I. That's it."

"Sure, OK. You and me against the world, right?"

"You better sync your mind to what's going on in the real world, Walker. The country will heal after the loss of Locke. But our democracy will crumble into a pile of salt and scatter to the winds of history if we allow anyone to subvert the will of the people and declare himself a 'Supreme Leader Chosen by God.'"

He spits out the words as if they're choking him.

"You see that, don't you," he pleads with me. "You can't put the peel back on a banana. If Locke takes power tomorrow, the democratic experiment flatlines and it ain't comin' back. Not tomorrow, not ever."

I shake my head. "How many times did you practice that speech this morning?"

"Did I lay it on too heavy at the end?" he asks. "I was worried about that."

"Jesus, you talk so much. Please get to it," I beg.

"Once Knox is sworn in as the next President of the United States, he will be there to peacefully and legally transfer power to the rightfully elected successor. If we are successful today, President-elect Drew Hayden will be sworn into office two weeks from now, and our democracy can continue to fumble its way forward."

The eloquence of his words can't mask the genius of his madness. But madness in any form is still madness, and now it's my duty to stop him.

CHAPTER 34

January 7, 2029
Occoquan Regional Park, Lorton, Virginia

THE OCCOQUAN REGIONAL Park won't open for another couple of hours, but the Congressman rolls past the gate and into the recreation area like it's his driveway.

"You set up a meet with a bunch of skinheads in a bougie area like this?" I ask.

"Boo-gee? What the hell is boo-gee?" he asks.

I laugh out loud. "Jesus, old man, *bougie* means upper crust, you know, bourgeoisie? This area is soccer mom heaven."

"We're just here to cowboy up before we meet the esteemed members of the SOA," he says. "SOA is—"

"I got it, Sons of the Apocalypse." I need to have my head examined. "What is it with you people? How the hell did white supremacists become a protected class in your upside-down administration?"

"That's a little above your pay grade, isn't it?" he asks.

"Obviously," I say. "The public adulation of ghastly politicians is a phenomenon I will never understand. Your *Polyester Messiah* spends far too much time pitching himself to the masses as some sort of savior. Study your history, Deac. Every tyrant who has ever subverted the will of the people did it under the guise of saving humanity."

"Which is why his term is up today," he says.

I step out of the car as he pops the trunk. I take a quick inventory.

"I'll take the Python and the Glock 34," I say, looking inside his cache of weapons in the trunk.

"This is more of a shotgun job," he says to me.

"Good, you take the Mossberg, and I'll take these," I say, breaking down and inspecting the Glock I pulled from the trunk.

"Forgot who I was dealing with." He laughs out loud.

I check the rounds in the Colt Python. "Hydra-Shocks?"

He nods his head. Every bit of this feels wrong. I feel like a high school kid whose friends decide it might be fun to steal a cop car. It doesn't sound or feel real. My life is becoming someone else's story. I don't know what the Congressman has planned, but any connection to this plot would forever stigmatize my daughter, ruin my family and everyone I've ever come into contact with.

The trip to Brandywine Bay from the park takes a little more than fifteen minutes.

Deacon Lobdell weaves his way down the gravel boat ramp leading to the abandoned Brandywine Pavilion. Three men are gathered around two battered pickup trucks thirty yards off to the left with the Occoquan River at their backs. The Congressman pulls his Mustang to a stop about twenty feet in front of a sleek good-looking Audi sedan with diplomatic plates. Tactically speaking, a terrible place to stop.

"Cover me," he says, coming to a stop and jumping out of the car.

I step out of the car door but stay behind it, keeping the Glock at my side. I block out the scent of rotten eggs emanating from the heavy smell of the morning river when I spot two bodies in the grass to the right of the Audi.

"Congressman, a word?" I call out urgently, stopping him ten feet from the Mustang.

The Congressman holds up one finger, signaling one moment to the men huddled by the pickups.

He takes a few steps back toward me but does not turn around. "Yes, ma'am."

"Two bodies, multiple gunshot wounds. They appear to be of Mideastern descent," I say scanning the area for any other participants in this morning's illicit activities.

He calls out to the men by the truck, "Ya'll been busy this morning! Why don't you quit playing peek-a-boo over by those trucks and come join me by the bodies. The sun's getting a little high in the sky for my likin'."

"Contact," I bark loudly at the Congressman. "Automatic weapon, man in the riverfront gazebo."

I've already moved to my right to avoid the Audi that would obstruct my field of fire. The Glock is trained on his center mass. He's forty yards due north under a frilly white open gazebo that's seen better days. It's a suicide forty-yard dash he can't hope to win unless he discards the AR-15 he's holding.

"Both of ya'll lower the goddamned weapons! We're all friends here," implores the Congressman with authority. "That youuuu, Zachariah? You don't wanna play footsie with this girl—she'll drop ya like a sack a shit 'fore ya'll can blink."

The bedraggled man with the automatic weapon is wearing what might have once been a blue-checkered heavy flannel shirt. It's full of holes and black greasy oil stains. I can only imagine what it smells like. I'll stick with the breakfast river stench on toast. His ginger handlebar mustache is unkempt and his leather face is battered from a lifetime of sun and wind.

My breathing slows down as I slip into combat mode. Without moving my head, my eyes check the three men to my left, watching their hands. So far, they haven't moved a muscle and seem more interested in watching the conflict unfold between their comrade and yours truly.

I know what handlebar is thinking. He likes his odds. He has the high ground. A woman with a pistol forty yards away is threatening his manhood and men like him always have some fatal point to prove.

"Zach. You got five seconds to place that weapon on the deck and you can walk away," I say, knowing all too well that he'll shed his mortal coil long before his deadline expires. He made his decision when I trained my Glock onto him.

He jerks his weapon up as two quick shots punch into the left side of his chest and eviscerate his back on the way out. His eyes are wide as if focusing on something in the distance. It's a look of incomprehension as he's blown off of the gazebo and lands on the tranquil bank of the gentle Occoquan River.

My Glock is already pointing at the other three men awaiting their next life choices.

"Hold your fire!" screams Lobdell. "What the hell is wrong with ya'll?" His wrinkled forehead looks like an escalator going down to his nose.

Neither man makes the slightest move toward their weapons. They carefully walk toward the Congressman as if all is well. The four men speak softly to one another, and I look for nonverbal cues. They look nervous, but not hostile. I've already determined which one I'd be forced to put down next if things go awry.

The Congressman turns to me. "Would you mind waiting in the car for me? On the driver's side? You're making these jittery boys hyperventilate."

I nod my head, watching them as they all walk toward the pickup trucks. I guess it's your funeral, Congressman. There's nothing I can do to protect him sitting behind the wheel of a car except watch.

I cautiously back my way to the car. There's no way I'll show any of these men my back. I slowly lower myself into the car, start the engine, and sit behind the wheel. I should already be on my way, with or without Deacon Lobdell.

I roll down the window to listen to the congressman berate the men in front of him.

"And I asked you to do a simple goddamn job, and now we got a goddamned slaughterhouse on the beach!" the Congressman yells at them. "Get rid of the car, get rid of the bodies, and get your stupid asses back up to Crystal City and be ready to move!" He moves over to the cab of the closest pickup truck, flings open the door, and grabs two large flat and very heavy FedEx packages off of the passenger seat.

He's heading back to me when he calls over his shoulder to one of the men, "Move it, dummy!"

He gingerly places the packages in the trunk and opens the passenger-side door of his prized Mustang GT. I guess I'm driving? Lobdell starts banging away on his phone and without looking up says, "Damn inbreds."

I back the car up slowly.

"Remind me about my job title again, Congressman. Hit man? Enforcer? Wait, I got it. Fixer?"

"Some damn fine shooting, Walker," he says still hitting the keys on his phone. "Let's move. Head north, please."

This deal is getting worse by the second and I find the Congressman's nonchalance around death unsettling. But I'm the one who put that man down, so I'm in no position to pass judgment. But this whole thing wreaks of insanity.

Monday traffic heading into D.C. is going to be horrendous. The destination I have in mind would take thirty minutes with no traffic, but during the Washington rush hour crush to get into the city, there's no telling how long we'll be on the road.

I swing onto I-95 North with my mouth hanging open because not only is traffic moving, the road is practically deserted. Overthrowing the government and ordering the National Guard to shoot up the Capitol must have led to some kind of government shutdown. Since the Congressman isn't running his mouth for once, I come to an executive decision. Breakfast.

Thirty minutes later, the Congressman looks up from his phone-induced coma asking, "Where the hell are we?"

"McLean, Virginia," I answer.

"I can see that. Why are we in McLean?" he asks with a slight edge to his voice.

"Because that's where the McLean Diner is and that's where I'm getting breakfast," I say.

"I live fifteen minutes from here," he says. "But I don't frequent the strip malls in the area."

"I know, Congressman. Ya'll are high class," I say with a smile.

We walk into the no-frills diner and take a seat at the very back facing the front window with the smell of burnt coffee hanging in the air. He's on his second cup when two generous platters of food appear in front of us.

"That's some spread for a strip mall diner," he says.

"You need to get out more, Congressman," I say, looking at an array of cheesy eggs holding the line against a frontal assault by the biscuits and gravy coming in from the north. The rush of sausage gravy has already overwhelmed the hash brown potato cubes. It's a carbon copy of the breakfast Reggie Devereux ordered during our early morning meetup in Arlington. Things are looking up.

"Last meal for a condemned woman?" asks the Congressman watching me plow into my breakfast. "I'm not trying to be a chauvinist and I mean no offense, but how in the Lord's good name can you eat like that and have such a . . . um . . . a pleasing and athletic figure?"

I ignore him, that question has been boring me to sleep for more than twenty years. The Congressman is only halfway done with his meal while I pick off the last remnants of egg yolk with a broken piece of rye toast.

"You know I can't be part of your plot. I get it, you want to stop the President, but this isn't the way," I say, dabbing the corners of my mouth with a napkin. "You have zero chance of success. We're just wasting time," I say.

He takes a slow sip of coffee and stares at me.

"You're delusional. This is a half-cocked pie-in-the-sky pipe dream," I say, warming to the subject.

"It's OK," he says, spreading his hands open to my comments. "Please continue."

"I put more planning into making a salami sandwich. You don't wake up one morning"—I suddenly lower my voice—"and say, 'I think I'm gonna pop the President of the United States later this evening.'"

He nods his head in understanding. "Mizz Walker, I've been planning this 'half-baked' endeavor every morning, noon, and night since the President and his people decided to overthrow the government and seize the Presidency. I've spent more than a hundred hours working out the finer points of this operation," he says, scanning the restaurant again.

"The reason this plan has a chance to work is because no one is expecting any trouble. There's no chatter—the FBI, the federal DHS, and the CIA are asleep at the wheel on this one. I know because, as you stated to me, I'm a ranking member of the House Permanent Select Committee on Intelligence, and as you also pointed out to me, 'I'm the Chair of the Counterterrorism, Counterintelligence, and Counterproliferation Subcommittee.' So you might want to consider that I have some inside knowledge of what the government deems to be a threat."

Then he smiles. "Is my plan reckless? 'Course it is. A hundred things could go wrong, just like everything went wrong for us in Benghazi. Good people died, and we lost a United States Ambassador in North Africa. But the difference between Benghazi and the Capitol attack yesterday is that we knew the terrorists were coming. No one knows we're coming, Walker. No one suspects a dang thing. The nation is still in shock from yesterday, and that's why the time to strike is now. Not tomorrow, not the day after. It has to happen during the President's speech tonight."

"You just referred to 'us' as 'terrorists.' You know that, right?"

I watch the server pouring coffee at another table across the restaurant.

"So how do I fit into your grand plans?" I ask. *And how can I put a stop to them?*

"I'll give you the down and dirty and you tell me what you think," he says watching me.

"You got a name for your suicide mission?" I ask.

"I do," he says quietly. "But no one except the two of us will ever hear it. I'm calling it *Operation Blowback*."

"The unintended adverse results of a political action?" I say, nodding my head. Better get an extra bed ready for him in the psych ward. I smile again despite myself. This guy is a real piece of work.

"We have the Ws covered," he says. "The *who, what, when, where,* and *why.* In his grand wisdom, the President has decided that as a *Law and Order President*, he's going to make his grand announcement right in front of the J. Edgar Hoover Building to show people how much he cherishes the rule of law."

"*The FBI Headquarters?*" I hiss quietly in complete shock and disbelief. "Right there on Pennsylvania Avenue? Who the hell came up with that half-assed idea? It's a choke point wedged between 9th and 10th Streets. It's a worst-case scenario for defenders and the perfect place for an ambush."

I shake my head at the catastrophic—no, the monumental—stupidity of such a decision. "Seriously, who's running point for these people?"

An impish grin spreads across the Congressman's face before he looks down and stirs some cream into his coffee.

"You? No way." I stare at him with my hand over my mouth. "OK, it's brilliant. Brilliant! How the hell did you pull this off?" I ask, wildly impressed, but suddenly terrified of the man sitting across from me. "Where did you get the inspiration?"

"Lincoln?" he says simply.

"Lincoln?" I parrot back. "Of course, Honest Abe was assassinated at Ford's Theatre, just a block away from J. Edgar's Headquarters," I say, seeing this man in a totally different light. He's more devious and more ruthless than I thought possible.

"How did you pitch it to the President? Let's box you into an indefensible position next to Lincoln's final resting place while you try to flush away the very democracy he died to preserve?" I ask.

"Something like that," he says.

"No, sir, I want to know how you convinced this moron and his people to green light this location and wedge the President of the United States into a *kill box*."

"Like you said, the President will be boxed in on three sides with the J. Edgar Hoover Building directly behind him. If we can coordinate a synchronized assault and sprinkle in some MILDEC, then we can achieve our objective."

MILDEC is the acronym for military deception.

"So you're planning a series of countermeasures and diversions to distract his multiple defenders and rapid action forces while gunmen terminate the President's command?"

"God save the king," says Congressman Lobdell.

"So, Congressman, you wanna tell me who's gonna pull the trigger?"

CHAPTER 35

January 7, 2029
Theodore Roosevelt Island, Washington, D.C.

APPARENTLY, I LOST my driving privileges after breakfast because as we headed south on the George Washington Memorial Parkway, I was back in the passenger seat. The Congressman had gotten a text message causing him to furrow his brow and cast several suspicious glances in my direction just before we left the diner. It appears I'm getting the silent treatment, and I'm welcoming it with open arms.

After everything I've experienced during the last forty-eight hours, my mind embraces any respite from human interaction. I feel a little bout of sleepiness wash over me when the Congressman pops up with yet another example of using thirty words to say what he could communicate in just five.

"We have an emergency meeting," he says pointedly. "Someone powerful. Wants to see both of us together. Care to venture any guesses as to the identity of this person?"

My mind races trying to piece together the accusatory tone of his voice, and I can only think of one *powerful* person I know on his side of the aisle.

"Cecilia Danforth?" I reply.

Judging by his expression, I nailed it. He's obviously shocked and even more dismayed than he was before. Answering the question was apparently an unforced error on my part.

"Well," he says, his voice turning deadly serious. "Normally, I try to take such startling revelations in stride, Mizz Walker, but today is not that day. Would you care to enlighten me as to why President Terry Locke's stepdaughter and Chief of Staff has requested the pleasure of our—and I mean *our*—company in a discreet location?"

"Don't know and I really don't care," I snap at him.

The mask of the Congressman's cool demeanor evaporates and a sheen of perspiration appears on his forehead despite the cool temperature inside the vehicle.

"Well, I suppose we should go see what's on her mind, shouldn't we?" he says turning off of the GW Parkway onto Canal Road.

What does this woman want now? How can this day get any more bizarre? This is hard-core *Twilight Zone* material. My workday kicked off with a bang when we drove up on a pair of dead diplomats who did or did not pass explosives to God's White Militia who then delivered them to a sitting member of the House of Representatives. And to top it all off during breakfast, the same Congressman confesses to me that he wants to involve me in a plot to kill the President. I'd call that a full day at the office—and it's not even nine o'clock in the friggin' morning! And don't get me started on yesterday.

And why Canal Road? I guess we're taking the scenic route to this clandestine engagement. After eight minutes of tense silence, we pull into the empty parking lot at Theodore Roosevelt Island. I've been here twice before with Abby. She actually renamed the place "Exercise Island" during her first visit with me when she was only four years old. We had taken a mommy-daughter road trip up to D.C. from Roanoke.

The only access to the island is a pedestrian bridge, so there's little chance of a convoy of government SUVs rolling up on us. However, the island is a forest unto itself, so there are plenty of places for an ambush.

I try to stay on task, but my mind drifts away to Abby and our adventures here. She thinks the giant statue of the funny exercising man is a riot. The *exercising man* as she calls him is a bronze seventeen-foot-tall statue of Teddy Roosevelt, and through a child's eyes, I can see why she thinks he might be squeezing in a workout in his full-length frock coat. One hand is straight up in the air while the other one is by his side. I wish I were here with Abby right now instead of having to meet with plotting politicians engaging in espionage and conspiracy.

"Are you planning on joining me for this excursion, Mizz Walker?" asks the Congressman, jolting me out of my thoughts.

We cross the pedestrian bridge onto Roosevelt Island and, according to the lines on the map, we have left Virginia and entered the District of Columbia. He leads me directly to the edge of the Roosevelt Plaza. There's a tall woman in a Lululemon running outfit stretching by a decorative stone fountain to the right of the exercising twenty-sixth president of the United States. She's about sixty yards away, but I can see her long blonde hair spilling out of a stylish knit cap—that's her. Her personal security teams are making their presence known and they don't look happy to be here.

"Good morning," announces Cecilia Danforth as we approach her. A raw winter wind slices through the trees causing her to tense up to ward off the cold. She shivers and rubs her gloved hands together. "You two are out and about early."

It's a statement, not a question.

"Cora Walker." She says my name but looks at the Congressman. "Is she part of the problem or part of our solution?"

"Mizz Danforth, I find myself at a disadvantage regarding your personal familiarity with Mizz Walker," he says expectantly. "Would you care to elaborate on the nature of your relationship?"

"Cora Walker and I go way back. Don't we, Cora?" she says, smiling at me.

I suppress the urge to turn and run. When you discover a basket full of snakes, it's best not to reach your hand inside and fish around hoping for something good to happen.

"Hard to believe you ditched my job offer to work for this knuckle-dragger," she says with a laugh. Her next sentence is completely drowned out by the deafening sounds of jet engines. This island is right on the flight path for aircraft heading into Reagan National Airport. After the deafening rumble subsides to a gentle roar, Danforth finishes her sentence.

"Did you negotiate a decent clothing allowance?"

I nod pleasantly, but I still have no idea what the hell is going on or why she's here.

"I have passes for both of you," she says. "You've both been electronically cleared and have full access in and around the J. Edgar Hoover Building this evening for the President's speech. Just click the link in the text I just sent both of you."

"You mean your stepfather?" I gasp, unable to suppress my look of shock and horror. I sit down on the bench near the fountain, the frigid stone instantly numbing my hands. She's in on it? She wants to murder her stepdad? There's no way in hell.

"What?" she says looking away from me and fixing a death stare on the Congressman. "You didn't tell her about the operation?"

"I did," he says flatly. "But to protect you, I didn't tell her about your involvement. She didn't have the need to know."

"Well, she knows now," she says looking at me. "Is my involvement going to be a problem, Cora?"

I stand up, anger clearing my head and pushing me forward. "I haven't agreed to anything, Cecilia," I say, using her first name for the first time. "I'd prefer being waterboarded rather than trying to keep up with the two of you and all of your scheming."

"Do you have a line on Speaker Vasquez?" she asks.

"Is that spy talk for, *do I know where she is?*" I ask feeling my temper flare.

Down, girl—these people are evil, but there's no reason to look desperate.

She smiles at me. The cold has reddened her cheeks in contrast with her perfect white teeth.

"I don't know where the Speaker is," I say flatly.

"Well, we will need her back in town after tonight's regime change," she says, devoid of any emotion.

"Regime change?" I say, my mouth hanging open again. "That's your stepfather."

"That *was* my stepfather," she says with striking aplomb. I don't have the imagination or vocabulary to describe the words that just came out of her mouth.

"I'm sure you two have a lot of planning to do," she says. "I just wanted to touch base and let you know that things are coming together on my end. Congressman, a word in private, if you please?"

They walk off together, and I'm left alone with the growing dread of my own thoughts. I guess it's all just business as usual in Washington D.C. Even if it means sacrificing your own stepfather to the wolves. And in this tragic circumstance, I'm playing the part of the wolf. I watch her talking to him, she's so at ease, just taking a stroll and catching up with a friend on a crisp winter morning.

I've met tyrants, warlords, rapists, and even suicide bombers. The worst humanity has to offer, but I've never met anyone quite like this woman. I thought Congressman Lobdell was bad; Danforth is in a league of her own.

I wander over to the statue of Roosevelt. He's by far my favorite President of all time. I wonder what the Rough Rider would have to say about all of this? I know what he'd say, *"You're being set up to take the fall, woman. These are powerful people and you, Cora Walker, are the pawn and they will sacrifice you quicker than you can say, 'Bully!'"*

I know all too well that I attract violence and death. Like a shark, it can smell me from miles away. I've never killed anybody in my life who wasn't trying to do me harm. At least that is what I tell myself. Do most killers have a fail-safe switch like me? A built-in catchphrase to justify their ungodly actions?

I was a teenager the first time I took a human life. An older man was trying to rape me when I accidentally killed him. I cut down scores of attackers in Benghazi, but they were engaged in a full-out assault against the compound I was defending and had murdered an American Ambassador.

For the most part, when I became a mother, I thought I had left behind the world of violence. I thought the killer inside of me was dead, but she was biding her time, and growing stronger. I found that out a few years ago when my daughter was kidnapped and held hostage in the Blue Ridge Mountains surrounding Roanoke, Virginia. I cut a murderous path through the kidnappers until I was able to bring Abby home safely. My reality is forever entrenched with the echoes of the dead that populate my garden.

Despite my transgressions, I've never killed anyone in cold blood. Does the President deserve to die? Of course he does. But does that mean I should be the one to execute him? Can I kill someone who isn't trying to murder me or bring harm to someone I love? It's true that the President is in the process of smothering our American democracy, but I could never justify killing him to myself. I still struggle with the death of every person who's stopped breathing by my hand. Different victims with different faces are never far away. I can't atone for my sins or make amends for the lives I have taken.

But what would happen to my soul if I took the life of someone who wasn't trying to kill me? Wouldn't that make me a serial killer? Am I living in denial? Am I a female Ted Bundy? My thoughts scatter as another airliner scrapes the trees over Roosevelt Island. Screaming jet engines lay waste to the tranquility of the island for the millionth time. Cecilia Danforth approaches from my left-hand side. She is the last person in the world you want sneaking up on you.

"Cora, walk with me for a moment." Her voice is barely audible over the diminishing rumble of the fleeing aircraft. She gently takes my arm and leads me past the fountain toward the edge of the woods. I stiffen at her touch and struggle not to run away screaming.

"I want to talk to you about this evening," Danforth says smoothly. "I know we're putting you in an impossible situation, but I'm going to protect you."

"You're going to protect me? I'm sorry, I don't understand," I scoff.

No one can protect anyone—she must secretly drink more than her stepdad.

"Let me rephrase—if you survive tonight, I will do everything I can to protect you," she clarifies.

"I'm not doing anything tonight," I say turning around to rejoin the Congressman. What the hell am I supposed to say to that mess?

"Cora," she says forcefully, stopping me in my tracks.

My blood runs cold and as a blunt instrument, I must tamp down the urge to lash out at her. I stop and stare into her eyes just to see if I'm brave enough to do it.

"I know you don't care about yourself," she says. "You don't fear death. You care only about the people and country that you love. I respect that. But what I want you to really know is that if you don't survive the attack, I will protect your family from the fall-out. They will never have to live in the shadow of an assassin."

Violence ebbs from my pours as I step into her personal space, nearly causing her to stumble backward.

"And how do you plan on making that happen, Ms. Danforth?" I say, spitting my words. "How do you plan on keeping my family safe when you two broadcast to the world that I was involved in a plot to assassinate the President?"

"By controlling the narrative," she says without hesitation. She doesn't back down at all and actually moves closer. I can smell her complicated perfume as the steam from her breath drifts past my face.

"I've compiled an extensive dossier on you. It's already documented that you've been secretly working for the President and would lay down your life to protect him. It fits the narrative, fits your personality and your entire personal history. You're a fiercely loyal and passionate defender of democracy who made the ultimate sacrifice to save him. Total continuity from the cradle to the grave."

It takes some time to digest what she just said to me. I feel so conflicted and yet, strangely grateful. Is she lying? I don't know

who to believe or who to trust. I know I'm a fool. Trusting this
woman is the equivalent of a death sentence. But will she still protect me after I thwart her attempt to take out her stepfather?
Stupid question.

"Why would you do this for me?" I ask, lost in a crush of
unchecked confusion.

"I have no idea, Cora Walker. Maybe you represent everything
America should strive to be. And not what it actually is," she says.

"When did you decide to do all of this?" I ask.

"The day I met you, Cora Walker."

CHAPTER 36

January 7, 2029
The Watergate Hotel, Washington, D.C.

I'M A SUCKER for a view. Even on a frigid morning like this high above the Potomac River. The Key Bridge seems to be floating on top of the icy fog rippling across the river. My morning run seems like ages ago. Congressman Deacon Lobdell and I stand side by side on the rooftop of the Watergate Hotel staring down at the rising sun reflecting off the water. Such a beautiful setting, a place to help someone make peace with their God if they happen to have one. If I were truly committed to saving President Locke, the most prudent course of action right now would be to grab the Congressman and toss him off the roof. Problem solved.

Short of that, I have to gather as much information as I can about the Congressman's plot if I have any chance of derailing it. It's not like I can report his plans to anyone. Who would believe me? It would be his word against mine. I have every reason in the world to kill the President, and Lobdell stands to gain nothing.

This is my first time at the Watergate Hotel although I've seen it from the road any number of times. I thought the history of this place would mean something to me, but I would take a hundred Nixon cover-ups over one Terry Locke. I soak up one last look, staring down at the light traffic coming into the city from Virginia, and follow the Congressman back inside. Using his key card, we go down one level. The elevator door slides open leading us into a darkened hallway.

"Watch your step," he says as we step into the blackness and the door slides shut behind us. He reaches to his left and flips on a light switch. Fluorescent lighting flickers for a moment before crackling to life. The room is stuffed with tables, umbrellas, pitchers, trays, and everything else a restaurant would need to stock an outside dining area. It's also a fire hazard and would never pass any fire code inspection.

He leads me to the end of a room on the right with a dead-bolted door marked CHEMICAL ROOM. There's absolutely no reason for a chemical room up here. We walk inside, he bolts the door behind us, and we have to slide behind a boiler with our backs against the wall before coming to a nondescript door with another dead bolt. He unlocks the door leading to what looks like an office bunker with a large ornate conference table, full-size refrigerator, and a fancy coffee maker. The amount of money that goes into these intelligence community setups staggers my mind.

"I need to make a quick call," I say.

"Not from this room," he says. "It's tech proof, no signals, no wires except the electricity that powers the table outlet, fridge, and coffee maker."

"That reminds me," he says, placing his briefcase on the table and opening it. "I had someone clean out your belongings from the Speaker's Chambers this morning. Your handbag is behind the driver's seat in my car and the rest of your materials are locked up in a safe place."

"My bag's been in your car all morning?" I ask.

"Sorry," he says. "Busy day."

He pulls out two small stacks of paper, takes one, and slides the other over to me.

It's a Google Map printout of the J. Edgar Hoover Building littered with tiny numbers in circles. The second sheet of paper has the key corresponding to what each number on the map represents. It's a schematic on how to assassinate a president broken down into twenty-four steps.

"It's a three-pronged assault," he says. "At eight twelve p.m., a timed diversionary explosive device will detonate at the northeastern corner of 10th Street and E Street. This will be the signal for you and other parties to engage your targets. You at the southeastern corner of 10th and Pennsylvania Avenue while your counterparts will initiate contact at the southeastern corner of 9th and Penn."

"Engage my targets?" I ask quietly.

He nods his head and the room falls silent again.

"Deac, I have to tell you. I will not, under any circumstances, attack any law enforcement officers. The President can rain down hell on this nation for the next twenty years, but I will not injure a single police officer for any reason. I saw enough battered and brutalized cops yesterday to last me ten lifetimes. Your people committed the worst acts of violence against the law enforcement community I've ever seen in my life." I turn apoplectic with rage reliving what I witnessed yesterday.

"I will not be part of it. Any of it."

"I agree with you," he says. "One hundred percent."

I silently dare him to lie to me, but my anger is already ebbing away.

"So, that's it? I can go?" I laugh quietly. "That's it?"

"Hardly," he says grimly. "Your role has nothing to do with confronting the police or the Secret Service."

"So what—you need me to dazzle them with a little shimmy and my cute smile?"

He laughs out loud. It was a tension breaker. Maybe it's what we both need.

"Your role in this is the most complicated part of the op," he says. "I'm setting you up, Cora Walker, and leading you right into a deadly ambush."

"Of course you are," I say shaking my head. "I always get the crap jobs." But, for some reason, I always end up volunteering for them.

"I've hired a hit team from the Sons of the Apocalypse, the men you engaged this morning, to run point at the corner of 10th and Penn. They were a four-man team, but after your display of marksmanship this morning, there are now only three remaining," he says.

"Not funny," I bite back.

As usual, my interjection falls on deaf ears.

"They are devout loyalists to President Locke. They're going to be tipped off about a potential deadly threat against the President an hour before he is set to address the nation. Their only job, their entire reason for living, will be to identify a rogue female D.C. Metro Police sergeant and shoot her down before she can bring any harm to the President."

"And they will be under the impression that I'm a real police officer coming to take out President Locke?" I ask.

"Absolutely," he says. "This is a win-win for them. They hope to bask in the glory of saving the President's life. And if they have to shoot a cop to accomplish that task, it's an added bonus."

"This doesn't make sense, none of it," I say.

"Once they make a positive identification, they're going to draw down on you," he says. "What you do next is between you and your creator."

"And *then what*?" I ask him.

"Let me worry about then what. You focus on the people trying to kill you," he says, ending the conversation. "Anything else before I burn these?"

"The only way to gauge true intelligence in its purest form is the ability to promote a better future," I say staring at him. "Is that what you think you're doing here?"

Silence is the only answer I'm going to get.

I take a long last look at the map without really seeing it. I don't need a map. I picture the area in and around the FBI Headquarters Building in my mind, the planters, the location of the windows, and how the sidewalk juts out too far onto Pennsylvania Avenue. The Justice Department will be right behind us with teams of snipers watching the event from above.

I can't tell what the objective is here. But I have to be there. If for no other reason, to protect the President from what he so richly deserves.

He gathers up the printouts and drops them into a heavy metal trash can lined with a solvent that smells like nail polish remover. He watches the ink float to the top of the liquid before lighting a match and dropping it inside. The chemicals in the can cause the contents to burst into flames.

"Smoke detectors?" I ask.

He shakes his head no, watching the smoke billowing up from the receptacle. He uses a pen to stir up the mixture in the can until he's satisfied that all traces of his treason have been forever wiped from existence. Five minutes later, we're back at his Mustang deep in the deserted parking garage underneath the hotel. I look at him over the roof of his car and say, "Where did you say my bag was?"

He reaches behind the driver's seat and pulls out one of my few prized possessions. God help me, I love handbags and this one is my favorite work companion of all time. It's a handcrafted Hammitt tote with pockets galore for everything any woman could possibly desire. There's even a slot for my water bottle. So help me, I love this thing—it's a perfect marriage of genuine leather and suede. The only problem is, it's of no use to me anymore—it's nothing but garbage now. God knows what GPS trackers or tracers have been sewn into the bag or sprinkled in with the contents. I'm gonna miss this thing.

"Let's just see if anything is missing," I announce unceremoniously, dumping the contents of my bag all over the back seat of his prized possession, his stupid 2008 Mustang GT.

"Damnit, Walker!" he says watching me dump my crap all over the place. "No one messed with your bag. They brought it straight to me."

"It's yours now, genius," I say. "Keep it!"

My eyes fall on a football-size item wrapped in light blue tissue paper that came out with the rest of the stuff I dumped out. *What the hell is that?*

I pick it up, tentatively noticing the haphazard wrapping job. Someone appears to have used an entire roll of Scotch tape to finish wrapping the item. I take a deep breath and hold the package lovingly in my arms. Taking my time, I gingerly unwrap it like a sacred sculpture. It's Pirate, Abby's revered stuffed tiger and her most treasured possession in the entire world.

"Hi, Pirate," I say choking up with more tears and emotion than I thought I was capable of. I turn around and lean against the car door, sliding down to the dirty garage floor desperately clutching Pirate to my chest.

"How did you get in there, you stupid tiger?" I ask. I stroke her ruffled fur gently, rocking back and forth. Jesus, why would Abby smuggle Pirate into my purse? What was she thinking? Goddamn it, I can't do this. How the hell can I stop this madness and save the President? I'm just a heartbroken mother with a stuffed tiger.

I stand up with Pirate in my arms and bark at the Congressman, "Where can I get some privacy and a cell signal?"

He stops to think for a moment.

"I'll drop you at Washington Circle North West," he says. "I can give you a few hours, but I need you at 15-hundred sharp, South Station Hotel at L'Enfant Plaza, Suite 1608. Get the key from the bell captain standing out in front of the Marriott next door. I'll text you the details. You can shower, eat, and relax there until we move."

"Swell." I say wearily.

The Congressman drops me off and speeds away into the traffic. I plop down on a bench with my stuffed tiger right smack in the middle of Washington Circle North West with the cold wind chapping my face. It's a traffic circle that has gorgeous tulips in the spring that surround a statue of George Washington mounted on a horse. There are no flowers now, just the desolate frozen earth and a forgotten bench with a stubborn morning frost that never bothered melting.

In another tragic plot twist of my life, I remember that President Ronald Reagan was shot about a mile up the road from here when he was coming out of the Washington Hilton Hotel. It happened several years before I was born, but obviously presidential assassination attempts are weighing heavily on my mind at the moment.

I pick the burner phone marked with the letter "A" and punch the redial key.

The phone rings six times. I look down at Pirate silently asking her if anyone is going to bother answering the damn phone. I put my finger on the end button when Cat picks up.

"Hey, girl," I say cheerfully.

"Oh my God, Cora," she says, panic rising in her voice. "What's the matter? What's wrong?"

"Nothing," I lie. "Everything is fine. I'm just checking in and hoping to talk to my little girl."

"Cora?"

"Please, Cat, I love you, but please just put Abby on," I say feeling the tears rake my salt- and frostbitten face.

"Hi, Mom! What are you doing? Are you coming to see me today?" Abby greets me on the other end of the line.

"Hey, baby girl," I choke out.

"Why?" she says instantly picking up on the tone of my voice. "Why are you sad, Mom? Why are you so sad?"

"I'm not sad, Abby," I lie again. "I'm just sooo tired. I just need some sleep. That's all. But I found something this morning that will really help me sleep tonight."

Abby squeals with delight. "You found Pirate in your purse, didn't you?" She squeals again. "You finally found her, right?"

"I did, sweetheart. And that was so sweet of you to share your tiger. But I'm a little bit confused."

"No . . . you're not, Mom," Abby says confidently.

"Slow down, sweetie," I say choosing my words very carefully now. "You've never been away from Pirate before so why would you send her on a trip with me?"

"'Member when I used to lose her all the time when I was just a little kid? You said Pirate will always find her way home. You know that. This time I sent Pirate with you so Pirate can bring you back to me!"

CHAPTER 37

January 7, 2029
Virgil's Memphis Barbecue, Washington, D.C.

I STARE AT my plate of picked over cornbread, not much of a meal, but I couldn't find my appetite. I look at a full-color advertisement for the Brisket Bash scheduled for this coming Wednesday. I wonder where I might be forty-eight hours from now.

I hit speed dial to contact Austin J. Barton, the man who picked us up from the Capitol yesterday and is keeping the Speaker in one of his safe houses.

Barton answers the phone on the first ring.

"Got a place close-ish to the Pentagon?" I ask.

"Define close."

"Under thirty?" I ask.

"Maybe."

"How maybe?" I ask. "Under forty?"

"Roger that," he says, breaking the connection.

I had more to say, but he's already gone.

This is the only burner phone I have left except for the Congressman's cell. I take out the battery, remove the SIM card, and snap the phone in half. Then I carefully stuff the phone's SIM card into a leftover piece of cornbread, never to be seen again.

I take out my last burner to make a call when I see the bartender approaching me. I close the phone and watch him walk. He's a cute young guy, maybe twenty-eight or so. He's got broad muscular shoulders to go along with his big puppy dog eyes that he flashes every time he approaches my table. He has a fresh pitcher of ice tea that he made for me even though the dining room is empty. He leans over me to refresh my oversized cup, and the citrusy smell of his faint cologne washes over me. Jesus, he smells so good. But sadly, I'm not here for the company or the ribs. Even still, I catch myself staring too long at his broad shoulders.

"Are you all by yourself? This is a pretty big restaurant to cover for one person, isn't it?" I ask.

"The manager left me to close up," he says. "Everyone blew out early because of the president's speech. All businesses need to be locked down in the area by four."

"Sorry, I seem to be your only customer," I say.

"Yup, we have the place all to ourselves," he says eagerly.

I look around the dining room curiously. "Well, since we're alone—Why don't you give me the ten-cent tour. Let me see the inner workings of a D.C. restaurant."

He looks at me with momentary confusion and then decides to go with it. "We're not in trouble, are we, Officer?"

Officer? Ha. I almost forgot I'm playing dress-up as a D.C. Metro Police sergeant.

"Nope. Just professional curiosity," I reply.

He shows me a few random pictures of celebrities on the wall and then leads me back to the kitchen where I spot the alarm system on the wall next to the manager's office, and the digital display is dark.

"Is your alarm system offline?" I ask.

"Am I going to get in trouble for this?" he asks.

"Just asking questions," I say smiling at him.

"We had more than a few false alarms during the past couple of months and the manager says it costs the restaurant 400 bucks every time the police have to respond. So we shut it down and are on the waiting list for a new security company."

He walks over to one of the coolers and opens the giant steel door. I notice that the office door is wide open. I peek inside and see an extra set of keys dangling on a nail by the door.

"This is the walk-in cooler and the freezer is over there," he says. "Are you headed over to Hoover for the President's speech?"

"Nope, done for the day," I lie, smiling back.

"Really," he says pausing and looking at me eagerly. "You wanna grab a drink with me? I mean, is that allowed? Not here, somewhere else."

I laugh. "You're sweet, but I have a long trip home this afternoon, and I need to get on the road. It's getting late."

He looks disappointed, but smiles walking me back to the table and struts off to retrieve the check. I'm guessing he probably doesn't encounter a lot of rejection from the opposite sex.

I drop a fifty on the table and exit onto the street. My next stop is the UPS Store a block north.

"We're closing in five minutes," a young woman with pink hair and a nose ring snaps at me, displaying another shining example of customer service and respect for law enforcement. I walk past her without a word and scoop up a rectangular box big enough for a football. I stop and stare at Pirate and stroke what's left of her fur one last time. I give the stuffed tiger a gentle kiss on the forehead telling her to take care of my baby before sliding her inside the box and sealing it.

I step up to the counter and hand the girl a twenty. "Will this go out today?"

"Yuppers," she says. "It's your lucky day. Truck will be any minute and today's a light day. Just a few envelopes and your box."

"Excellent," I say collecting my change. "Have a nice day."

Time to take out the Congressman-turned-assassin before he
gets his shot at the President. I quickly cover the two blocks to the
Brighton Hotel and join the throngs of Locke supporters behind
the police barricades watching the VIPs arriving for tonight's
inauguration announcement. Cabinet members, Joint Chiefs, and
other ardent supporters arrive in a parade of Mercedes, black cars,
and limos.

The area is rich with high value targets. Security is airtight. A
phalanx of police officers, Secrets Service agents, and undercover
Park Police line the barricades on both sides scanning the crowds
for anything even slightly out of place.

Regardless of the occupants, every vehicle is subject to a full
screening before anyone is allowed out of the car. Trunks and
hoods pop open as bomb-sniffing dogs circle every vehicle at least
twice. Secret Service agents with tactical search mirrors on sticks
inspect the undercarriage of every car looking for irregularities.

This is a double layer of protection, because the vehicles have
already undergone the same treatment at 7th and Penn Ave before
being allowed two blocks north to the Brighton Hotel.

There's a ton of firepower here. Most security personnel are carrying automatic weapons while the rooftops are teaming with
snipers glaring down below like gargoyles. Extracting the
Congressman without blowing a hole in his back is going to be a
challenge.

I push my way to the front, listening to the exchange between
the security and the occupants in the vehicle. The man in body
armor instructs each person in the vehicle to lower their car

windows one at a time before carefully scrutinizing their identification. The process takes forever and the line of traffic coils backwards like a worm on a hook.

It's OK with me, waiting for my target gives me time to focus. I have a sinking suspicion that the Congressman might already know I'm gunning for him. I'll stop him from killing the President, no matter what the personal cost. I force away any flicker of self-doubt. It's a distraction I can't afford.

Regardless of my beliefs, he can't honestly think that I would stand by and let him assassinate the President of the United States. When he first recruited me, he told me I'd be the nuclear option, but I never imagined it meant killing the President.

I secretly linked my phone to the Congressman's this morning, so I know he's one of the next cars up. I watch him carefully as he gets out of the car scanning the area. After passing through security, he immediately works his way inside the Brighton Hotel. Besides the main entrance, I found only two viable exits from the building, and they are buttoned up tight. I guzzle down a large bottle of Gatorade, watch and wait. I guess they're keeping people in the staging area until the last possible moment.

Congressman Deacon Lobdell walks out of the hotel and speaks to two of the people manning the front entrance. He laughs and slaps the back of the man on his left and is escorted to the far side of the barriers. He comes through a checkpoint and is on the street walking quickly toward the Hoover Building. The crowds are beginning to thicken. It takes only a moment before his phone appears and he begins punching away at the screen.

My phone buzzes in my hand.

"Are you in place?" he asks.

"Trick or treat," I reply. "Don't turn around."

He stops in place, remembering the last time I used that line on him in the subterranean Capitol Garbage Tunnel. He pushes his earbuds in a little deeper. And begins to scan the immediate area.

"What's on your mind, Bronco?"

He's trying to buy time.

"Do you believe me to be a woman of my word?" I ask.

He answers my question with dead silence.

"Slowly, like your life depends on it—and it does—look to your left."

He turns his head slowly as I press the barrel of my .38 special into his ribs on his right side.

"Let's go back the way we came," I say conversationally.

"If I refuse?" he asks.

"Then we go out in a blaze of glory," I say simply. "You have two seconds to comply."

He starts walking. "Have you thought this through?"

"Walk," I say, the gun tucked into my pocket, but pointing directly at the spine of the Congressman.

"You're insane," he spits, shaking his head.

Three eager-looking men approaching the Hoover Building spot the Congressman and converge on him. This might be the end of the line for both of us.

"Great day for America, isn't it, Congressman?" says the pudgy man with the ill-fitting suit.

"We're going to make some history," he says, pumping their hands enthusiastically. He's looking for a way out, but deep down, he knows there's nowhere to hide from me.

Their mindless banter is finally over and the Congressman excuses himself.

"Left down D Street. Pick up the pace, please," I instruct. "Where the hell is your security?"

"Why don't you tell me?" he says.

We pass the Brighton Hotel on our right and continue down the street back to the restaurant where I had lunch. Twenty minutes later, the Congressman is securely bound to a chair that is anchored to one of the tall permanent shelves in the walk-in cooler back at Virgil's Barbecue.

"I need details, Congressman," I ask searching his eyes. "I know I'm supposed to be the decoy, but then what?"

He starts to say something and then chuckles. "What the hell are ya'll thinking, Walker?" His Southern twang always comes back when he's under duress. "What in God's name do you hope to accomplish with this stunt?"

I check my watch; the President is set to speak in an hour. I answer his question with my own: "How many teams do you have? How many people do you have back there? What's the plan?"

"We reviewed the plans this morning, didn't we?" he asks innocently.

"Are you the trigger man?" I ask.

"You're protecting the wrong people for the wrong reasons. You've turned your back on the country when it needs you the most. You're embracing the terror that's gripped our nation since 2024 and prolonging it indefinitely. Your belief system is upside down."

"*My belief system?* You want to assassinate the President of the United States?" I say. "You're lucky I don't cut you to pieces."

"Let your conscience be your guide, Walker," he says. "You're going to ruin everything. Saving the president will drive a stake into the heart of our democracy. The country will fall under the iron boot of a tyrant, and you'll be dead or rotting in a cell."

"I was under the impression that we were going to work together to make sure that didn't happen?" I ask, staring into his eyes looking for some spark of reason.

"The only way to save our democracy is to eliminate the greatest threat this nation has ever known. But you failed. You failed me and you failed the American people, and worst of all . . ." His voice trails off.

"Finish," I say shoving the .38 under his chin.

"You failed yourself," he says pushing his chin down hard onto the gun. "Do what you need to do, Walker."

I don't know what to do. He stops and looks at me pleadingly. "It's not too late, Walker. Untie me. We can do what needs to be done and bring our country back from the brink. You and me. One last mission."

I have to get back to the Hoover Building and the President's speech. I tap the Congressman's phone in my pocket. Maybe it can help me unlock the deeper secrets of his assassination plot.

I stuff a cloth into his mouth and whisper into his ear, "Gotta get back to the dance."

CHAPTER 38

January 7, 2029
J. Edgar Hoover Building, Washington, D.C.

I COMB THE Congressman's phone while I stand at parade rest listening to the D.C. Police Watch Commander. He has a large map pinned to a city police wagon. It's a three-block grid of the area surrounding the Hoover Building. The top of the map shows the Metro Center Train Station with a red X emblazoned across it.

"There are five roving CT—Counter Terrorism—Sniper Teams on the roofs here, here, and here." He points using a laser pointer. "The following Metro Stations have been locked down until tomorrow morning: Metro Center, Federal Triangle, and Archives-Navy Memorial-Penn Quarter. No one in; no one out. Crowd control's gonna be a bitch. We are not expecting trouble but be vigilant. At this point, we're not hearing any chatter about any counter protests. And they really can't breach the perimeter here anyway."

He puts his hands behind his back and says solemnly, "We're missing more than two hundred officers after yesterday's massacre at the Capitol."

He lets that sink in for a moment before continuing,

"The National Guard is on standby and staging at 9th and E," he says pointing at the map again. "Don't let your frosty feelings for the Guard interfere with what we're here to do this evening."

He motions over to his left.

"Turn around and look north. You can see them forming at the intersection up there," he says. "Questions? Concerns? Comments?"

I reflect on the carnage I was caught up in twenty-four hours ago at the Capitol Building and our narrow escape from the President's National Guard. Our "Tyrant and Chief" became just the third president in American history to suspend habeas corpus last night so he could illegally imprison several members of Congress. Lincoln did it to stop the government from being overthrown during the Civil War. Bush Two did it after the terrorist attacks of 9/11. Legally speaking, not one of those three Presidents had the legal right to do what they did, but obviously they didn't let anything so trivial as the rule of law interfere with their plans,

I think back to the first time I completed my S.E.R.E.—Survival-Evasion-Resistance-Escape—Training at the FBI Training Academy in Quantico. The U.S. Army head shrinkers—psychologists—swore to the special program trainers that they didn't believe it was possible for my heart rate to skip past 120 beats per minute no matter how much duress they put me under. I'm definitely not that woman anymore.

I have always intuitively understood that casual indifference in a city setting is the perfect disguise whether you're stalking a target or being hunted. Animal strength, speed, and cunning can only take you so far. Infinite patience and purging yourself of any visible sense of urgency are the most valuable qualities an urban hunter has at her disposal. A little visit from Lady Luck never hurts either. You must take advantage of her when she sneaks up, but you can never count on her coming your way.

The government-controlled news cameras are all lined up in a row. The semi-free national press has been barred from the area and will have to rely on the news feed coming from government-edited footage.

At 8:04 p.m., I force a set of plugs deep into my ears. Only eight minutes until the diversionary explosion is set to go off around the west side of the FBI Building. President Terrance Locke struts out of the Hoover Building like a Roman Emperor surrounded by security and several of his Locke and Load Legislators. By basking in the glory of the President's extremism, these leaders are now prisoners of the monster they helped create.

I look for the men that the Congressman sent to ambush me. They could be anywhere. The crowds are pushing in behind us and I worry about the collateral damage when the shooting begins, but I'm in the deep end now with nowhere to go but forward.

Four minutes to go. I spot at least two men eyeing me from behind the steel barriers surrounding the President and everyone inside. I can't be sure if it's the men who are looking for me. I'm only forty yards away. I could put both of them down instantly, but I don't know if they're the right men who've been tasked with killing me and that would be cold-blooded murder. I see one man reach inside his coat, but I'm fraught with indecision. I can't risk shooting—my thoughts are forever silenced as the force of an unimaginable blast rocks the entire city block, mowing down every person on the west side of the Hoover Building and blowing out hundreds of windows. Shards of glass and debris rain down everywhere like a volcanic eruption as the entire city shudders from the pummeling shock wave.

A massive cloud of dust and smoke races down 10th Street and plumes up over the top of the Hoover Building seconds from crashing down on top of every one of us. Mass hysteria ensues as a thunderhead of death and blackness rumbles forward. Old videos of the collapsing Twin Towers flash through my mind as several people in front of the Hoover Building turn to run, but there's nowhere to go.

I plop down on my butt, yank off my police hat, and smash my face deep inside of it. I shove my head between my knees, just as a wave of white-hot viscous dust blasts into every one of us, snuffing out the screams of every living thing around me. The concussion bowls me over as the city slips into a macabre silence.

I curl up into a fetal position, keeping my face welded into the thick fabric of the hat, praying for the cloud to pass. More images from 9/11 intrude upon my thoughts. Countless videos of people trying to outrun the debris cloud that swallowed them up as the World Trade Center collapsed all around them.

Sickening pain scurries up my spine causing me to go rigid. If I had been speaking, I would have bitten off my tongue. My eyes sting like I've caught a face full of battery acid. Murky lungs plead for fresh air. My chest constricts. The world spins underneath me as the blackness offers the gentle comfort of a child's embrace.

My mind goes offline, comes back fast, and then sputters before disorientation sets in. Where am I? The temptation to give in to sleep and give up is overwhelming. I cough, feeling shards of glass pinpricking holes in my esophagus. Am I sick? I lick at my lips trying to moisten them, but my selfish mouth offers no moisture. The coward in me screams for shelter, but I have no idea where the hell I am.

I'm trapped in an impossibly deep well void of light and sound.

"Momma?" I hear a faint voice from the top of the well.

I feel panic rising. Abby needs me. How can I climb out of here? "Abby?" I whisper. I stop and listen for her to call again. Nothing. Abby isn't here. I'm in Washington.

My brain flickers slowly to life, trying to reboot while I tamp down the terror of lying blind and exposed in the middle of a blast zone. The fog in my head is trying to take over, but conscious thought is slowly fighting its way to the surface.

"Oh my God, what has he done?" I silently cry out. My face is still buried inside the policeman's thick service cap, terrified of what I might see if I ever come out.

I wonder how many people the Congressman just murdered in the name of his version of democracy? Lobdell lied to me. This was no diversionary explosion. That blast was some type of military-grade bunker buster. A savage double military explosive designed to destroy targets buried deep underground like the ones used during the Gulf War.

I gradually move into a sitting position, keeping my eyes and face buried into the hat. I blindly grope my tactical vest, feeling for my riot goggles. The ones I should have already been wearing. I fish them out and get them ready. I squeeze my eyes shut, causing hundreds of marble-sized white flashbulbs to pop beneath my eyelids nearly causing me to vomit. I take another moment before yanking off the hat and snapping the goggles into place, ripping out a handful of my hair in the process. I keep my eyes closed until I'm sure the goggles are on tight and then open my eyes. I should have kept them shut. I'm not prepared for the carnage in front of me. I take shallow breaths, trying not to scream.

Bodies are scattered around the area covered in a coat of thick grayish ash. The taint of sulfur and chemicals cauterizes the blood flowing freely from my nostrils. My scalp is singed in several places and my throat catches fire with each breath. I shake my head violently, sending a plume of hot dust out of my hair and into the air just above my head. I'm a punch-drunk fighter and I can't stand up.

I feel gentle hands on my body and I'm in no shape to resist. Police officers on either side of me in full riot gear help me to my feet. Their goggles and full facial shields saved them from the sandstorm that just savaged its way through us. Their voices sound far away as they help me to my feet. I try to see through the ash cloud hanging limply in the air to see if the President is OK, but a viscous fog obscures my view of the podium. I'm sure his service detail rushed him into the safety of the Hoover Building seconds after the blast.

Everyone within a hundred-yard radius is coughing, spitting, and choking up the dust they inhaled when the cloud washed past us. Injured people are strewn everywhere and several of them have blood trickling out of their ears and noses. The initial shock wave blew out a lot of eardrums. By far, the people who were right in front of the Hoover Building fared the best because they were protected from the shock wave and the plume of debris. They're still shrouded in soot, but none of them seem to be seriously hurt. Thanks to a stiffening breeze, the brunt of the dust storm seems to have already moved on to points south.

My combat awareness slowly comes back online like a flickering light bulb. I have to locate the hit team the congressman sent to kill me. They were likely spared the brunt of the explosion. I spot them for a second time but luckily, they haven't found me yet. Wrong—they have me.

My blood turns slushy as I reach for my sidearm. No joy—I got nothing. No weapon. Must have lost it when the blast bowled me over. I drop to the ground scrambling low and searching for my Glock. I see my weapon four feet away just as two of the assassins sent to kill me bring their weapons up to fire. I roll toward my gun, flinching as four gunshots split the air, causing a renewed panic on Pennsylvania Avenue. I can't make sense of what happens next. Several men behind the barricades crumple to the ground.

A police officer speaks frantically into his radio as five other officers in full riot gear keep their weapons trained toward the men who were about to shoot at me. The police officers must have spotted the gunmen drawing their weapons and put them down before they could fire. But now everyone in and around the FBI Building has a new and potentially more deadly problem. The gunshots have caused a secondary wave of panic and anxiety in the wake of the explosion.

More than twenty Secret Service Agents are now pointing their weapons at the group of police officers with me who just gunned down the attackers. The policemen identify the threat and aim their weapons back at the Secret Service Agents.

I look to my left and see President Locke pinned to the ground with at least two Secret Service agents on top of him. He's frantically trying to stand up, but the agents are keeping him down. I can't begin to understand why the agents haven't evacuated the President back into the safety of the J. Edgar Hoover Building.

"Get the President back into the building," I try to call out, but the effort sends my chemically burned throat into a coughing fit.

To make matters worse, nervous National Guard Troops are pouring in from 9th Street sweeping aside the barricades and blocking the President into a corner. It slowly dawns on me that the most deadly and unnecessary gunfight in American history may be taking shape right in front of me.

The disoriented Secret Service agents can't seem to decide which is the greater threat to the President's life—the National Guard Troops or the D.C. Metro Police. First responders are boxed out of the area to the east and west while the National Guard has completely gummed up everything on 9th Street with their ill-advised advance. Tenth Street is littered with the victims from the initial explosion so everyone is staying put for now.

I can't believe these people haven't sought shelter for the President, but then it hits me. Reinforced bomb blast doors have sealed off the J. Edgar Hoover Building, cutting off President Locke from any means of escape. The Polyester Messiah is stuck here with the rest of us. Just as Deacon's plan called for, the President is being held hostage in an inescapable *kill box*.

Yesterday, President Terrance Locke brought war to the United States Capitol. Today, through a series of missteps and blunders, he's started a new war and he's pinned facedown at the front of the battlefield.

The National Guard begins a deadly push inside the barricades to rescue the President. The people inside the closed-off area begin stampeding and trampling one another to escape the advancing soldiers.

"Do not come any closer," yells a Secret Service Agent into a bullhorn. "Stop where you are or you will be fired upon."

Automatic weapons come up on both sides, and it looks like the Secret Service and National Guard are on the verge of a colonial-style face-to-face musket engagement, but this one will be fought with automatic weapons. And then I realize, the simple brilliance of the Congressman's plan to terminate the President. If members of the Secret Service or the National Guard begin shooting, the President will almost certainly be killed in the crossfire.

D.C. Metro Police Officers exchange confused and concerned looks as the Watch Commander issues hand signals and orders them to stand down and fall back. He's a smart man, no reason to get in the middle a shooting war between the Secret Service and the National Guard.

I scan the entire situation unfolding in front of me when both sides start screaming at each other. "Drop your weapons! Drop your weapons! Hold your fire! No one shoot. Drop your goddamn weapons—that's an order!"

What I don't hear is anyone issuing the order to "Stand Down." If someone can't figure out a peaceful resolution in the next sixty seconds, the FBI Headquarters will become a shooting gallery.

Too much testosterone and a dizzying deficit of common sense are often the flashpoint for far too many of the world's armed conflicts. A reflection catches my eye as I look up at the J. Edgar Hoover Building. A huge chunk of a broken window damaged by the explosion seems to be teetering about twelve floors up.

I watch it break free and tumble down in slow motion. Despite his sins, despite his evil, my only wish was to save the President of the United States, but as I watch the huge chunk of glass somersaulting toward the earth, I know his reign of terror is about to end. The air erupts with the sound of a thousand breaking bottles near the President, causing everyone in the immediate vicinity to open fire.

At long last, the chaos-President is getting his wish. Unchecked gun violence is raging in the streets of our nation's capital. Even with my earplugs, the sound of the gunfire is deafening. Bodies drop all around the Commander in Chief. President Locke jerks several times as stray bullets rake his body.

The President and his party have a sinister *go-to* statement after every mass school shooting. When the parents come to collect the bullet-ridden corpses of their small children, they try to explain away the gun violence they made possible with the line "thoughts and prayers."

I turn my back on the massacre and whisper over and over, "Thoughts and Prayers. Thoughts and Prayers!"

CHAPTER 39

January 7, 2029
National Mall, Washington, D.C.

I TRUDGE ACROSS the National Mall still lit up for the holidays as sporadic bursts of gunfire echo around the city. However things turned out at the FBI Headquarters behind me, the face of our democracy has been reshaped forever. The defenders of our republic chose to worship the Mad King instead of upholding their oath to defend the Constitution of the United States. Perhaps their reward will be in heaven or points farther south.

The role I played in whatever happened this evening will likely land me in a cell for all eternity or perhaps some sniper will mercifully turn out the lights for me. At this point, I don't have a particular preference.

I try unsuccessfully to remember that pain is only a state of mind as I hobble forward. Every step forward sends burning embers up the base of my spine. My right hip has burns from the ash and my ankle is a mess. L'Enfant Plaza is only a few hundred yards ahead. I wonder if the mass-murdering Congressman has freed himself yet? His blatant disregard for human life is appalling, and I feel an uncontrollable urge to snatch the last breath from his body.

I fish around my tactical vest without looking, stumble, and tumble to the ground. I lie there on my back with my eyes closed panting like a dog trying to orient myself. I resume the search in my vest and I'm finally rewarded with a tube of ibuprofen or what soldiers like to call "ranger candy."

I fumble with the childproof cap and promptly stuff a handful of white tablets into my bone-dry mouth. I try to swallow them, but my throat is so parched I have to chew them instead, leaving my mouth full of a choking, chalky residue. I lie there on the frozen ground for another few minutes gagging on my ibuprofen snack while struggling against the urge to go to sleep.

The pills only make the dizziness worse, but I finally raise myself and stagger back in the direction of the hotel. People gape at me in abject horror as I stroll into the luxurious lobby of the South Station Hotel. I'm still dressed in the D.C. Police Uniform although I doubt anybody can identify it through the gray dust, debris, and blood caked and cooked all over my body. I expected my appearance might cause a commotion in the hotel lobby, but oh my Lord!

"Officer, Officer! Can I help you?" asks a hotel manager running up to me. "Can I do anything to help you?"

I whisper into his ear and he nods, looking at me with great concern. "I'll get that right up to you. Can I help you into your room?"

I wave him off and stagger over to the hotel elevators and punch the UP button. I feel like a giant crocodile watching people part like the Red Sea to give me plenty of clearance. I'm rewarded with an elevator all to myself. I walk into the Congressman's four-bedroom penthouse suite and rip open the full-size fridge snagging three huge bottles of water. At the same time, I decide that if

Lobdell does come back here, I'm gonna get answers from him by whatever means necessary. Unless, of course, he kills me first.

I stroll into his master suite walking over to the giant bathroom sink. I nearly topple over in horror as I catch a glimpse of the filthy bleeding face staring back at me in the mirror. I examine the woman in front of me and wonder who she really is and what she's become. God knows I failed the President.

There's a huge gash on my right cheek that's caked shut with ash and dirt and my bottom lip is swelling like a water balloon. My right forearm is gonna need stitches, and I know my ankle is badly swollen underneath these combat boots. I stop and take a long look at the living nightmare staring back at me. I didn't look this bad after a ten-hour firefight in Benghazi. No wonder people were grabbing their kids and running for the hills when I ambled into the hotel lobby.

I turn on the cold water in the sink, take a huge gulp from a water bottle, rinse with it, gargle it, and spit it out. Disgusting chunks of dust and bloody flesh from my mouth hit the sink and scamper down the drain.

I repeat the same action again and again before I'm actually ready to drink. My throat's on fire but that doesn't stop me from slamming the last twenty ounces of water and cracking open a second one. This time, I suck all thirty-two ounces down and wander over to the Congressman's bed.

I slump back onto his California King size bed and pull a pillow over my face to protect me from the mess I'm about to make. I raise my right combat boot in the air and blindly fiddle with the laces of the boot until it's untied. I cough up another nasty nugget of dust phlegm from the explosion.

As I peel the boot off, copious amounts of dust and filth spill out all over the bed and blanket the room. By the time I'm completely naked, it looks like someone slashed about five industrial vacuum bags full of soot and gravel and shook them out all over his suite. I look at my handiwork and hobble to the minibar looking for something to soothe my throat. I don't drink alcohol unless it tastes like chocolate, but I grab a tiny random bottle with amber liquid and slog it down. The taste is awful, but it works almost immediately to numb some of the pain thrumming though my battered body.

I begin a long, tremulous walk to the bathroom, not able to put my full weight on my ankle. I turn the shower jets on as hot as I can possibly stand them. There's a prominent stone bench in the shower. I gingerly sit down and aim the jets at my body and drift off into a half sleep letting the hot water pound and cleanse me of my sins. I don't know how long I stay there, but the hot water never falters.

I absently pad out of the Congressman's room wrapped in a hotel bathrobe and fluffy slippers. I turn to look at the devastation I left behind in his room. It looks like another bomb might have exploded directly over his bed. I close the door behind me and retrieve my personal phone. I call Cat's burner phone while trying desperately to clear my raw throat.

After a few rings, Cat answers the call. "Snowflake?" she whispers into the phone.

"Hey, you," I whisper back.

"Why are you calling on your real phone? Why are you whispering? Are you OK?" she asks, questions tumbling out her mouth.

"I have a sore throat and I can't really talk that well," I say honestly.

"What are you doing?" she asks.

"I'm sitting in a luxurious suite at the South Station Hotel at L'Enfant Plaza curled up in a stunningly comfortable terry cloth robe," I say.

Cat chuckles over the phone. "Fine, don't tell me where you are, just tell me you're OK."

"I'm OK. I'm alive and the nightmare may be winding down," I say.

"Have you heard the news?" she asks seriously.

"What news?" I ask.

"The President is dead," she says.

"What do you mean *the President's dead*?" I ask already knowing the answer to the question. The first President of the United States to die by friendly fire.

"There was a drone strike at the FBI Building and then some sort of gunfight and the President was killed," she says.

"My God, that's awful," I say. That's not even close to the truth, but obviously I can't tell her that over the phone. I'm not sure I can ever tell her anything about what happened tonight. So it's official, the Polyester Messiah is no more.

"So what's happening now?" I ask, walking over to the television. I point the controller at the TV and change my mind. I have enough horror floating around my head to last me three lifetimes.

"Vice President, Sebastian Knox is going to be sworn in at 22:30," she says. "He says his thoughts and prayers go out to the people who died in the drone strike and the others who were killed in a shootout with the terrorists."

I shake my head—*thoughts and prayers*.

"Domestic terrorists?" I ask.

"No one is sure yet," she says.

"I just wanted to check in. Tell Abby I love her. Stay put until you hear from me."

I break the connection and fill up the sink with cold water when the doorbell chimes. It must be the soup and hot tea I ordered from the manager. Thank God.

"Just a second," I say, not loud enough for anyone to hear me.

They can wait at the door for a minute. I'm just about to shove my face into the cold water when the doorbell rings again. Screw it. I shove my face into the water trying to rub the sickness off of my face. I note that some of my skin is actually flaking off into the sink. I walk over to the door when someone on the other side kicks it open. Three operatives decked out in tactical gear with guns drawn form a triangle formation around me. Well, that didn't take long.

"Hands high," commands the man closest to me.

I follow his request.

"Good, now kneel," he says.

Fat chance—I'm in a bathrobe.

"If I have to squat, spread, and show you my goodies, make sure your orders are to kill me," I say hoarsely. "Because if you expose me to this third-world indignity and I survive, I'll track you down and feast on your heart."

He looks at me in surprise and then at the members of his team.

"Bank on it, Chief," I say.

The resident badass changes his approach and allows me to get dressed. The reality is that I'm not a shy girl at all, but if you want to humiliate me because I'm a woman, you and I are gonna have to figure things out the hard way. The four of us go down the back freight elevator as a room service waiter pushes past us with my soup and hot tea. Not cool.

I sit wedged between Thing 1 and Thing 2, but I'm too sore to do anything except lean my head back and close my eyes. We drive for about ten minutes, and I'm pretty sure we didn't cross any of the bridges into Virginia, so we must still be in the District. The driver gets a call and speaks quietly into the phone. I can't make out what he's saying and I don't care. I assume they're taking me to meet the Congressman for my interrogation and execution.

"Miss Walker," says the driver, "I am to extend my sincerest apologies to you. Time was of the essence because the District of Columbia is now under a mandatory forty-eight-hour period of martial law. We were not told the nature of your pickup. We were told only to take you into custody and that you were likely armed and dangerous."

"Am I under arrest?" I ask.

"What?" he asks, confused.

"Ammm . . . I under arrest? Simple question. What the hell are your orders? Just kill me and get it over with."

"No, ma'am," he says.

"Fine. Just tell me where we're going and who's holding your leash," I snap.

I look out the window. We're heading north and coming up on Chevy Chase, Maryland.

"Ma'am, the Chief of Staff wants me to take you wherever you want to go with her heartfelt apologies. However, she would sincerely appreciate it if you would accept her hospitality and consider spending the night at her private residence, since you will not be able to get back into Washington D.C. tomorrow because the city is on lockdown."

"Cecilia Danforth?" I ask.

He nods his head.

"Just get her on the phone for me." She must be suffering from separation anxiety.

"Ma'am, she's at the private swearing-in ceremony for the Vice President," he says as we pull up to a spectacular mansion. The place looks like a palace, but I'm looking for peace, not luxury.

"Fine. Take me back to my hotel and back to my room. Tell the Chief of Staff that if she wants to talk to me, she knows where to find me."

I've had enough politics for one lifetime.

CHAPTER 40

January 7, 2029
L'Enfant Plaza, Washington, D.C.

I'M BACK IN the same hotel lobby, but it's deserted this time. A markedly different experience from the people who were gaping at me when I waltzed in covered in muck and death two hours ago. I amble up to the Congressman's room in a daze. The key card unlocks the door, but before I can reach down for the handle it flies open and I'm looking into the barrel of a gun.

"Get that thing out of my face before you hurt yourself," I say, shoving the weapon aside and limping into the room.

I know the Congressman has to shoot me. He has no choice. It's his only play. I'm a loose end he can't afford. He looks like death. I should have locked his ass in the restaurant freezer instead of the walk-in cooler. He keeps his weapon trained on me.

"Busy evening, Congressman. Let's see. You blew up a city block," I say as I pour myself a stiff orange juice from the refrigerator and grab a banana. "You've replaced Tim McVeigh as the deadliest domestic terrorist in American history. He's the madman who slaughtered almost 200 feds in Oklahoma City, right?"

He nods his head, refusing to meet my eyes.

"They'll be sifting through the rubble for days," I say, staring at him. "I've never met a mass murderer on your scale before."

He walks over to the bar and pours himself four fingers of whiskey. He slops half the drink down his shirt, looks at me, and pours another. My disgust for the man shakes me to my core.

"Was that your Unabomber Manifesto?" I ask. "If you're going to shoot me, get on with it. You have to kill me. You just butchered what? Maybe two hundred Americans? More? Human life means nothing to you. Pull the trigger, Congressman. Clean up your mess, little man."

He looks at the gun in his hand and places it on the minibar. That's the fatal misstep of a man who is not thinking clearly.

"Do you even know what a diversionary explosive is? It's like a pipe bomb or, I don't know, maybe an M-80. You took out a city block, you son of a bitch!"

He stares at me like an idiot.

"Do you like to blow things up or watch people burn? Please, enlighten me."

"I swear," he says as his voice cracks. "I had no idea how powerful that explosive was." He sloshes some of his drink onto the carpet.

"Great, you're not a mass murderer, you're just a moron who plays with bombs? Perfect."

"It wasn't the right explosive. Something happened! She must have switched it out or used both," he says.

"*Sheee?*" I ask.

"Aahona—the suicide bomber—she must have switched out the explosives. It's the only thing that makes sense," he says.

"*The suicide bomber?* You said you were going to use a timed device?" I say, but then I understand. "That's why the bomb exploded four minutes early. It wasn't a timed device; it was human error. She got nervous or maybe she tried to pull the suicide vest off?"

He nods his head as the madness of his actions sucks me into a stupor. We sit there in silence for three long minutes.

"Aahona?" I ask. "Libyan?"

I close my eyes tightly, already knowing the answer to the question.

"Do you even know what *Aahona* means?" I ask him.

He shakes his head no.

"*The first rays of the morning sun*," I say, trying to stop my head from spinning. I take another moment. "And the dead men at the Occoquan River—let me guess—Libyans too?"

He nods again.

"And your suicide bomber? Any connection to the Benghazi attacks?"

"She was ten years old when her father was killed attacking the CIA Annex we were defending in 2012," he says.

"And you recruited her under the guise of avenging her father?" I ask.

He nods his head again.

"Why me, Congressman? Why choose me? You're always a step ahead—did you anticipate that I'd grab you before your assassination attempt to try and stop you? Give you an alibi?"

He turns away and looks out the window at the smoke still dominating the night sky over Washington.

"Of course you did. I was just the goat tethered to a pole." I'm all out of clever speculations.

I snatch his gun off of the minibar, flip the safety off, and point it at him from a comfortable distance. I tap the trigger guard, willing my finger to pull the trigger and air him out. Exactly 5.3 pounds of pressure is all it takes. Empty the clip into him and make the world a better and safer place. But that's exactly what he wants. A quick way out. A clean and merciful death that he does not deserve.

He sees me in the reflection of the glass pointing the gun at him. My hands are rock steady, but my mind is afire. He wants me to put him out of his misery.

He turns around and appraises me with pleading eyes.

"Tell me why you recruited me?" I ask.

He leans against the window silently. I look past him into the night sky for a long moment. I feel the bloodlust emanating from my pores. Searching for justice when there is none to be found. I want to avenge the innocents he slaughtered tonight. My finger caresses the trigger, knowing what must be done, but I also understand that letting him live with the horror of his actions is a different kind of death sentence.

"You should use this after I'm gone," I say, waving the Glock in front of his face and gently placing it on the glass table between us. "I'm not cleaning this up for you. You know what to do. Ease it underneath your chin and finish this."

He doesn't have the courage to look me in the eyes. I take out my phone, send a quick text, and head for the door.

"We're not done," he whispers.

I ignore him and gather my things to leave.

"We have unfinished business, Mizz Walker," he says raising his voice almost to a shout.

I walk over to the minibar, plop his cell phone into a half-full ice bucket, and leave the room without a word. Congressman Lobdell, I sentence you to spend the remainder of your tortured existence pursued by an army of ghosts.

CHAPTER 41

January 7, 2029
L'Enfant Plaza, Washington, D.C.

I EXIT THE elevator leaving the Congressman to ponder the legacy of his atrocities. The three-man kidnapping squad who are now apparently at my beck and call are waiting dutifully at the curb for me. I shoo one of them out of the passenger seat and with a grunt painfully pull myself into the front seat.

"Cross the 14th Street Bridge and take me to Pentagon City Mall, please. You know where that is?" I say, trying to keep my eyes open. I need this day to end.

"D.C. has been locked down tight, ma'am," says the driver. "No one in, no one out."

"Don't you work for Cecilia Danforth?" I say, staring aimlessly out the window. "Figure it out."

He spends the next twenty minutes at a massive roadblock trying to get clearance to leave Washington D.C. while I drift in and out of a restless sleep. I snap awake with a start when the driver returns to the vehicle. It looks like he finally talked our way past the barrier and into Virginia.

I instruct the driver to drop me off at the bus stop in front of the Pentagon City Mall. After a heated debate, I finally convince Danforth's hit squad to leave me in peace. I crawl out of their vehicle, nearly losing my balance, and amble over to the bench at the bus stop. Danforth's team is conflicted by my orders, but finally relent and hop the ramp back to Washington. I'll probably freeze to death before my ride shows up tonight, but right on cue, a red Toyota 4Runner rounds the corner.

"Ghost Rider," says the driver, my dear friend Austin J. Barton. "Pickup, party of one."

He watches me with concern as I stand up slowly and limp, but knows better than to ask me if I want help. I struggle into the passenger side of his ride. He seizes me the moment I plop down next to him and suffocates me with a desperate bear hug that nearly snaps my spine. He holds me for thirty seconds, and I hug him back fiercely. It's the first time we've ever hugged each other. He slips the SUV into drive while I recline the seat all the way back to rest my eyes for just a moment.

When I open them, we are sitting in my driveway in Chantilly, Virginia, and I know I've been out for a while.

"How long have we been here?" I ask groggily.

"Only about two and a half hours." He chuckles softly.

"What's wrong with you, Sheriff Bart?" I ask. Except for my father, this is the only man I've eve been able to count on. From the day we shook hands in Benghazi, he's been a rock.

"There's no way I can ever thank you for all you did and the risks you took," I said. "You got us out of the Capitol, protected the Speaker, and played a huge role in saving our nation."

"Aw shucks, ma'am," he says, making fun of me.

"C'mon, the spare bedroom is always ready," I say, reaching for his hand.

"I really can't," he says his deep voice rattling the windows of the 4Runner.

"Don't make me beg," I snap at him. "I don't want to be alone right now."

"Are you a danger to yourself? Are you having suicidal thoughts?" he says, mocking me again.

"I can see you've developed quite a personality," I say as we climb out of the vehicle. Every muscle, every bone, every fiber of my being is in pain. He comes around and silently offers his arm. I surprise myself by accepting it and letting him help me into the house.

I show Bart the spare room as he assists me to my room and gently lowers me onto the bed. I'm asleep in seconds before being jolted away by the horror of the past two days. I feel an all-encompassing exhaustion in my body, but sleep is no longer interested in me. I fumble with my phone and look at the screen to unravel the most recent version of last night's events being offered by the twenty-four-hour news cycle.

I'm rarely shocked when I read the news anymore, but these damn journalists got me good this morning. The fiction they write and tales they weave, where do they find the time? I comb over the fractured fairy tale describing last night's carnage in Washington. This epic saga would leave H.G. Wells shaking his head in creative envy.

What was originally thought to be a drone strike in the heart of Washington D.C. might have been the work of suicide bombers with ties to the far-right group known as the Sons of the Apocalypse. President Terrance Locke, who had been in failing health due to a heart condition, suffered a fatal heart attack brought on by the explosion that shattered hundreds of windows in the area. Authorities are conducting a "blast analysis" and warn that the death toll will rise in the coming days as searchers continue to comb through the rubble. If you have a loved one or know somebody who attended the President's speech and have not heard from them, you should contact your local law enforcement.

Of course, the President was actually killed in a deadly shoot-out between two government agencies that were sworn to protect him. But that will morph into one of those wild conspiracy theories President Terrance Locke was so very fond of. I take a long, deep breath and continue reading.

Rescue workers are still sifting through the debris at the sight of the explosion and using K-9 units to search for survivors. According to the latest count, more than 282 people are dead and at least 191 are unaccounted for.

Twenty-one Secret Service Agents and thirty-six National Guard Troops were killed during a secondary explosion, also allegedly triggered by the same right-wing extremist group. The Federal Bureau of Investigation has already arrested several members of the Sons of the Apocalypse as the investigation begins to ramp up. President Knox and the Justice Department have stated that this attack was a one-time occurrence and that the group has been neutralized and is no longer a threat to public safety. Flags will be flown at half-mast for the rest of the month to honor the loss of our President and the brave men and women who perished by his side last night.

I must have missed the second bomb blast due to all the automatic weapon fire being exchanged between the National Guard and Secret Service, but when the government controls the news feeds, I suppose any fable has the potential to become reality. I was standing right there. It's nothing short of unbelievable that Deac found a way to pin all of this carnage on the Sons of the Apocalypse. That's obviously why he pitted me in a gunfight against the SOA members who had direct contact with him. With friends like him, enemies are nothing more than an afterthought. Now that I think of it, it was also the Congressman who made the final call that only government-controlled film crews would be permitted to record last night's event and now he's fanning the flames of what is likely to become the greatest cover-up in American history.

I press on.

Upon confirmation of her stepfather's death, the President's Chief of Staff, Cecilia Danforth, ordered the Justice Department to rescind the arrest warrants that had been issued for Vice President Sebastian Knox and the Democratic Speaker of the House, Sarah Vasquez. President Sebastian Knox was sworn in last night as our nation's Forty-Eighth President at a small ceremony in the White House naming Cecilia Danforth as his Chief of Staff.

Danforth must live on energy drinks and cocaine. Just last night, she coordinated an assassination, shut down the Justice Department, attended a Presidential Inauguration, and tried to kidnap me because she wanted some girl-time.

President Knox went right to work overturning President Locke's Emergency Executive Order that led to the arrest of more than thirty senators and congressmen during the invasion of the United States Capitol. They were all freed and told to report to Capitol Hill no later than 10 a.m. this morning.

I look at my bedside clock; it's just a little after nine.

President Knox worked with his team through the night, gathering members of Congress to proceed with the Election Certification Process that he will preside over. This will be the first time in American history where a sitting President will oversee the certification process that is scheduled to begin at noon Eastern Time.

My phone buzzes in my hand, causing me to jump. I close my eyes and answer it without looking.

"Walker," I croak, my voice barely above a whisper.

"Good morning, Cora," says the Speaker.

"Good morning, Madame Speaker," I choke out through an aching throat and pounding skull.

"Are you sick, Cora?" asks the Speaker with concern in her voice.

"Just a little sore throat," I answer.

"I can hear the pain in your voice, Cora. So please don't try to speak, just listen," she says. "I wanted to tell you in person, but this will have to do for now. Thank you," she says. "I mean it. The nation owes you a debt of gratitude that can never be repaid, and so do I."

"Thank you, Madame Speaker, that means a lot to me," I say. What I don't say is that except for saving her life, I didn't accomplish anything. As a matter of fact, I've been part of one of the greatest failures in the history of covert services. During my watch, not only was the President of the United States assassinated, but also hundreds of people perished at the hands of a suicide bomber. If that's not the very definition of an abject intelligence failure and dereliction of duty, I don't know what is.

"I don't want to see you back in this office until President-elect Hayden is sworn in on the 21st. He actually told me he's very interested in making your acquaintance," she says. "But enough politics. I wanted to have you over to my place for dinner some time when you're back on your feet."

"I would like that," I say feeling the guilt of the dead press down upon me.

"OK, Cora. Ah . . ." she's goes quiet again for several long seconds, and I wonder if she's hung up. "I'll never forget what you did for me."

She breaks the connection. I tiptoe over to the spare room, but the sheets have already been stripped and the bed has been left in immaculate condition. There's a small note on the bedside table.

It was great seeing you last night! Sheriff Bart

He is a man of few words. Jesus, the old softie even made the coffee before he left.

I pad into the kitchen to grab a mug when I hear the garage door open. I limp down the stairs, and as the door to the garage bursts open in front of me, I freeze in place, coming face-to-face with my little girl.

We stare at each other, matching sets of eyes drinking the other person in. I can't risk a single blink, fearing she might vanish in front of me if I'm hallucinating. I scoop her up into my arms and spin her around as Abby squeals at the top of her lungs.

She helps me upstairs until we make it to the living room. She gingerly places her hands on each side of my face, inspecting the damage from last night's explosion. Ever so gently, she presses her forehead against mine and begins softly crying.

"I have you, baby," I whisper through my tears.

"I know you do, Mommy. I knew you'd come back," she says softly kissing the gash on my cheek to make it better. "I knew you would."

ACKNOWLEDGMENTS

First and foremost, I must thank my wife, Gina. Without her enduring faith and unwavering support, this book would not have been possible.

A shout-out to my nuclear-powered daughters, Maddie and Savannah, for keeping Daddy on his toes at all times. They never tire when I prattle on about new concepts for my books and are always happy to contribute ideas of their own.

And a special thank-you must go out to my mom and mother-in-law, Mary Anne Adams and Denise Martin. They are both authors in their own right and have been essential in my writing process, contributing their ideas, guidance, and interesting perspectives on multiple topics.

I'm forever grateful to the Watchung Writers Group and our fearless leader, Pat Rydberg, who set me on the proper path of personal writing accountability. This amazing group of people perpetuated my desire to present them with a fresh chapter for every new meeting.

Katie Taillon, a heartfelt thank-you for inviting me to the writers group and always being the one who picked at the thread of every chapter I've ever written.

Susan Edwards, your parallel journey and support in the writing process was essential to the completion of this novel.

Thomas Melore, your unique perspective always helps me take another look at my story from a different point of view.

Vivian Fransen, your keen eye for grammar and structure helped temper my impatience during the proofreading process.

Nicole Burdette, your input and interest in Cora Walker along with your enthusiasm for my storytelling was and is a constant source of motivation for me.

To the three professors who played such a significant role in my education and helped shape my worldviews on history, politics, and journalism at George Mason University.

Scoobie Ryan, the Associate Director of the School of Journalism and Media at the University of Kentucky, you taught me the most important life lesson that shaped me as a journalist and as a human being. You were the first person to grade me on effort instead of content, an edict that has guided me throughout life.

Despite the fact that Roger Wilkins was a civil rights champion and a Pulitzer Prize–winning journalist, I had no idea who he was when I took my first class with him at George Mason University in the1980s. However, his exuberance and vast intellect on civil rights issues still guides me to this day. The world was a more complete place with him in it.

American historian and Robinson Professor Shaul Bakhash sparked my lifelong interest in Middle Eastern affairs. His efforts to teach me to tie the Koran and the evolution of the Muslim world into current events was a gift to me that I can never repay.

And, finally, I would be remiss if I didn't thank Professor James Daly at Seton Hall University. He wasn't a college professor in the 1970s; he was my seventh-grade social studies teacher who fueled my passion for American history and social justice. He was famous in the High Bridge, New Jersey, school system for making his students present oral reports several times a semester. His unique style of teaching helped me fall in love not just with social studies, but also with the art of public speaking.